Books by Ash Penn

Single Titles

Rent Mate

Rent Mate

ISBN # 978-1-78686-152-8

©Copyright Ash Penn 2017

Cover Art by Posh Gosh ©Copyright 2017

Interior text design by Claire Siemaszkiewicz

Pride Publishing

Published in 2017 by Pride Publishing, Think Tank, Ruston Way, Lincoln, LN6 7FL, United Kingdom.

Pride Publishing is a subsidiary of Totally Entwined Group Limited.

RENT MATE

ASH PENN

Prologue

The flat was small but relatively clean. Flimsy metal art sculptures and sepia city prints littered the magnolia walls. Further cheapness showed in the laminate flooring and flat-pack furniture, much of the latter mismatched for shade. A large flat-screen TV sat in one corner next to a tatty bookcase crowded with DVD boxsets and dog-eared paperbacks.

"Can I get you a drink?"

Roy switched his attention to the young man standing in the center of the room. "What do you have?" he asked, knowing full well his favorite twelve-year-old malt was out of the question.

Button lowered his head, as shy and awkward as if he were the visitor. "We have some vodka," he said, sweetly unassuming. "And my flatmate also has some beer in the fridge. Fosters, I think."

Lager. Roy suppressed a shudder. "What are you having?"

"Nothing for me. I'm not thirsty."

In the four months since they'd met, Roy had never known Button to touch a drop of alcohol. He claimed to be teetotal, but Roy could never be certain how much of Button was real and how much an act. That was half the reason he'd insisted they spend their evening here. It was far more difficult to conceal one's true self at home.

Nothing Roy had seen so far indicated that Button was anything other than how he appeared. A beautiful, innocent young man who sought affection in all the wrong places, often with the wrong kind of men.

Right there was the other reason Roy had forced this invitation, to save Button from such a dangerous existence.

He planned to once again make the offer that had been turned down twice already in the past month. The offer of safety and financial security, in return for complete exclusivity. The reason Button was so resistant to the idea remained a mystery, but now was not the time to raise that particular topic. Not when Roy's eagerness to please was raised enough already, albeit trapped within the confines of his underwear.

He cleared his throat. "Then perhaps just show me to your room."

"Yes. Of course."

Button led the way down the hall, trailing his fingers along the wall as the ragged hem of his jeans grazed the fake wooden floor. Every now and then, Roy caught a glimpse of faded pink soles. The shade reminded him of the boots his wife had recently bought their granddaughter.

A waft of shame brought him to an instant standstill. As he put out a steadying hand, his palm flattened against something smooth and waxy. A poster. Attached to a door. A picture of a naked man reclining in a barn, surrounded by hay. His slim, sinewy body gleamed in oil. His cock stood fat and erect as he lay on his back, propped up on his forearms, a flirtatious smile poised on his lips.

"Roy?" Button stood farther down the hall, lifting his pink soles one after the other in a nervous, stationary march. "My room's this way."

Roy gestured to the door. "Whose room is this?"

"Just my flatmate's. Why?"

"He not home?"

"No. I told you, he's out. *All* night."

"Oh, yes." Roy gripped the door handle. "That's exactly what I thought you said." A creature who displayed such filth in the presence of a naïve young man like Button definitely required further investigation.

"No!" As soon as Roy opened the door, Button rushed to his side and clawed at his arm. "Please don't go in. He wouldn't like it."

Well, then. It was just as well Roy didn't give the vaguest of shits what the owner of this room did or did not like. The door opened into shadows.

"Roy, please!" Button's fingers bit deep into his arm as Roy reached inside for the light switch. "Don't."

With a flick of his finger, a sickly yellow beam illuminated a single bed, unmade, and a chipped chest of drawers spilling clothes. Obscene posters served as wallpaper, a naked male featured in every one. Sometimes two or more together. Fondling, copulating. All in full, glossy color.

The vague scent of old, sweaty clothing hung in the air. A bottle of supermarket scotch sat on the chest of drawers. Roy headed toward the bottle with an aim to helping himself. Anything to help with the shock of this obscenity. And most certainly unbranded scotch would suit his palate better than lager.

"Don't touch that." Button tugged on his arm again. "He'll—"

"He'll what?" Roy picked up the scotch and examined the contents. Half empty.

"He'll not like it. This is his private room." Button leaned close. His breath whispered across Roy's ear and cheek. "Please, let's go to mine. I'll definitely make it worth your while. I promise."

Those two softly spoken words burned straight to Roy's cock. He instantly let go of the bottle and Button was equally as quick in returning it to pride of place on top of the chest of drawers.

As Roy allowed himself to be gently coaxed from the room, he stepped over a grubby pair of jeans topped by a pair of skimpy underpants. Having held a mental image of Button's male flatmate as a huge Neanderthal, dim and unwashed, the underwear suggested a man no bigger than Button himself. Not that size mattered here. Having perused the man's bedroom, there was no way Button could continue living in the company of such a perverted specimen.

7

The next room Button took him to was not as he'd had envisioned, either. Pale pink walls, a double bed with a velour pink headboard and a dressing table littered with odd bits of cosmetics.

He picked up a lipstick. "Do you use this?"

"Sometimes." Button claimed the lipstick back. "I like to dress up." He flashed a perfectly innocent smile, though he'd never demonstrated the slightest hint of cross-dressing before. He dressed much the same as any other boy his age. Scruffily casual, except for those tatty pink-soled shoes. Perhaps they were the giveaway. Or perhaps the only reason he dressed up was on the instruction of clients. Further thought on exactly how many clients Button entertained was a mood-killer he'd rather not waste time contemplating.

Instead, he reached for his tie. "Take off your clothes."

Button's innocent smile fell away as he kicked off his shoes and unfastened his fly. He stripped quickly and efficiently, until he stood shivering in the center of the room with his clothing scattered around him.

Roy focused on the boy's subdued penis and puckered scrotum. "Cold?"

"A little. We don't have the heating on at night. It's too expensive." Button cast his lashes low in a blatant theatrical turn, then lifted them again along with his lips in the sweetest of dimpled smiles. "You'll warm me up, though, Roy, won't you?"

"I certainly will." Roy closed the distance between them. His cock throbbed solid as a heartbeat in his pants. "You're so beautiful." He raised a finger to the curve of Button's cheek. "So very vulnerable."

The soft touch, or perhaps softer words, stole Button's dimples. His smile fell away. "I'm not. I can take care of myself."

Roy didn't believe that. But he wouldn't push the matter. Not yet. Instead, he leaned close and pressed a kiss to Button's naked shoulder. The sweet-smelling skin twitched beneath his lips. Resisting the urge to bite and mark the flesh as his own, he pulled back and started unfastening his shirt. "Go lie down for me."

Button scampered to the bed and settled down on top of the quilt.

"You do realize," Roy said, discarding his shirt, "that despite your continual rejection, I still fully intend to have you all to myself."

"No, Roy. I told you I—"

"I know what you said. And while this flat is more than I expected, the person with whom you share is less so."

"I can handle him. You shouldn't worry. I'm happy here. Really."

"But if anything were to happen—"

"It won't," Button said quickly. "Even if it does, you'd soon forget about me with your wife and children and grand—"

Roy rushed forward. He pushed his hand over Button's still-talking mouth. "Stop." He'd made a mistake ever talking about his family, and never did so with any of the others. None made him feel as lazily content when they were lying in each other's arms as Button. "That particular subject is closed. Understand?"

Button's pupils shrank to pinpricks, but he nodded all the same.

"Good." Roy let his touch fall away. "We'll talk some more later."

He trailed a fingertip down the boy's narrow breastbone and smooth belly all the way to the deliciously half-erect cock. He wrapped a fist around the shaft, which obediently twitched and swelled further under his hand.

"Hmm." Button raised both arms above his head in a languid stretch. His lips formed a thoroughly wicked smile. "Fuck me."

Roy chuckled, allowing his irritation at Button's vapid nature to fall away. "Ravenous nymph." He indulged a few more languid lengths before reaching toward the bedside table. "Where do you keep the provisions? In here?" He pulled open the top drawer and reached in. His fingers brushed against something smooth and sleek, yet hard. It took a moment to realize what, exactly, he was touching. "What in the world is this doing here?"

Button instantly paled at the sight of the large sex toy thrust in front of his face. "It's not mine."

"Then to whom does it belong? And what's it doing in your room?"

"Um..." Button flailed, evidently grasping for a lie. "I think someone must have put it there as a...a silly gift."

"A silly gift from whom?"

"Possibly... Oh. My flatmate?"

"Are you asking or telling me?"

"Telling." Button bit his lip. "He must've put it there. As a joke."

"And why would he do such a thing?"

Again, Button hesitated a touch too long. "Well. It's probably his idea of a joke. I told him I was bringing someone home tonight. Someone special, I mean." His cheeks flushed a delightful shade of rose. "He would have put it there while I was out. He doesn't like queers."

Roy raised an eyebrow. "Despite the odious posters on his walls?"

"Well, he's self-hating. And he doesn't like me because I'm too...too..."

"Feminine?"

As the word hit the air, Button's face contracted. His skin flushed and his lips drew back from his teeth. "F—" He seemed to catch himself, and his expression smoothed. "What?"

Roy gestured around the room. "Judging by all your pretty things."

"Yeah. I mean, yes. That is why he hates me."

Roy rose from the bed and carried the dildo to the white wicker bin by the dressing table. "You wouldn't have to concern yourself with such behavior if you'd allow me to take care of you. I'm even willing to negotiate on price." After dropping the thing in the bin, he returned to the bedside table and opened the next drawer down. "All you'd have to do is remain exclusively mine for the duration of our agreement." He pulled out a condom and some lubrication. "Prepare yourself for me."

Button accepted the provisions without a word. He tore the packet of lubrication open with his teeth and squirted a generous amount onto his palm.

Roy finished removing his clothes then laid them on the chair by the dressing table that was littered with odd bits of makeup. Perhaps Button wore such greasepaint for other men. Perhaps they preferred him dressed like a doll. Until Button belonged to him, he wouldn't stop wondering about the elusive others.

A lusty groan vibrated the air and Roy's full attention sprang back to the bed. Button writhed on the mattress, working his tight little hole with ruthless vigor. His spine arched. His toes curled. His cock flared dark red, leaking dewy drops from the exposed head. Far too close.

"Enough."

Button lowered his hips to the mattress and withdrew his fingers from his body. Raising both hands to bars of the headboard, he waited. Knees to his chest, wantonly irresistible.

Roy climbed onto the bed and plucked up the strip of condoms. They wouldn't require such inconveniences when Button belonged to him. Indeed, when that day came to pass, the boy would spend the majority of his time awash with their spent passion.

For now, though, Roy tore a foil packet from the strip and rolled the latex over his erect cock in a ritual he preferred to take care of personally. The scent of the eager boy tingled up his nostrils, along with the clean wisp of laundry freshener from the sheets.

He clasped the backs of Button's slender thighs and guided them over his shoulders. Going up on his knees, he ignored the arthritic crackle through his bones and speared deep into Button's body.

"Ahh." Button squeezed his eyes shut. "Please...slow down. You're too big."

In other whores, Roy would accept the request as part of the spiel. But Button was different. Genuine. He demonstrated a naivety that could not be faked, especially like this with the pain of entry frozen on his delectable face. As he bucked and squirmed and twisted, Roy clamped down on his hips to keep him still. A grip tight enough to leave marks for the next man who took his place.

* * * *

Afterward, with Button's semen slicked between their bodies and his own tied off and discarded in a litter bin along with the sex toy, Roy slipped his fingers along Button's breastbone then pressed the tips to Button's slack lips. "Clean them," he said, his voice a throaty whisper.

He watched, fascinated, as Button licked ticklish patterns over his flesh until not a trace of semen was left.

Only then did Roy relax back into the mattress. Button immediately curled into him, all sweaty and pink with exhaustion. Roy held him as he wished to hold him every morning. An impossible fantasy, even if his offer was accepted. He and his wife no longer shared a room, but she fully expected him to share their lives.

He gave the slick furrow of the boy's spine a tentative caress. "I leave tomorrow." With his business here concluded, he couldn't extend his stay without invoking a certain kind of wrath from his wife.

Button snuggled closer. "Will you look me up when you're back in town? Or just look up me, if you prefer."

"I'll call you." Roy shifted position and rolled Button over. He leaned in to steal a forbidden kiss. As usual, when their mouths were close to making contact, Button snapped his head left. Keeping his lips well out of reach.

Anything else Roy requested was granted without hesitation, but their lips must never touch. No matter. He'd claim that plump mouth at his every whim, soon enough.

"There won't be others inside you tonight?" he asked as Button squirmed beneath him.

"No. You've worn me out." Button wriggled. Not in erotic encouragement, more in a determined effort to free himself. Roy held him until he stilled again. "I'll just sleep when you've gone," he said, face still turned aside.

"And tomorrow?"

Button slumped beneath him. "I am what I am, Roy. Can you please get off me now? I can't breathe."

Roy rolled away. A chill shivered over his skin. He left the bed and retrieved his jacket from the chair by the window. When he took out his wallet, his heart wilted at the sharp gleam brightening Button's eyes.

"There's an extra fifty here." He counted out five tens. "It's yours. On the condition you give some more thought to my offer. An apartment in the city, a generous monthly allowance and the odd bonus if you please me. Which I'm sure you will. All I ask from you in return is complete exclusivity." He offered the cash, just beyond reach. "Think about it. Yes?"

Button pushed out his bottom lip. "Fine."

"Good." Roy edged closer.

Button snatched the money and slipped the notes under his pillow. With his money safety tucked away, he watched with keen eyes as Roy dressed.

Once settled into his jacket, Roy approached the bed with every intention of indulging his final wish for this evening. Bowing close, as if to utter a quiet goodbye, he grasped Button's exposed upper arms and pinned them to the bed.

Button opened his mouth.

Roy plugged it with his tongue.

He tasted wonderful. No traces of alcohol or cigarette tainted his breath. Just mellow clean flavors to explore. Roy thoroughly probed every delectable inch of that alluring—

if uncooperative—mouth and, when he drew back, the depth of the kiss continued to tingle over his lips.

He might even have risked another had he not looked up and met the sudden toxic clouds shrouding Button's eyes. So thick and dark, his own reflection resembled a slathering predator leering right back.

With a blink, the predator dissolved to the distorted but still rugged features he greeted in the mirror each morning.

As the boy's eyes once again steadied to their usual clear transparent blue, Roy stepped back rather more quickly than was appropriate. "I'll contact you shortly for my answer." He forced a casual stride to the door. "If that's all right with you."

"No."

Roy opened the door. "What did you say?"

"I said no. My answer will always be no." Button drew the covers over his head and disappeared into their depths.

With one final look at the boy hunched naked under the duvet, Roy flipped out the light and closed the door. Rather than head outside, he retraced his steps to the flatmate's door. He tore the obscene poster in two before discarding the pieces on the floor.

Chapter One

Liam West had just finished a ten-hour stint at the hospital and wanted nothing more than to crawl into bed and cocoon himself under the duvet for the next week. But first he had to speak with Katie. What had happened between them yesterday afternoon had nagged at him all the way through the night shift. So much so, he'd lost his temper at a couple of drunken revelers who'd turned up at A&E bruised and bloodied as a result of a fight. Prior to that, he'd had to wheel a twenty-year-old girl to the morgue.

After putting the kettle on, he went to Katie's door and tapped rather than knocked. Anything to avoid the wrath of Martin, who hated to be woken before ten. Woe betide anyone who interrupted his beauty sleep. Not that he needed much, the vain little shit.

"Katie? Can we talk?"

No answer.

It occurred to him then that when she'd stormed out yesterday afternoon she might not have come back. She'd already stayed out four of the last five nights, so one more wouldn't make any difference. He knocked again, harder. "Katie? You awake?"

Silence.

Liam opened the door.

Sunlight seeped around the partially open blinds and threw a sharp beam across the bed. Highlighted in this radiant glow was the flutter of golden eyelashes spread upon a pale cheek. Beneath a button nose, full lips rested together and formed a petulant pout that may or may not have been the result of collagen injections.

Wait a minute.

What was he doing staring at Martin Bailey's lips? Especially when those lips were pouting in his best friend's bed. Liam forged inside the room, ready to eject the bastard short shrift. Then the golden lashes flickered open.

Martin lifted his arms in a lazy stretch. The move elongated his torso, displaying the fine arc of his ribs and the smooth dip of his taut belly. From there Liam's attention was drawn to where the covers met his groin.

Wait another minute.

Was he *naked* under that quilt?

"Liam?" Martin slurred, suggesting he'd been in the midst of a deep sleep. "What're you doing here?"

"You're starkers in Katie's bed, and you ask me what *I'm* doing here?"

"Katie's..." Martin looked blearily around. "Oh. Hell." He pushed the quilt aside and swung his legs out of the far side of the bed.

Liam flipped on the light.

Martin threw an arm across his eyes. "Man. You have to do that?"

"Yes." Liam clenched his teeth. "Why are you in here? What's wrong with your own bed? And where's Katie?"

Ignoring every question, Martin stood and stretched both arms high above his head. As he did so, Liam's gaze fell to the small, pert peach of his backside. Dark patches bloomed on the pale skin, harsh blobs that looked very much like finger-shaped bruises. "Have you had someone here?" he asked the bruises. "A..." What were they called? Customers? Clients? *Johns?* "A punter?" Liam clung to the word with both hands. "You had a punter in here?"

Martin didn't laugh at the term, but neither did he offer up an answer. Instead, he bent to pick up his clothing as if Liam had ceased to exist. As he did so he let out a pained groan and pressed a palm to his belly.

"What's wrong?" Liam asked, knowing he shouldn't give a shit. Especially after finding the bastard in his best friend's bed. But he couldn't ignore the fact Martin was in pain. And considering those bruises, and what he did for a living, Martin's pain must get pretty bad at times.

"Nothing." Martin straightened, using the bed post as support. "It's just the bloke from last night." His blue eyes shimmered from under a mop of tousled hair.

Liam's rage dissolved. What the hell had gone on in here? "What happened, Martin? You can tell me." He edged another step closer. "Did he hurt you? Or...?" Or worse?

"He..." Martin sucked in another sharp breath. "God, Liam. He..." His plump lower lip trembled, then parted from his equally plump top lip to form a manic grin. "He's got a cracking great knob on him. Knows how to make thorough use of it, too. My arse is flaming like a Catherine wheel on bonfire night."

Every bit of sympathy Liam held in his body boiled away. "You are a sick, fucking..."

Martin let out a cackle of ear-grating laughter then reached under the pillow. He spun around, waving a shock of notes in the air. "Not bad for half an hour's graft, eh?"

Half an hour? The steam from Liam's anger thinned to disbelief. There was as much there as he earned in a week. How fair was that? Then again, thinking back to the bruises, the money wasn't so great.

"Where is she?" Liam asked as his temperature once again set to simmer.

"Who?"

"Katie. Who'd you think?"

"I reckon she spent the night with her boyfriend. Her well fit boyfriend, from what I saw."

"You've *met* him?" That Katie had broken her promise to stay home last night was bad enough, but paled into insignificance when contrasted with the fact that Martin had met this elusive new bloke of hers.

"Yeah." Martin idly flicked through his takings. "Why?"

Liam paused. He refused to show just how much of a slap in the face that was. "So while she's out you thought you'd, what? Take advantage of her absence? You really are pathetic." Liam itched to shake a sense of decency into the little shit. But there wasn't much to grab a hold of except his half-erect cock, and Liam was keeping well out of the way of that thing. "I want you out of here. Now!"

"All right, big man." Martin raised a dismissive palm. "No need for the 'tude." He set about gathering the rest of his clothing from the floor, then paused in the doorway on his way out. "You reckon you could give the sheets a rinse through? They're a little...crusty."

Liam surged toward him, fists clenched, but being twice Martin's size meant an unfair advantage right from the off. And since Liam despised violence more than he despised Martin, he stood there and seethed instead while Martin continued down the hall like nothing was up other than his dick.

"And I mean out," Liam yelled, trying not to stare at the pert cheeks of that perfect, if bruised, arse. Out of the flat and out of their lives. For good.

"Then have a word with Katie." Martin flashed another exaggerated grin from over his shoulder. "It's got to be unanimous, or I'm going *no*where." He disappeared into his room then, and slammed the door behind him.

Martin placed his earnings into his night-table drawer then lowered himself gingerly to the bed. Falling asleep in Katie's bed had been a mistake, a big one. He'd only used her room because pink suited his alter-ego's personality. Feminine, chic fairy lights and a patchwork quilt beat wallpaper made of porn stills and the half bottle of whiskey sitting on his chest of drawers.

As he made to rise from the bed, he caught his reflection in the full-length mirror hanging on the door. Martin Bailey — all bedhead and bloodshot eyes. But if he fluffed up his blond hair and lowered his lashes, if he parted his lips and licked them until they glistened, then there was Button. The sweetly innocent sap hardly clued in about sex, and forever oblivious of the effect his young body had on the men who were willing to pay to explore it. The kid Roy wanted to buy and keep purely for pleasure.

Like that was going to happen. He couldn't play the naïve piece of fluff twenty-four-seven. Mainly because his pathetic alter-ego's saccharine willingness to please pissed him off no end. He'd taken his frustration out on Liam this morning and now would have to heal the atmosphere. He liked living here, more than most of the other places he'd stayed. But before he did anything else today, he needed that shower.

Standing under the hot water jets, he cleansed the grime of his job with a generous slather of Katie's strawberry shower gel. She never minded him using her things, unlike Liam staring daggers across the Weetabix of a morning. Liam minded he dare breathe half the time. Granted, breakfast was usually dinner time for them both, but, no matter what time of the day or night, the sad fact was he and Liam would never become friends.

He'd grown to appreciate the big guy over the past few months of living here, despite the constant complaints and not-so-subtle digs about his job. However hard he tried, he wouldn't be able to wear an eternal grin for minimum wage in a supermarket. He could smile for a two hundred quid shag, no problem. He could please any man on a fifty quid blow job. He'd perfected the art in cheap hotel rooms and narrow alleyways for going on almost three years now, and before then in the privacy of his home.

Not all his punters were totally undesirable, either. Roy had his good points. He was never violent or overtly kinky. He insisted on bringing Button to orgasm every single time. A lot of others weren't so generous. Even so, last night Roy had become extra pushy, extra keen to claim Button's flesh as his own.

After switching off the water, Martin wrapped a towel around his waist. Bath rather than hand. Usually he'd deliberately parade around in a much smaller towel just to flaunt himself in Liam's company. Irritating the big guy had proven to be quite the leisure pursuit lately. Precisely the reason he'd not-so-casually dropped meeting Katie's latest boyfriend into the conversation. In reality, their introduction had been little more than a brief hi and bye when passing in the hall, but Liam didn't need to know that.

Martin grabbed his toothbrush and scrubbed the remnants of Roy's taste from his mouth, then made his way through to the kitchen. Liam was sitting at the table nursing a coffee. He might be fuming like a midsummer's dung heap, but he smelled much nicer. Sweaty but clean, with a frisson of some ocean-themed aftershave. Aesthetically, he wasn't too bad on the eye, either. Tall, broad and black-haired, he exuded a soothing presence. A quiet, underlying strength, a protective presence that Martin liked. A lot. Mainly because Liam was totally straight and remained so even when wasted. Every now and then, though, Martin liked to wobble the boundaries to see how safe his walls were. The reason he found Liam's smoldering presence quite so warming was best pondered another day.

He set five crisp ten-pound notes on the table then pulled out a chair. Perhaps he should have dressed first, but this bad atmosphere needed tackling sooner rather than later.

Liam eyed the notes. "What's this?"

"An apology." Martin fixed on his brightest grin. "I shouldn't have taken Katie's bed, and this is my way of saying sorry."

"Fifty quid's worth of sorry?" Liam swept the cash to the floor. "I'm not your pimp, Martin. You can't pay me to keep my mouth shut, either." He powered to his feet. Fists pushed to the table, knuckles big as bolts. "In fact, I've got a good mind to show you exactly what I think of you."

"Go ahead." Martin pushed back his chair and stood, too. "I can take a fist. Just be aware I charge an extra hundred for the privilege." He stuck out his chin and readied for the glancing blow he probably deserved. Not that he believed

Liam would cave his face in, bolt knuckles or no bolt knuckles. Liam just wasn't the violent type. His gamble paid off when Liam slumped in his chair and picked up his mug.

"Will you tell Katie?" Martin resumed his seat. His adrenaline fizzled to a sickly slither of nerves. Katie wouldn't want him to leave, would she? She was an easygoing girl, but there had to be a limit to even her level of acceptance. Using her bed to entertain his clients wouldn't go down well, no matter how close their friendship.

Liam hunched his shoulders. "Depends."

"On what?"

"The reason you did it."

Like that's any of Liam's business. "One of my regulars wanted to see where I live. He's been hassling me for exclusive use, and I—"

"Exclusive use? What does that mean?"

"Just that he wants to buy me. Like, full-time. So I'd get to be with him and no one else."

"You mean he wants to *own* you?"

"No way. I ain't nobody's slave." Martin scowled. "I just thought if he could see that I don't live in squalor with a bunch of junkies and rapists, he'd stop worrying about my living conditions and—"

"You could've used your room for that. You could've made do with a single. In the past I've had to…" Liam shut his mouth.

"You've had to what?"

"Nothing." Liam dragged his mug closer. "We're talking about your bedroom habits here, not mine."

Only because Liam probably didn't even have any bedroom habits. Not past his right hand, anyway. For as long as they'd known each other, Liam had never brought anyone back to shag. He'd never brought anyone back, ever.

"Roy—that's my punter—he clocked the naked meat pinned to my door and wasn't impressed. So I had to tell him my room was my flatmate's, AKA, yours."

Liam spluttered a mouthful of coffee halfway across the table. "You told your trick that porn infested hell-hole was *mine?*"

"You mind?"

"Of course I mind, dipshit." Liam pushed out of the chair and fetched some kitchen towel from the roll on the wall. "Like anyone is going to believe you kip in a pink fairy grotto, anyway." He swiped the towel across the puddle but only succeeded in spreading it further. "You're not that camp."

"I ain't camp, full stop." Martin bit down on his anger. Trying to communicate with Liam was a total waste of time, as always. But he owed an explanation. Wouldn't be an acceptable one, but it would be the truth. "I'm not. But Button is."

Liam paused his mopping. "Who's Button?"

"Me. Sort of. He's, like, a persona. Button's seventeen. A dumb twink who swaps bum fun for cash 'cause he's too thick to work a proper job."

"Sounds like you, never mind this Button character." He deposited the soggy towel in the bin. "Apart from you being twenty-one and a long way from dumb, that is."

He'd take that as a compliment, even if dumb probably referred to his mouth rather than his intelligence. "Yeah, well, in my line of work, the younger and more inexperienced you appear the more you can charge and the more the blokes are willing to pay. They lap it up, trust me."

"I don't doubt it." Liam shot him another disapproving look before sitting back down. "How old are they, then? These blokes who pay fake seventeen-year-olds for sex. What about him last night?"

"Dunno. Sixtyish."

"Sixtyish?" Liam's disgust flared again, in full uniform regalia of the likes not seen since some passing neighbor had thrown up in the hall directly outside their front door. "You bring sick old fucks who like teenage boys to mine and Katie's home, then give them what they want in Katie's bed?"

The earlier compliment meant absolutely nothing if Liam thought this of him now. "I only brought Roy back, and he ain't even that sick a fuck." Roy treated him with respect. Roy also fucked hard enough to bruise, but the bruises were of the energetic, not the violent, variety. "Seventeen is legal. I could play younger if I wanted, but I got my principles, too."

Liam snorted out a laugh.

Martin chose to ignore it. "Roy's harmless enough and he tips well."

"Yeah, well. Whatever he is or isn't"—Liam stabbed a finger down on the table—"you bring any more of your desperado perverts here, and I will throw you out myself. Personally. Rental agreement or no rental agreement. Understood?"

"Sure. I get it." Martin slipped from the chair to the floor and set about gathering his money together. He stuffed the cash into his pocket then levered himself upright. A fresh spark of fire seared through his pelvis and he couldn't prevent a whimper that made Liam's upper lip curl in distaste. Now there was an expression he'd caught on a variety of different faces over the years, and was more than used to ignoring. "Time I was going, anyway. There's a half price breakfast down the pub with my name on it."

Chapter Two

The bloke wouldn't quit staring. Martin sat at a table with a full English but couldn't get comfortable under such keen attention. His audience of one was dressed in a sweater and an unflattering tan jacket that looked as though it had been dragged kicking and screaming from a charity shop skip. He also had a habit of staring at people within his direct line of sight.

Martin sawed into an overcooked sausage and raised the fork. Again, he met with the stranger's steady stare. Enough was enough. He picked up his plate and shifted to a booth.

With the weight of the unwelcome attention gone, he coaxed his mind to where he'd spend the rest of the morning. He'd take roses today. A bouquet made up from the fancy florist in town. Thanks to Roy, there'd be extra money in the bank this week. Enough to take tonight off, even. With the dull yet constant ache in his arse, even one night off sounded like heaven. And he could use the time to try to make up with Liam. If such a thing were possible. Offering money in exchange for silence had been his second mistake of the morning, especially after flouting his ill-gotten gains not ten minutes before. Liam had morals. It was easy to forget there were people around who did, especially when he fitted in so much more easily with those who didn't.

He finished his breakfast in peace then checked his watch. Nine-thirty. If he ordered the roses now, he could pick them up before catching the bus.

First things first. He needed a wazz.

When the bathroom door banged open then shut behind him, he didn't think anything of it until he'd zipped up and turned around.

Tan jacket guy stood directly between him and the exit, dragging the ugly taint of nicotine closer with each step.

"How much?" the guy asked, his voice rough and as cracked as his jacket.

Martin inched back. Playing innocent was his best bet. He clenched his right hand into a fist, though, just in case. "How much what?"

"Twenty now. Twenty after." Tan Jacket drew out his wallet and extracted a note. He nodded toward a stall.

Martin moved to the sink to wash his hands. A craggy face glared beyond his in the mirror. "Got no idea what you're talking about, mate." *Did he exude 'rent boy' like a cheap aftershave?*

"Then how much will it cost?" Tan Jacket's stare was cold and harsh. Not the look you gave to someone you wanted to fuck. Or pay to fuck. He'd seen that exact expression before. Mainly as a kid, on various 'uncles' before they'd smacked him one. The guy laid the money down on the counter beside the sink then added another couple of twenties. "Eighty enough?"

Martin's hands were wet, but he didn't fancy showing his back again to use the dryer. "Enough for what?"

"A blow job."

Straight to the point. That was positive. If this guy was a cop, that line would be taken as entrapment for sure. The money sat on the counter, and since he could rarely afford to turn down ready cash he decided to play along. On his terms. "One hundred."

"Just for getting my cock sucked?" The guy let out dry chuckle. "You're having a laugh, kid, aren't you?"

Martin drew back his shoulders. "Before ten on Wednesday morning it's a hundred. If you can't afford me, you know what you can do." He nodded toward the exit.

"Right. One hundred it is." Tan Jacket once again drew out his wallet. He muttered something that might've been 'you greedy little sod', but Martin couldn't be sure so let the

25

comment pass.

He took the money and replaced the notes with a condom. Sometimes he didn't bother for a blow job but didn't want to spill his breakfast by gulping cum right on top. For a hundred quid, he'd usually be expected to swallow.

Tan Jacket gave the condom a wary look before gesturing to a cubicle. "In there."

Martin slipped the cash into his pocket then headed inside. Sideways, so he could keep an eye on his latest punter. He didn't trust the bloke any more than he'd trust a starving dog with a plate of freshly cooked sausages. Although, in this situation, he remained very much in charge of the sausages.

Tan Jacket followed him in and locked the door. As the confined space filled with the stench of stale nicotine, Martin checked the floor. Clean and dry, so at least he wouldn't ruin his last decent pair of jeans by kneeling in a puddle of piss.

When he reached for the man's fly, long gnarled fingers clamped around his wrist.

"What'd you want me to do, mate?" He looked up. "Suck it through a straw?"

"For what I'm paying, I just decided I want more."

"Not for a lousy hundred you don't." Martin tugged back on his wrist. A full fuck was double and he wouldn't risk it here at this time of day. "Let me go, shithead. Or you'll be sorry."

The grip on his wrist tightened. "Will I?" The guy rammed a bony forearm hard across his chest, and drove him up against the cubicle wall. Nicotine breath seared his skin, fogged his nostrils. "Teetering on the edge of the gutter? Like hell. You dived in head first a long time ago. Didn't you, skank?"

"What?" Martin focused on the face in front of him. Lean but haggard. Like a lean slice of bacon left out of the fridge too long. Had they met before? He tended to remember smells better than faces, but there were so many smells, and so many faces in his past, sometimes he couldn't pick one out from the masses.

"No, kid, you don't know me." Tan Jacket leered closer, apparently having read his mind. "I don't know you, either, but I know what you are. And that's enough."

"Enough for what?" Martin bit his tongue. He already regretted the first time he'd asked, so why ask it again?

"Enough for what's coming."

Martin's heart lurched. He'd been in this situation before but never in such a confined space. Didn't mean he'd make for a willing punch bag, though. Focusing his strength in his right thigh, he brought up his knee. Usually this worked a treat, and the threat went down like a cold bucket of piss. This threat, however, had somehow known what was coming and twisted, deflecting the blow to his hip rather than the squidgy sac of his scrotum.

"Nice try." The guy's rancid breath scoured Martin's face. "Let's see if I can go one better."

Martin squeezed his eyes shut. Braced for a set of hard knuckles slamming into his cheekbone. When nothing happened, he cracked open an eye. The predicted fist hovered in front of his nose, threatening to forge forward and make a mess of it. Or worse, his teeth. A nose could be fixed on the NHS. Teeth were another, more expensive, matter.

"Wait." He bit down on the harsh blade of a coward's way out. "A fuck is two hundred. Cash up front." Despite his earlier bravado, he couldn't afford to damage his looks. "Just leave off with the physical crap."

"Hmm." The guy's voice softened. "That's better. Except… oh, yeah. I just remembered. I'm no faggot after all."

Before Martin could think about sighing with relief, a flesh-colored blur powered into his stomach and he went down chasing the bile spewing out of his mouth.

A loud bang echoed around his brain, followed by a waft of cool air. The cubicle swam. Nausea seared the back of his throat. The stench of puke hung heavy in the air, flavored with grease and the acrid tang of tinned tomatoes. He forced open his eyes in time to see a retreating set of denim clad legs and a tatty tan jacket bearing an image of a pistol in silhouette, smoke puffing thickly as if the barrel was a cigar.

Martin lowered his cheek back to the floor. What a dumb fuck. Why chase an extra few quid when he'd already made enough for the week? Greed was a dangerous regret, and contempt had rolled off that wanker in waves. He inched into a sitting position and probed his ribs. His chest burned when he took in anything but the shallowest of breaths.

Crawling from the cubicle, he gritted his teeth against the flames burning up his ribcage. After using the nearest basin to haul himself upright, he checked his face in the mirror. Thankfully he found no evidence of injury. Just a trail of puke from lips to chin, easily washed away. Nothing for Sandra to worry about when she saw him. He'd have to go home first, though, and change before ordering those flow…

Shit.

With his heart thrashing in his already aching ribcage, he patted down his pockets. His wallet was still there. A quick check confirmed every note was accounted for. Why hadn't the guy snatched the cash back? Unless he got off on bashing queers for fun and preferred to pay in order to ease his conscience. Weirder things had happened. One thing was for sure. There had never been the slightest possibility of sex. This was purely about getting bashed.

The main door swung open. Martin almost dropped his wallet. But the man who inched through had to be seventy if he was a day. He glanced at Martin, noted the wad of cash and the sick-stained sweater, and shuffled to a cubicle. The bolt snapped across.

Martin pushed his wallet into his pocket then splashed his face with clean water. He might stink like a bad Saturday night, but he'd walk out of here with his head high even if pain pulsed from his ribs to his pelvis and dictated he should limp most of the way home.

Chapter Three

Liam opened his eyes, startled awake by the finishing ding of the dryer. He'd fallen asleep at the kitchen table. Unwashed dishes sat piled high in the sink and the light on the washer-stroke-dryer glowed green.

Rousing enough to stand, he decided to put the sheets on the bed before Katie came home. Then he'd wash and go to bed. His spine ached. As did the crick in his neck. Not to the mention the proverbial pain in the arse that had to go. But Martin Bailey wasn't going to take up any more of his thought processes this morning. He had more productive tasks planned.

He'd just reached Katie's room with an armful of clean linen when the front door flew open. Martin staggered in, backed up until the door closed again, then leaned heavily against the wood.

"What's the matter this time?"

"Nothing." Martin pushed off the door, trying for casual, but Liam had caught the discomfort in his breath. The bitter stink of puke drifted down the hall, which even the potent fragrance of the fabric conditioner couldn't mask.

"Have you been working?"

"Mind your own fucking business." He stepped inside his room and slammed the door behind him.

Great. If that was what he wanted, forgotten already. Liam returned to Katie's room and set about remaking her bed and tidying whatever had been disturbed. Before he left he glanced into her litter bin to see if it needed emptying. It did. Of a used condom and a sex toy. A dildo, if he wasn't mistaken. Once again, rage tightened his chest. Another line had been crossed, and this one he wasn't prepared to ignore.

Bin in hand, he strode down the hall to Martin's door. The wanker inside had lost all rights to a cursory knock. He pushed the door open. Martin immediately fell back onto the bed. Bare-chested, another bruise shadowed his ribs. A bruise he hadn't had that morning. A bruise he'd probably been studying in the mirror on the back of his door.

"What happened now?" Liam asked, eyeing the discolored skin.

"Nothing." Martin sprung up off the bed and went to his chest of drawers. "You can't just barge in here." He brought out a clean sweater and yanked it down over his head. "I pay rent. This is my private space."

"You mean like Katie's room is her private space?" Even as Liam asked the question, he became distracted by Martin's slender back. Prominent shoulder blades flexed beneath a fine layer of creamy skin. Such a contrast to the bruises blooming across his lower spine and arse. "Why'd you let them do that to you?"

"Do what? Shit happens in any job. I bet you get enough abuse from the pissheads every Saturday night, and your wafer-thin wage packet definitely ain't worth the trouble." He pulled the sweater down then dropped onto the bed. "What do you want, Liam? If it's just to be a nag again then—"

"This." Liam set down the bin. "I could have left this for Katie to find. I don't think I'd have had much trouble persuading her to throw you out of here if I had."

Martin kicked off his shoes and lifted his legs up on the bed. "You still can, if you want."

"I will, then." Liam wished he'd spoken with more conviction. If he had, perhaps Martin's lips wouldn't have tilted as they did to form a strangely enigmatic smile. They were too pink for a guy's. Pillowy and puckered, as if in anticipation of a kiss rather than the smack they were due. Still, since he'd obviously been battered enough for one day, Liam turned his attention to the rest of the room.

The posters in here weren't as tasteful as the one on the door. Most of them were made up of erections and arses and men writhing with other men on ludicrously large beds. Some of the images were so sharp he could see the sweat beading their skin and the nail marks etched into their backs.

"You like?"

Liam jerked back from a particular picture of a muscle-bound bloke on all fours, a much smaller and fairer partner buried balls-deep behind him. "They're depraved."

"So you got no pussy gracing your bedroom wall, then?"

Liam let out a slow breath. "Of course not."

"Just a bikini shot of Katie in a collage tastefully entitled 'Wishful Thinking', right?" Martin laughed, a nasty, mocking sound that set Liam's teeth on edge. "Come on, big man, even *I* know you're wasting your time there."

Something delicate and fragile withered inside Liam's chest. "What'd you mean?"

"Let's just say, I've clocked the way you look at her, and how she looks at you. And I got to say, your looks and hers are in no way compatible."

Was that a not so subtle way of saying he'd be punching above his weight with Katie? He didn't care if Martin thought him ugly. What he cared about was his secret passion for Katie not being a secret. And if Martin had read the signs, he might as well have advertised on every billboard in town.

As he turned his back to protect the effects of the possibility blooming on his cheeks, his attention snagged on a half empty bottle of scotch sitting on the chest of drawers. He picked it up. Odd. Why would Martin keep alcohol in his room when he didn't drink?

"Put that down."

"What?"

"The bottle." Martin swung his legs to the floor, his full attention fixated on the scotch. "Put it back. *Now*."

"It's half-empty. I thought you didn't drink."

"I do. Occasionally."

"Katie says you don't. And I've never seen you touch so much as a beer."

"Does it matter?" Martin's gaze flickered over him before returning to the bottle. "It's mine and I asked you to leave it alone. You can leave me alone, too, unless you want Katie to know who's the star of your wet dreams at night."

Liam hoped the breath he'd sucked in hadn't carried to Martin's ears. He could deny the accusation as much as he liked, but he'd be wasting his time. If Katie thought his love might not be entirely of the platonic variety, their relationship would change. One day Liam would be the one she asked to leave.

"Fine." He set the bottle down, grasping for a shift of focus. "But tell me. If the money's so good for selling yourself to all and sundry, how come you're living here with a hospital porter and a primary school teacher? If you can make more money in an hour than I do in a week, why don't you ever have any?"

Now he came to think about it, that was an extremely good point. Martin wore old, faded clothing which was, more often than not, riddled with holes. He ate the cheapest of supermarket basics, usually made up of porridge and baked beans, and he traveled everywhere on foot or by bus. He lived like a pauper, when he should he living like a footballer. Or a politician.

Martin stared at him. "The dildo's Katie's."

"*What?*"

"Roy found it in a drawer and assumed it was mine, but it wasn't. Just saying."

Just lying, more like. Tainting Katie with his deviancy. Well, that wasn't going to work. Liam had known Katie most of his life. They knew almost everything about each other and sex toys were definitely not the kind of thing she'd want anywhere near her. "You're a lying, pathetic piece of shit." Liam stabbed a finger at Martin's too-pretty, too-smug face. "And I will tell Katie. *Everything.* Just as soon as she gets home. Whatever it takes to get you out of here."

Martin rose from the bed. "You want me out, big man?" He stepped up close. Close enough they were swapping breaths. "*Throw* me out."

Liam let the full impact of his most venomous attention slide over Martin's body. "Then I'd have to touch you, and I wouldn't want to get my hands *that* dirty."

A casual line, and Martin had much smarter comebacks queued up in that big gob of his. But, for some reason, he didn't use them. Instead, he plucked the used condom from the bin with his bare hand. "I'll go take another shower, then. Least that way, I'll be clean on the outside."

"But we're not done here yet." For one thing, the dildo still sat in the bottom of the bin, all pink and painful-looking. Had Martin used that thing last night? Or on the other man, or on himself? Or —?

What the hell was he wondering for? Steering his mind to cleaner territory, he snatched up the bin and moved into the hall. There was something on the floor. Two pieces of paper. From a magazine, by the looks. He turned them over to reveal two sections of the naked man Martin usually had pinned on his door.

Had Martin done this? Doubtful, considering how much joy he got from displaying the thing despite Liam's objection.

Not that it mattered. Their flat was much better off without such lurid decoration. He tossed the thing into the bin with the sex toy then decided to catch a few more hours' sleep. When Katie came home, they'd have a proper chat. About best friends, new boyfriends and soon-to-be-ex flatmates.

Chapter Four

Visiting hours at Oakland House were flexible. Martin usually made two or three mornings a week. The house stood about a mile out into the countryside and had been converted into a nursing home from its former status as country manor.

Sandra had a room on the second floor overlooking the car park and drive. It was a large, comfortable space decorated with fresh, bright watercolors. Sandra was in a chair at the window. The mid-morning light caught her pale hair and highlighted the strands in a rich shade of gold.

"Hey," he said softly, notifying her of his presence before he came in and laid the flowers he'd bought for her on her lap.

She touched the cellophane with long, spindly fingers and studied the blooms as though they were precious diamonds. He always brought a gift, either flowers or a DVD, though he could never be sure how effective the DVDs were. She liked animations the best, because of the bright colors. Probably the reason she liked her flowers so much, as well.

After examining her gift, Sandra turned her smile upon him. She always smiled when he visited now, far more than she ever had before the accident. She showed him more affection, too, but he had no right to feel warmed or comforted in any way. She only loved him now because she didn't remember why she shouldn't.

"I thought you'd like to go out today," he said, gesturing beyond the window. Out back, there were a couple of acres of garden to explore. They usually had tea and cake in the café on the ground floor afterward. Sandra seemed to enjoy that just as much as their frequent walks to the village down the road. "I reckon it'll rain later, so we'll just stick around here for today. Next time, I'll hire us a taxi and we can go see a film or something. What do you think?"

A tap at the door sounded behind him. "Hello, Martin. Oh, what beautiful flowers." The care assistant stepped up to the Sandra's side and admired the bouquet. "Sandra, you'll have a rose garden all to yourself in here soon."

That was true. A new bouquet sat on the chest of drawers. A dozen or more scarlet heads with long, slender stems. The roses filled the room with a warm, fruity scent as fragrant as any air freshener.

Sandra's sister usually sent flowers about once a month, rarely accompanied by a visit, but these must've cost way more than her usual ten or so quid. Was there a special occasion he'd missed? It wasn't her birthday. He couldn't recall Sandra's sister sending something so elaborate at any other time.

"Who sent these?" He gestured to the roses. "You know?"

"I'm afraid I don't, no. If there's a card, we usually stick it on the vase."

Martin turned his attention to the plain glass vase. No card. Sandra's sister always wrote a note. No one else sent her flowers. Or anything else, for that matter. They'd arrived here by mistake, but he wouldn't say anything. Sandra would get upset if they were taken away now.

Instead, he gestured to the wheelchair in the corner. "Is it okay if we go for a wander into the village?"

"I don't see why not. Let me sort the flowers and I'll rope someone in to help her get ready." She gathered the bouquet from Sandra's lap and made her way back toward the door.

Martin unfolded the wheelchair then grabbed a tissue from the windowsill. Then he resumed his seat and dabbed the drool from Sandra's lips.

* * * *

Being tucked up in his bed rather than slumped at the kitchen table didn't help Liam find sleep. Martin Bailey swirled around his brain like an obnoxious turd that refused to flush. As he gave up trying to chase the ghost of sleep, he reached the decision that the turd would have to be manually expelled. *Today.*

He was all set to start packing Martin's belongings when the front door opened. This time, it was Katie who barged through. She looked disheveled, her dark hair flowing loose around her shoulders rather than the elegant bun she usually wore for work. Her lips were smudged scarlet. Her cheeks were pink too, but not from makeup. She was done up for a night out in short skirt and a low-cut top under her short leather jacket. She hadn't been wearing that outfit when she'd stormed out the afternoon before. She'd still been dressed for work then.

"Who died?" Katie asked, squinting at him from down the hall.

"What?"

"The face on you. What's the matter? Aren't you supposed to be in bed?"

"Aren't you supposed to be at work?"

"Nope." Katie kicked off her shoes. "I called in sick." As if on cue, she straightened and clamped her hand over her mouth. Then charged into the bathroom. The sound of retching filled the silence. Another thing Katie and Martin had in common. They both stank of puke.

Liam lightly tapped on the door. "Are you okay?"

"Completely," came the choked reply.

"Do you want a coffee?" Strong and black, if she'd been on the razzle all night enough to be suffering the effects at three the following afternoon.

"Lovely." More retching followed. The sound of the toilet flushing indicated she was done.

Liam hurried to the kitchen.

He'd just set a couple of coffees on the table when Katie shuffled in, her face far paler than usual. She took a careful seat and wrapped both hands around the mug. "Thanks, hon."

"Another heavy night?"

"Hardly. Only the flicks followed by a single glass of wine." Judging by the state of her, and not for the first time lately, he should assume this was another lie. "I either had a dodgy curry, or I'm..." She bit her lip.

"You're what?"

"Developing an allergy," she said weakly.

"To alcohol?" She'd been sick a lot recently. Usually when she came back from whatever she'd been doing the night before with her new boyfriend. He wouldn't think about what else might be making her sick of a morning.

"On one drink? No, Mr. Snarky Pants, I don't have a hangover."

Her glare was too hot to hold, so Liam refocused on the table. "I thought you'd have come home last night. So we could talk this morning."

"We're talking now, aren't we?"

They were, sort of. And hopefully their conversation wouldn't drop to the depths that it had yesterday when he'd found out about this new boyfriend she'd been keeping secret for weeks. He'd definitely have to be more restrained when it came to digging around for information on who exactly this latest loser was. "Martin said he met your boyfriend last night."

"You and Martin are talking?"

"Not exactly. He just couldn't resist mouthing off." And they'd get to Martin later. "Why haven't I got to meet this guy yet?"

"Because you'd hate him. It's your default position. Like I said yesterday, you've hated every boyfriend I've ever had."

Liam hunched his shoulders. "That's not true."

"Name one you've liked."

Was she issuing a challenge? She'd never been overrun with boyfriends, but those she did have didn't last long. She always went for a type. Narcissistic, arrogant show-offs. None were ever good enough for her.

"Kevin Barnes," Liam said with a touch of smug triumph.

"We were fourteen," Katie reminded him. "Hardly counts. Besides which, you went right off him as soon as he and I started dating. Didn't the pair of you get a two-day suspension for fighting it out after football practice?"

"No," Liam said thinly. "It was rugby." That particular fight had had nothing to do with Katie, had it? He couldn't remember. But if Martin had so easily picked up on the reason behind his protective streak, had Katie, too? He didn't think he could look her in the eye ever again if she found out, especially as he'd always known she would never return his feelings.

"The reason I haven't brought Robbie to meet you is because I like him too much to scare him off with your overprotective father routine."

'Overprotective father' stung. They were the same age. Or was she saying he was old beyond his years, and not in the intellectually wise way?

"You let Martin meet him." There was nothing prematurely wise about his jealousy. He sounded like a sulky child. Not without some provocation, though, since Martin was taking his place in everything. Including an introduction to this new boyfriend *Robin* or whatever his name was.

"That wasn't pre-arranged. He just happened to be here while I was picking up some clothes."

"But you two are close, considering you've only known him ten minutes." Did he sound jealous? He couldn't help it, as much as he was being irrational.

"Yes, well." She looked away. "He's easy to talk to."

"And I'm not?" They discussed everything together. Or had. Which was another reason he didn't want her getting close to Martin. There were things he never wanted that malicious rent-a-gob to know.

"He's got a different perspective, hasn't he? On blokes, I mean. With his line of work and everything. He gets to examine them in greater detail." In any other circumstances, Liam might have laughed. But Martin wasn't funny in the slightest. Not in an amusing way.

He could hardly tell her about wanting the cuckoo in their nest out now. She'd apply the same reasoning as she had to this new boyfriend of hers and break out some home truths. The fact of the matter was that he just didn't like her being around men. Even gay men. That might make him a jealous and unreasonable prat, but didn't change a thing as far as Katie was concerned.

"You're not arguing." Katie tilted her head. "I'm not sure if that's a good or bad sign."

"Would there be any point? You like him no matter what I think."

"I didn't mean Martin. I meant about you hating my boyfriends."

"I don't hate your boyfriends." He sipped his coffee and hoped she'd swallow the lie as easily. "I just don't think you have great taste in men."

Her voice tightened. "What?"

He'd been too blunt. Said the wrong thing. Now he'd have to backtrack, or risk making matters worse. "It's not you. It's them. You just attract the wrong sort of bloke."

"The wrong sort?" Katie's cheeks flushed. "What does that mean, exactly?

"Well, you know." Liam swallowed. This could get out of hand rather quickly if he wasn't careful. "It's just the guys you go out with tend to be out for what they can get rather than—"

"Is that a roundabout way of telling me all I'm good for is sex?"

"No. Of course not!" *How the hell had she jumped to that conclusion?*

"Are you *quite* sure about that?" Judging by the ice in Katie's tone and the sharp, rhythmic clack of nails on the table top, this conversation had started to go very wrong, very fast.

"I'm sure. But you have to admit the relationships you've had never last. And it's always you who ends up hurt because of it. I'm worried about you, that's all."

"Right." The tension showed no sign of easing in her voice. "I suppose if you had your way you'd be choosing my men for me. Because I obviously haven't got a clue." She stood, anger plain in her stance. "You want to meet Robbie, fine. But one wrong word, one veiled insult, and that'll be it for us. Do you understand?"

'It'? A two-letter word had never sounded so ominous. He couldn't work out if she meant 'it' for sharing a flat, or 'it' for their friendship. She'd just threatened to put another bloke first, before him. They'd always promised they wouldn't do that. No bloke more important than him. No girl more important than her. He'd yet to test his side of the bargain, seeing as he'd yet to meet anyone he'd want to get serious with. "I'm not sure I do. What do you mean, exactly?"

"I don't know." Her shoulders dropped, and she raked a hand through her already untidy hair. "I just...don't know." She sat back down. "I'm sorry. I know I'm quick to fly off the handle recently. I'll ask Robbie here since you're so keen to meet him. How about Sunday? I'll cook."

Liam wasn't keen. Unless keen counted as wanting to see her dump another new man who'd be useless and hurt her as others had in the past. He hoped she was being careful. That this bloke was such a terrible cook that he'd given her food poisoning every morning and not... He wouldn't go there.

"Whatever." Neither could he summon the energy for keen.

"Good. I'm going to have a lie down and hope this headache clears. We'll talk more tonight." She kissed his cheek before she left. The familiar honeysuckle scent of her perfume swirled around him and almost made him feel as if 'it' didn't mean anything at all.

Chapter Five

The atmosphere hadn't lightened any by the time Martin stepped back through the front door, armed with a bag of fish and chips for two. Katie was home, earlier than usual. She'd discarded her shoes and bag in the hall, and Liam had probably presented the case for the prosecution already. By this time tomorrow, he might well be out in the cold. So there was even more reason to enjoy this one night off while he still could.

He took a wrapped parcel containing his early dinner and sat down in the lounge. Liam had a box set of *Breaking Bad* in the bookcase. He'd keep amused by starting from the beginning.

"Get your filthy feet off the coffee table." Liam appeared in the doorway, wearing an expression not dissimilar to the one he'd worn after catching Martin in Katie's bed.

Martin focused on the tops of his trainers, which were far more gray than white now. A series of holes edged the worn pink soles, and a speck of mud now grazed the glass surface of the table. He shifted his feet to the floor and made a mental note that the time had come to invest in a new pair of shoes. "I got you something from the chippy. In the kitchen, if you're interested."

"I'm not."

He'd change his mind when the irresistible aroma of freshly fried fish batter had a chance to permeate the air. Liam was big on food and there was a lot of him to feed. "Suit yourself." Martin nibbled a chip. "Katie home, then?"

"Yep." Liam grabbed the remote from the coffee table. He switched on the TV then fixed his attention to the screen like he was all set for the evening.

So much for the box set, then.

The big guy wasn't going to make this easy, which was obviously the intention. Martin focused on chewing while applause from some quiz show thundered in the background. "You working tonight?"

"Nope."

"Same." Small talk was pointless around Liam but, since only just gaining an appetite back, he'd be damned if he'd let anyone ruin his dinner like they had his breakfast.

Following a few minutes of furtive side glances, Liam got up and went into the kitchen. The microwave hummed for a couple of minutes, then he returned with a plate of fish and chips. "You did say I could have this?"

"Bought it for you, didn't I?" Martin tried not to look smug. "It's a peace offering."

Liam sat down with his prize. "A bribe, more like. Hasn't worked, though. I'm still going to have a word with Katie about getting you out of here." He pushed a chip in his mouth then returned his attention to the telly.

Going to have a word? So, as yet, nothing had been said. That was probably more than he deserved. He made a mental note to check the local property sites, just in case. Best to keep one step ahead, so life didn't fuck him in the arse too hard and often. Unlike his job.

"I meant what I said." Martin stared into his barely touched dinner. "I won't bring no one else here."

"Makes no difference. I didn't want you here in the first place, especially after I found out what you are."

"I never tried to hide that." He used to, in other places. Sometimes the lie caught up with him, but he'd gotten a good vibe here from the off. Katie had conducted the interview. Her uncle owned this place and she and Liam rented from him. Their previous flatmate had moved on, so choosing a new one was supposed to have been a joint decision. Katie had made a unilateral one and told him he could have the room right there and then. Which probably went some way to explaining why whatever he did rubbed Liam up the wrong way, even when doing something nice like buying dinner.

When Katie had asked after his line of work, he'd already prepared a lie. A waiter in an all-night café. Vague enough he didn't need to give names and no one would go checking. They'd got on so well together he'd decided on honesty. She'd thought he'd been joking at first, then she'd shrugged and said 'whatever floats your boat'. All he had to do was pay the rent on time and check Button at the door. To date, he'd managed to follow only fifty percent of the rules. But at least they were the most important fifty percent.

"This flat is not a knocking shop." Liam slapped the arm of the chair. "It's mine and Katie's home."

"I know."

"I don't think you do, else you wouldn't have done it." Liam snatched up his empty plate. "You finished?" He gestured to the half-eaten food nestled in the paper on Martin's lap.

"No. And I'm sorry." He looked away.

Liam grunted. "You should find another job. Even sweeping the streets must be better than letting blokes do whatever they like to you."

"I don't let them—"

"Afternoon, gentlemen." Katie came in, dressed in her pajamas, and flopped down on the couch. "Ooh, are you done? I'm starving." She swiped a cold chip from Martin's dinner and rested her head on his shoulder while she ate.

Liam noticed and tossed him a couple of daggers. "I'm going down the pub."

"Oh. Then I'll see you later." Katie lifted another chip from the wrapper. "Needs ketchup." She got up and disappeared into the kitchen.

Liam's daggers lengthened to swords. Swords customized to flamethrowers. He whipped up a gale as he stormed down the hall and out of the front door, which he shut none too gently behind him.

Katie returned with ketchup in hand. She glanced around the room. "He gone already?"

"Yep."

"Typical." She upended the bottle over the chips. "You ever had a guy offer to cover you in sauce and lick it all off?" She angled her eyebrows, her smile mischievous as she resumed her seat.

The powerful taint of tomatoes wafted up Martin's nose and brought with it a memory of that morning in the pub toilets. He so wanted to let the ordeal rest now. "None that could afford to pay what I'd charge. I hate the smell of ketchup."

"That's what it is with Liam, you know." She tugged the paper from his lap to hers.

"He hates the smell, too?" Who knew they had things in common after all.

"No, buffoon. Your job. Liam's moral. He went to Sunday school as child. Never missed a week."

That explained a lot. Those religious types always poked their puritanical noses into other people's business. "He thinks I'm a pervert. Like I might taint Saint Katie with my freely available wiles."

"If your wiles were free, I doubt there would be so much of an issue." She gnawed on a crisp piece of batter. "But it is an issue you should deal with sooner rather than later."

"I fucked up last night." Literally. "Liam would call it being disrespectful."

"That's what Liam's grandfather might call it. What happened?"

"I brought a punter back." If he didn't do this, Liam would. He'd rather she heard the raw truth from him than the exaggerated version from Liam. "A paying client. Since my bedroom's a mess, I used—"

"Liam's?" She let out an odd laugh. "No wonder he's extra pissed off at you today."

"Not Liam's room, no."

As the color drained from Katie's face, the heaviness of

regret settled over him. She folded the paper around her food, scrunching it up in such a fashion that the contents would be mashed to pulp in no time. "Oh. He didn't tell me."

Was Liam in trouble now? That hadn't been the intention. He needed to fix that before she got the wrong idea. And he definitely wouldn't mention the dildo Liam had found in the bin. Not unless she noticed it was missing, anyway. "He thought that you were better not knowing because of how you'd feel."

"Then why mention it now?"

The hurt seeping out of her made him wish he'd kept quiet. Liam wasn't to blame. This was all him and the fear of losing Roy's custom. "Because I wanted you to understand Liam's not the bad guy."

She looked up, defiance flaring through the hurt and disappointment. "I know Liam's not the bad guy. I love him, and there's nothing anyone could do or say to change that."

He should have kept his trap shut. This was why he didn't do the friendship thing. Too many complications he couldn't afford. "If I could have a week or so to find a room, that would be great. If not, I'll go before Liam comes home." He didn't have much, and preferred it that way so when the unexpected happened he was only ten minutes from being packed.

Katie grabbed his arm as he rose. "If I were to ask whether you had any intention of repeating what you did last night in my room the answer would be not a chance, wouldn't it?"

Martin sank into the couch. "It was a one off. I made a mistake, and it won't happen again." He meant every word. He wouldn't risk bringing a punter here a second time. He'd been an idiot to let Roy talk him into it in the first place.

Katie placed her hand on top of his. "Let's think of what happened as a mistake and move on. No harm done, is there?" She smiled, and the gesture appeared genuine. "The bed was second hand when I got it. It's probably seen all sorts of action in the past."

Martin wasn't sure if her being nice was better than her demanding he get out of the flat this minute. "Liam was right, though. I did invade your privacy. Bringing work home with me was never going to make a fan out of him, was it?"

"Or me. But even I wish you'd pick something else to do with your life. You're better than you give yourself credit for."

No, he wasn't. She wouldn't think so either if she knew what he'd done. A lifetime of whoring couldn't make up for his crimes. But that was his secret. One he'd take to his grave. "If you say so."

"I do. And since I don't want to go into lecture mode, that's all I'm going to say on the subject." Her serious face lit with another smile. "You want to watch a film? There's popcorn in the cupboard."

Easy as that? A bit of honesty and he was safe again. Oh, yeah, he'd definitely been thrown out of worse places for less.

Chapter Six

Liam was weaving his way home from the pub when he plowed into a tall, bony bloke hanging around the bushes at the corner of the building.

"Sorry, mate," Liam said, although technically he'd been the one backed into.

The bloke spun around. "No, you're all right. My fault." He ducked his head and finished zipping up his jacket.

He looked like he was waiting, like a taxi driver who had come to take Martin far away. Right. Like that sort of luck ever landed Liam's side of the fence. Besides which, even cabbies had better taste in clothing.

As Liam walked away, he chanced a look behind. The jacket sported a picture on the back. Hard to tell in the dark, but it looked like a pistol with smoke puffing from the barrel. If confirmation were needed that the jacket was the ugliest piece of clothing he'd ever set eyes on, that was it.

Katie and Martin were curled up together on the couch, watching *The Woman in Black* and hiding behind a large bag of microwave popcorn. The four pints he'd necked down at The Stag numbed him to the poisonous effects of the cozy sight. He belched before dropping into the armchair.

Katie clutched Martin's skinny arm and buried her face in his shoulder. "I hate when the dead kid climbs out of the swamp. I'm closing my eyes. Let me know when it's over."

Liam's shoulder offered broader protection, but Katie wasn't over here with him. She didn't so much as look at him.

"Popcorn?" Martin offered out the bag with a too-bright smile. A smile Liam couldn't read. Sincere wasn't a word connected with Martin. Of course, it might help if those lips weren't so full or perfectly shaped.

"No." Liam fixed his full attention on the dead boy traipsing from the swamp to the big old dilapidated house. The kid reminded him of Martin a lot. Cruddy, dirty and very unwelcome.

Katie's phone buzzed. She leaped off the couch in her haste to drag the thing from her dressing gown pocket. "Hello? Really? Whereabouts?" She primped at her frazzled hair. "I can't. I'm in my pajamas. What, *now?*" A giggle. "Fine. You twisted my arm." She hung up. "Sorry about this, guys, but I'm going to have to suspend the rest of movie night. I have a better offer." She straightened her robe and pushed her feet into her pink slippers. "How do I look?"

"Tired," Liam muttered.

"Robbie's downstairs. You don't mind, do you?" At least this time she directed the question at him rather than her new bestie.

"Would it matter if I did?"

"Actually, no. I would invite him up, but that's best left until you're in a better mood. You remember about Sunday, don't you? You will be nice when you meet him?"

Why did she sound as though she expected him to grab this guy by the throat with one hand and twist the guy's nuts off with the other? In his fantasies, maybe. In reality, he was almost certain he'd be able to control the urge. "'Course."

"Good." Her smile surrendered to a frown. "But somehow I'm less convinced than I was before." She paused to brush a kiss across her BFF's peach-soft cheek. "I'll see you later, hon."

A kiss *and* a 'hon'. Liam didn't get anything more than a muttered 'Goodnight' as an afterthought from the doorway.

When she'd gone, he got to thinking about the bloke in the beige jacket outside. What if that had been his first encounter with the new boyfriend? The man had to be twice Katie's age and sported a dress sense even lousier than his own. The bastard smoked, too. He'd reeked of nicotine. And why wait so long to ring? He might have knocked on the door, come to that. Unless Katie had stuck a 'beware of the flatmate' sign on the intercom.

Martin didn't speak after Katie had gone. He made no sound apart from crunching his way through the popcorn. But Liam had plenty of things to say, and there was no time like the present to make a start.

"You've made yourself right at home here, haven't you?" Liam stared at the TV but kept Martin in the corner of his eye. He'd come up with a plan after that fourth pint. Since Katie had left them to it, now was the ideal time to cash in. Or out, as the case may be.

"About as much as you, I reckon, seeing as we pay the same rent."

Great. Martin had brought up the money subject without the need for a prompt. Taking the unintentional cue, Liam slipped his wallet from his pocket. He withdrew a mix of twenties and tens, placed them on the coffee table and waited for a reaction.

Martin eyed the cash and wondered if he should say something. Probably, he should. Since Liam had made such a grand gesture of fanning the notes out like a royal flush.

"Your half of the takeaway only cost five quid," was about all he could manage.

"It's yours if you pack up and leave."

Did he mean at this precise moment? Some hope of that. Martin slid a socked foot across the table, scattering the cash over the floor. The action lent him a faint sense of satisfaction, considering this was a complete role reversal of what had happened that morning when his fifty quid had ended up in the same place. "Two hundred is nowhere close to getting me out. Two grand and we could talk."

Liam smashed his fists down on the chair arms. "Don't you think I'd offer you *ten* grand if I had it?" He pushed to his feet. "You'd be out already if I told Katie how I found you this morning. That's most of my wages you got there. You'd better take it. We're never going to get along, and if I had to ask Katie to choose who she'd want to share with, we both know she'd pick me."

Martin raised an eyebrow. "You sure 'bout that?"

"Yes."

No doubt at all in his mind, then. Liam was right. Katie would always side with her best friend and unrequited lover in the end. Wasn't even worth mentioning that Katie had forgiven him for last night. Liam wouldn't see things any differently. No one had offered him their life savings to up and leave before. He'd been thrown out of places. He'd left places in the middle of the night with the rent due the next day. But having someone offer him cold hard cash to disappear was a first he didn't care to repeat. "Is that your plan, then? To hit Katie with an ultimatum? You or me?"

"If I have to."

Martin gestured to the bank notes on the floor. "You could've done that without offering the cash. Which, coincidently, is my going rate for a shag."

Every muscle in Liam's substantial body tensed. "Don't even bother to go there."

Martin fended off a triumphant smile. He didn't feel much like celebrating. "Relax. I don't fuck people I like, anyway."

Liam opened his mouth then closed it again. "What?"

"Yeah, so I think you're okay." He set the popcorn to one side then slipped to the floor to scoop up bank notes for the second time that day. "You got morals and principles. That's a good thing. You're also overbearing and kind of sanctimonious, but you'd make for a dead loyal mate. All I'm saying."

Liam snatched the notes from Martin's outstretched hand and rammed them into his pocket. "I'm never going to be your mate."

"You made that more than clear enough already." Katie and Liam's relationship was far more important than his stake in this place. Besides which, he made sure not to get too comfortable anywhere for long. His welcome always ran out, usually sooner rather than later. "I'll start looking first thing in the morning."

"You serious?"

"Yeah. I can't stay someplace I'm despised every minute of every day." He picked up his shoes and started for the door. "Even I ain't that insensitive."

"Where are you going?"

"Out. Since I'll need to find a deposit for another place, looks like I'll be working tonight after all."

Chapter Seven

Martin walked from the flat, head down, hands tucked into his pockets. A fine rain dampened the air like a sneeze, but he barely noticed. Liam shoving money at him had affected him more than he'd care to admit. Baiting the guy was one thing, but now he realized just how much this wasn't a game. Liam wanted him out and he had no real choice left but to go.

He'd never make one of life's good guys, but he could do good deeds occasionally. Or unselfish deeds. What was the word? Altruistic? Yes. He'd made an altruistic decision. He just wished he'd felt better about making it.

He'd had a proper home, once. Not perfect by any means, but it had been real enough. He'd had a family who'd loved him. Not in the right way, but love was love. Whatever problems he'd had as a kid were a ton better than those he had now as an adult. He didn't like living alone. He liked being around people. People who'd notice if he disappeared. People who'd consider him worth plowing up fields or dredging rivers for even if, in reality, they gave no more of a passing shit about him than they did a total stranger.

He sat on the edge of the quay with his feet dangling over the water. Behind him the day had dribbled to darkness, and he huddled in the shadows to watch the world go by. Across the thin stretch of water, several yachts were moored, their rigging clanking lightly with every flick of the breeze.

Later, he'd wander down toward the cycle track. Punters often gathered there in the trees looking for what the likes of him had to offer.

"Button?" A thin, youngish guy in glasses and a waterproof jacket stepped out of the murk. An uncertain smile caught in the light from the pub behind them. "Thought it was you."

Then again, punters often didn't even make it as far as the trees.

Martin dusted off Button's best smile. "Oh, hi, Chris." Chris probably wasn't his real name any more than Button was Martin's, but names didn't matter. Only intentions.

"Everything all right?"

"Yes, thank you."

"Are you working?"

Working to summon Button from the dark space inside him, but he didn't suppose that was what Chris meant. Chris was a regular. Sometimes they met on the track. Sometimes he'd get a call. They always fucked in his car, and Chris never lasted more than a couple of minutes, anyway. Easy money, he was. And that was always welcome.

"Not officially." He fluttered his lashes and willed a blush to ripen his cheeks. "But seeing as it's you…"

Chris squatted so close the murk of river water reflected in his glasses. He slipped a hand over Martin's thigh and squeezed. "I was hoping you'd be around tonight. I tried to call you earlier. Your phone was off."

Martin tightened his grip on the quay wall, nails gouging the moss-covered stone. "It needs charging."

"I'm parked nearby. We could…" At the clip of footsteps echoing along the quay, Chris whipped his hand away and yanked up his hood.

"Is something wrong?" Martin asked as the footsteps veered into the pub.

Chris shrugged. "My wife's been asking questions recently. She might be having me followed."

Martin looked past him at the vague blur of people through the pub windows. "Why would she be having you followed?"

"Because she suspects I'm having an affair."

Martin widened his eyes in the style of a shocked Button who definitely held morals not dissimilar to Liam's. "And are you?"

"Wouldn't dare." Chris grinned then pushed to his feet. "I'll meet you in the car park by the cycle track. Ten minutes?"

"Okay," Martin replied, but Chris was already melding with the shadows.

He remained where he was for a few minutes more, then started to make his way along the quay. He passed the new-build flats and followed the line of the river beyond the boatyard, where the hulls of dry dock yachts and cabin cruisers loomed from the shadows.

When he sensed someone behind him, he glanced back and caught the vague outline of a figure down the road. Too far to claim he was being followed, but the sensation was there, nonetheless. He'd probably picked up the paranoia from Chris, who was always way too jumpy for his own good.

He passed several used car showrooms at a trot rather than a stroll, then practically jogged to the unpaved car park surrounded by a heavy curtain of trees. The white people carrier was already parked at the far end. Chris stood by the open rear door, chugging on a cigarette.

Two hundred quid would be waiting on the rear seat, arranged over a towel to catch any mess. The towel wasn't needed. Button had yet to come once from Chris' clumsy ministrations.

After pocketing the cash, he crawled onto the back seat. Chilled air wafted over his bare backside as he slipped his underpants and jeans to his knees.

Chris wasted no time jumping in after him, then shoving a cold, dry finger up his arse. "You're not lubed."

Martin winced at the burn. He usually prepared in advance, but following that row with Liam he'd just wanted out of the flat and hadn't thought so far ahead. All he had on him was his wallet, door key and a strip of condoms.

Fortunately, his apparent lack of professionalism might do him a favor. He wasn't comfortable here now that he suspected someone had followed him up from the river.

"I forgot to bring any, but we could drive into town and get some." He widened his eyes and pouted, but Chris was too busy fumbling with a foil packet to notice. "You know how tight I am. I don't like it to hurt." He sniffed for effect. "We can find somewhere else to park up afterwards. Somewhere quiet."

"No." The word emerged as a low growl. "I can't chance being seen. I don't have the time, either. Now bend over."

Chris lunged. Martin twisted away. Past experiences had taught him a dry cock in an even drier arse chaffed like hell for days afterward. He pressed his rear to the seat. "Don't you have something else we can use?"

Chris swore under his breath. "A minute." He withdrew and stretched over between the front seats.

While he rummaged in the glove box, Martin sat up and peered through the window at the deserted car park. They were close to the trees, but he couldn't see anyone lurking in the bushes. No camera flashes that would indicate photos to be shown to Chris' wife as proof of her husband's infidelity. But then, if there was someone hidden they wouldn't want to be seen.

"Vaseline." Chris jerked back, wielding a jar. "That'll do, won't it?"

"I guess." Martin took the jar and opened it, determined not to relate the oily stink to Chris' baby. With the thick gel coating his fingertips, he reached between his legs and angled his hips. Slicking himself up with his jeans and pants lodged around his knees wasn't the easiest of tasks, but he managed to insert a couple of fingers before Chris gave him a polite but firm shove.

"Come on, Button. My wife thinks I've gone for a pizza."

Martin flipped over, resting his forearms on the seat and shoving his arse in the air. Almost immediately, the blunt end of Chris' cock prodded his entrance. He hadn't had much time for a good dousing with the Vaseline, and Chris never lubed up, so the burn of penetration spread from his arsehole to his hips. He buried his face in the seat and tried to ignore the milky whiff of baby sick.

As soon as he had a man inside him, a switch flicked off his head and he tuned out. He'd trained himself a long time ago, when sex had still physically hurt. Very few of his clientele had ever gotten him off, and Chris had never been one of them.

Chris pounded like a madman a dozen or so times then grunted and collapsed. His harsh breath pushed hard at the back of Martin's head. "I can't tell you how much I needed that."

Martin rested his cheek on his hands. His consciousness slipped, urging him home to a clean bed. But after tonight he wouldn't have the luxury of either. He'd need to sell a few times more tonight if he was going to make that deposit on a new place.

"You've not fallen asleep on me, have you?"

If only sleep would come as easily as Chris did. But all Chris was hinting at was that his time was up, his usefulness over. "I almost did." He sat and rubbed his eyes, Button style. "You know how much you tire me out."

Chris traced a delicate but cold finger under his chin. "Me and whoever comes before and after. Your beauty is enough to blind most of us to your bullshit, but I'm not that naïve. And the truth is, neither are you."

Martin flinched away. A trick penetrating his disguise was as powerful as a wielded knife.

"I've got to go." He opened the door and slipped out into the cold air, jeans and pants hugging his ankles.

"I'll be seeing you, Button." Chris climbed from the back, over to the front and into the driver's seat.

Martin fumbled to pull up his jeans as headlights flared. The engine roared. Chris lowered the window and tossed something out before reversing the car.

A sliver of moonlight beamed down from behind a cloud and highlighted the used condom in a puddle at his feet, bloated and half submerged in the mud.

Martin fastened his fly then sent a wish for the moon to stay high and bright as he started along the path through the trees toward the river.

The air prickled with a rain-chilled breeze. Anyone in their right mind would be at home. The reason he wasn't was because he'd pushed too far with Liam, and there was no use pretending—

"How much?"

The voice drifted up from the river. Martin squinted but couldn't see much of anything except blackness. The gentle slick of the water rolled in farther down the bank. The bushes rustled. A hand appeared, waving a couple of notes. If he were in a better mood, he might have laughed. Whoever that cash and that hand and that voice belonged to had been watching too many pornos. Or crime dramas involving murdered prostitutes, most likely.

He stayed on the path and wiped a hand across his face. *How much?* He'd heard those exact words many times before.

"Come on, skank. Haven't got all day. I need a seeing to. And fast."

Muffled laughter flitted through the trees to the left of the speaker. Two blokes. Not so amusing anymore.

Déjà vu exploded around him. The last time he'd heard that question had been that morning, in the pub toilets. The same voice doing the asking. He'd bet money on the hand belonging to an arm encased in a tan-colored jacket.

Two words struck his mind at the exact same time.

Fuck. Run.

He made two steps before powering into something far bigger and more solid than he was. He breathed in a lungful of nicotine and rain-scented sweater, then pulled back hard. No faces. Only trees and darkness. A thick, fat palm slammed over his mouth from behind. A broad arm clamped around his chest. He lashed out with his feet as he was lifted high off the ground.

Trees blurred past as he was dragged deeper into the shadows. The hand over his mouth stank of smoke and earth, stifling the scream tearing at his throat.

A wet mouth pressed to his ear. "You want to know what happens to dirty queers like you?"

No. No he didn't. Even if he could speak right now, he doubted his answer would count for much, anyway.

"We drown 'em."

Water splashed under his feet. Distant lights across the river blinked on and off. The chill soaked his shoes and the hems of his jeans. His heartbeat thundered around his body, seeking escape. There was none. He tried to dig both feet into the mud, but the ground tilted away. A heavy force struck the back of his neck. He went down, plunging into stinking ice-cold froth. A vicious grip embedded in his hair, forcing him forward, head first. Panic surged through him. Filthy water slicked down his throat. He thrust out his hand and grabbed water. And mud.

A fine haze of light blinded him. Warmth spread through his groin. He'd pissed himself. Instead of shame, he experienced only gratitude at the heat through the chilled water.

He stopped struggling. The terror seeped away, along with the searing pain in his chest and the cold biting his bones. He couldn't move. Didn't want to move. Just to float, unfeeling, while the world carried on without him. And there was nothing to mar this perfect utopia, except the irritating voices.

"We're supposed to scare him, moron. Not kill him. Now what the fuck do you know about CPR?"

"Not a damn thing. And even if I did, I'm not going near that with my mouth. God knows what I'd..."

The voice fractured. Martin gulped air and a world of sensation flooded in around him.

The wet. The mud. The cold. He couldn't see or move.

He could hear, but the voices had faded into the void. The silence was worse.

He rolled over and coughed into the soggy earth, damn near choking up a lung. When the coughing fit ended, the cold set in. He didn't know he was shivering until he realized he couldn't stop.

Chapter Eight

Liam lay on the couch, quietly dozing with the TV playing to itself. Something had woken him. Something separate from the TV. He could have sworn he'd just heard a knock at the front door. With reluctance born of interrupted sleep, Liam levered free of his chair. Katie might've changed her mind about staying over at her waster boyfriend's and forgotten her key.

He peered through the spy hole and found only the door opposite theirs. No one there. He opened the door on the off chance there had been a late delivery and expected to find a parcel on the floor.

Instead of a parcel, he found Martin hunched against the wall. Soaking wet and covered in mud. Pale hair turned the color of a grubby puddle. A watery trail led down the hall, starting, or rather finishing, where Martin had dropped.

If someone had told him half an hour ago he'd find Martin washed up — literally — after a night out, he would have sat there in his armchair with a smug grin. But imagining such a fate and seeing the results right here in the hall were two entirely different things.

Martin's eyes were half-lidded. The dirt staining his skin stank of river mud. A sudden cough punched the air.

"What happened?" Liam stepped outside and squatted at Martin's side. "Who did this? One of your customers?"

Another cough bounced up from Martin's lungs, this time accompanied by a spray of water. "Bugger off."

A dousing in the river hadn't improved his manners, but he didn't require an immediate trip to A&E.

"Come on." Liam tugged his shoulder. "Let's get you into

the shower. You stink like a week-dead halibut."

Martin's hands came up in a half-hearted attempt to bat him away, but he wasn't going anywhere. He often dealt with difficult patients at work and knew how to handle their flailing limbs safely enough. He sank to his knees and grabbed firm hold of a wet, bony shoulder.

"Leave me alone, you great fat arsehole." Martin gifted him a feeble elbow to the ribs.

"Listen, swamp boy." Liam kept his voice low. "I don't know what happened to you, and to be honest, I don't care." A lie, but he had little time to sympathize even if he had sympathy to give. "You think you're feeling bad now? Then imagine it's morning and all this mud you're caked in has set right through to your bones. If your intention is to give yourself pneumonia to cadge a few extra days here, don't bother. Katie's too caught up with this new dickhead boyfriend of hers and I'm not going to play your nursemaid, seeing as I can't stand the sight of you. You want to end up in hospital? I'll call an ambulance to cart you off. But once you're out, you don't get to come back." Harsh? Probably, but Martin would be a lot easier to handle if he cooperated rather than fought.

The speech must have sounded partway convincing, because Martin stopped struggling. "Feeling's mutual."

"What?"

He grabbed a handful of Liam's sweater and pushed his face closer. "Can't stand the sight of you, neither."

Glad they had settled things, Liam helped him to his feet. They made it to the bathroom, where Liam sat him down on the toilet lid. He kneeled at Martin's feet and removed both shoes and sopping wet socks. "What happened?"

Martin sat with his head bowed, hands forming fists in his lap. "You said you weren't interested."

"Did one of your customers do this?"

"No."

Liam teased a straggly weed from Martin's hair. If not a customer, the culprit must have been someone who didn't like the business he conducted. Hazard of the job, Liam supposed, like the bruises. "I've ended up in the river a time or two myself in the past. Usually after a night on the lash."

Martin raised his face "Wasn't chucked in." His nostrils flared. "Some fuck tried to drown me."

Drown him? For real? Unlikely, in Liam's world. But Martin didn't share his world. Martin skulked in dark places looking for things Liam would rather not contemplate. The reason he'd gone out tonight was to earn the money for a deposit to put down on another place. Because Liam wanted him out.

"Did you see who it was?" he asked, desperately trying to veer from the dark space that had opened up at the base of his stomach. A fathomless pit labeled Liam's Fault.

A wisp of emotion passed across Martin's face. Confusion? Puzzlement? Before Liam could fully interpret it, his expression blanked again. "No."

"What do you remember? Enough to give the police a description?"

"Police?" Martin leaped to his feet. He lost his balance, flailed around then slumped back on the toilet seat. "Not a chance."

"If someone tried to kill you, then the police need to know."

"If?" Martin spat the word. "There is no if. They held my face under the water. I couldn't breathe. I felt as if my lungs would burst and I'd die in sewage and that weren't the worst part."

"What was the worst part?" Liam wasn't sure he wanted to know, especially as his imagination supplied more than enough lurid details.

Martin sniffed. He kept his chin low and his words emerged barely audible. "That I didn't care, and no fucker else would, neither."

Since Liam had spent the best part of eight weeks wavering between begrudging acceptance and acute

64

dislike, he couldn't provide much to argue against. "You must have someone who'd miss you. Katie would, for one. If you disappeared —"

"That's what you want me to do."

"Not into thin air. Don't you have family? A parent or sibling or someone?"

"No. And I don't want none of your pity, neither."

Liam sat on his heels. "Good, because I reckon I'm about the last person to give you any."

Martin lowered his head again, looking smaller and more humbled than Liam had ever seen him before. "Just didn't realize 'til now even I don't give a shit about me, that's all."

That part of the conversation was best left where it was. Liam couldn't lie and make like he suddenly gave a shit. Martin would see clear through him. He stood and backed toward the door instead. "You want to get into the shower now? Don't run the water too hot."

He hung about by the open door, to double-check Martin wasn't going to sit on the toilet seat all night. But Martin didn't twitch. He didn't do much of anything except breathe.

Damn. Katie should be here to deal with this. Martin was her friend, her choice of flatmate. Her responsibility. But Katie wasn't here. She was out with her ageing loser of a boyfriend. Which meant either he was going to get lumbered with Martin, or Martin was going to get lumbered with him. Neither prospect appealed.

He'd witnessed the effects shock could have on a person. What sort of bastard would he be if he walked? Even if Martin swore blue murder he didn't need any help.

The shower wasn't hot enough to steam the air, but a slow uncomfortable humidity swirled around the small room all the same. Liam searched for his work ethic as he approached. "You need to take all this wet clothing off. You're not going to warm up until you do."

"Huh?"

Was Martin spacing because of the shock, or was he

mulling over the fact that he believed no one cared whether he lived or died? "Clothes off. Shower in. Okay?"

Martin managed a slight nod and didn't object when Liam helped slip the jacket from his shoulders. Next to tackle was the drenched sweater beneath. That task wasn't quite so easy.

"Too cold," Martin complained, hugging his elbows closer to his body soon as Liam exposed a couple of inches of belly.

"Not for long." Liam tugged at the sweater. "Can you at least try and help out?"

Martin made another weak attempt to shove him away. "Already told you to fuck off, didn't I?"

"You did. But as I said, I'm not nursing your pneumonia." Before he got the chance to object again, Liam whipped both sweater and T-shirt over his head.

Martin hunched over, drawing his arms close. His body looked unmarked, except for the earlier bruising. *This could have been a lot worse than attempted drowning.* Liam couldn't be sure worse hadn't taken place, but surely Martin would be in more of a state if that were the case? Although he must be used to strangers groping and using him, if anyone had hurt him in that way, wouldn't he be more reluctant to have his clothing removed? Might be a wise idea to check.

"The men who did this, they didn't do anything else? Nothing the police might need your clothes for." He couldn't ask outright, he dared not.

"No police."

"But—"

"Nothing else happened."

Ah, so he had understood the vague inquiry. "You sure?"

Martin fixed him with a stony stare. "I think I'd know."

He probably would, too. At least that was something. "Can you stand? There's no getting the rest of your things off if you don't."

Liam braced for a smart comment. None came. Martin's jaw was too busy chattering to waste time on comebacks.

With help and support, he got upright. There were only his jeans left to remove, and he could take care of those himself.

Martin kept his head bowed as he shoved his jeans and underpants down past his thighs. When he straightened, he revealed his subdued cock nestled against shaven skin. Even his balls were hair-free.

"Hey, straight dude. Why you staring at my dick?"

A sliver of light filtered back into Martin's eyes. Liam focused on the running shower to hide his rioting blush. "You got nothing I want to see."

Martin coughed again and clutched the sink as he stepped out of his wet jeans. "Calm down. I ain't questioning your sexuality. Straight guys look, too. It's a size thing, right?"

Did the question require an answer? Liam didn't know. The one thing he did know was that he'd stayed in this room about five minutes too long. "Seeing as you're more alert now, you can deal with the whole shower situation yourself. I'm..." He gestured to the door with his thumb.

"Don't run off." A naked Martin ventured forward, streaked in dirt, melding with the shadows ghosting the slats of his ribs. "I didn't mean nothing by it. Even if you weren't straight, I still don't fuck people I like."

Yes, he had said so earlier. Hadn't made much sense at the time, but now the statement warranted more serious thought. "What about boyfriends? I assume you like them."

"Dunno. Never had one."

"A boyfriend?"

"Nope."

"You only go with men for money?"

"Why? You wondering if you can afford me now?"

Liam twitched, refusing to give in to the urge to sprint for the door. "Not a chance."

"Go, if you're worried I might molest you. Now I remember why I don't ask no one to do me any favors." Martin climbed into the shower, flashing his small but compact arse before sweeping the curtain closed.

Instead of heading through the door as his senses

demanded, Liam leaned against it. He needed to demonstrate how he wasn't intimidated by sharing space with a naked rent boy. Even one who could be bought for a relatively small amount of cash and who claimed to have never had a boyfriend or fucked anyone he liked.

Martin wasn't the sort of person anyone could make sense of. He was a nasty bastard one moment and almost amiable the next. Now the intensely private Martin had told him things only friends should know. But they weren't friends, were they? Not when they could barely stand the sight of one another.

Chapter Nine

The water wasn't nearly hot enough. Martin craved heat as much as cleanliness. He twisted the dial as far as it would go in the hope of killing the chill of the river and the weird thoughts buzzing around his head. Such as that bizarre conversation he'd just shared with Liam. Where he'd practically admitted that if he didn't fuck for money, he'd still be a virgin.

Sometimes his lifestyle caught up with him. Not just the physical dangers, but the emptiness, too. Like tonight. He'd get over it, he always did. But Liam was waiting to ensure he emerged from the shower in one piece, and that raised his temperature every bit as much as the water.

He grabbed the nearest shower gel and lathered a blob in his hands. Steam filled the bathtub and curled around his head in a big puffy cloud. Leaning against the tiles, he ignored the chill and searched for the fuzzy space he'd taken refuge in when he'd thought he'd been about to die. Not the terror of drowning, but the freedom of what had come after. A tranquil place locked somewhere deep inside his mind. If he could relax enough he might find that sense of peace once again while the water rained down around him, surrounding him...

Heat gushed through his body. His brain simmered, his vision popped. Tipping sideways, he flailed for the shower curtain. His feet went out from under him and he landed hard in the bottom of the bath.

The steam evaporated. Liam stood over him, one hand on the shower curtain and the other on the shower's dial. "What did I tell you? You're meant to warm up slowly."

Liam worked in a hospital. He knew what he was talking about. Didn't mean he'd get any credit for it, though. He offered out a hand.

Martin looked away. "Fuck off."

"Make up your mind." The shower curtain rustled back into place.

"No. Wait. Liam?"

The curtain slipped aside again. A shadow fell over the bath. Liam's hands curled around his biceps and lifted him free of the bath as though he didn't weigh more than a bar of soap. Then he was gently guided backward toward the toilet.

"Sit down." A towel was shoved at him. "I'll put your wet clothes into the washing machine."

Martin sat. "I got some money in my jacket. Least, I did have." He didn't recall either of the two guys who'd attacked him groping around in his pocket. Not for money, or for any other reason come to that.

"In coins, I hope."

"No." Martin wiped the towel over his face. "A couple of hundred in notes."

"Hundred? Where did you...?" Liam gawked at the clothing as though he'd just discovered a decomposing rat nestled in the center. He picked up the jacket between thumb and forefinger. Perfectly fine to take the thing covered in river slime, but not so keen now the pocket contained a bundle of immoral earnings. Best not to mention he'd pissed himself.

"Ain't catching." Martin stood and tucked the towel around his waist. Shouldn't make a difference, seeing as he'd spent the past ten minutes naked. But with Liam wearing a face full of distaste, somehow it did.

"What isn't?"

"What I do for a living." Martin took the jacket, unzipped the pocket and removed the roll of soggy cash. "This came from a respectable married man. It's about as clean and normal as you can get." As he thrust the bundle forward,

Liam flinched. "You're such a fucking hypocrite." Martin returned to the toilet seat and began unrolling the cash. None of the notes were ripped or stained. They'd be fine once they'd dried.

"Why?"

Martin raised his face "What?"

Liam stepped close again, still armed with his clothing. "Why am I a hypocrite?"

"Because you want me out. And so I got to earn enough to find someplace else to stay. I know you'd sooner see me sat on the street with a begging bowl, but that ain't going to be much fun for me."

"I didn't say you had to leave right now."

Didn't he? Martin didn't remember so much about that. "I still got to make enough to put down a month's rent up front." He shivered. "Could you put the heating on?" He offered out the cash. "And dump this lot on the radiator to dry. Another couple of nights and I'll be out of your hair."

Liam's brow creased. "You're going out again *tomorrow?*"

Why does he sound so disapproving? It was hardly fair considering what had happened. "You can't expect me to go out again tonight. You try getting yourself half drowned and see how much you want to fu —"

"That's not what I mean." Liam snatched the cash. "You're not listening to me, are you?"

"I am on some level or we wouldn't be having this conversation. I just can't work out what you're getting at."

Liam turned away, cash in one hand and clothing in the other. "Doesn't matter. I have a feeling I'd be wasting my breath."

Probably so.

After Liam had gone, Martin cleaned his teeth and paused to study his reflection in the mirror. He half-closed his eyes, plumped his lips and found the mask Chris had seen right through. If others had too, then he was getting too old to play this character. What if acting vulnerable made him vulnerable?

Once or twice in the past he'd considered creating another alter-ego. Someone tougher and more street-savvy. Someone more believable. But he'd played this role for so long he wasn't sure he could become someone else so easily. Besides which, there wasn't a role out there more popular with his clientele than sweet, naïve almost-virgin. Tough street slut just didn't carry the same appeal.

He searched his pockets again, seeking a key that didn't want to be found. Either he hadn't brought it with him or he'd lost it in the river. Not that it mattered, since he wouldn't need a key to this place anymore, anyway.

He hung his wet jacket on the bathroom door then made his way to his room. He'd spend his time in here for the remainder of his stay, since even when he wasn't trying to piss Liam off he still managed to do so. There were only so many times he could take being looked at as though he were a scraping from a tramp's foreskin.

After discarding the towel on the floor, he climbed into bed and brought the covers over his head. Tomorrow might be a better day, but instinct told him it would be worse.

Chapter Ten

Liam found Martin's wet jacket hanging from the bathroom door. A bathroom devoid of Martin, who had cleared off to bed without a goodnight, let alone a thanks for helping out. Liam gingerly lifted the jacket from the back of the door with his thumb and forefinger. He'd add it to the rest of the things in the washing machine, after going through the pockets. That would prove a challenge in itself. Who knew what lurked inside?

In the kitchen, he gathered his nerve and delved inside the left pocket. There was something in there. A strip of condoms and a half-dissolved receipt. The condoms he'd expected and set aside, but the receipt warranted further inspection. If he squinted hard and angled the receipt toward the kitchen light, he could just make out a transaction for eighty-odd quid spent at a place called Floss's Florist. *Eighty-odd quid on a bunch of flowers?* This from someone who never showed much evidence of having any money and who reckoned he had no one to care about him.

Who could Martin be buying flowers for? He knew damn well if he asked he'd get accused of pawing through Martin's pockets. The best thing to do was go to bed. In the morning, he'd ask all the questions echoing around his brain. Only something told him if he got any real answers from Martin, he probably wouldn't like them.

He'd barely closed his eyes when a yell pierced the air. At first, he was half convinced he'd imagined the noise. When he heard the cry again, he sat up. Clad in his boxers, he swung his legs out of bed, stood and made his way out into the hall. He was most of the way to Martin's room when a third cry hit the air, this time more of a sob than a shout.

"Martin?" Liam tapped on the closed bedroom door. "You all right?"

No reply.

Pressing down on the handle, Liam braced for a tirade of abuse. Through the open door, he could just about make out a raised ridge under the duvet. The ridge shifted. Liam opened the door a shade wider. The hall bulb threw a shaft of light across the room, which shimmered across Martin's bare chest and wide, glassy eyes.

"Liam? What d'you want?"

"You were yelling."

"Was I?" He ran a hand over his face. "Must've been dreaming."

"That's what I thought." Liam wanted to make his apologies and leave, except an apology didn't sound right because he had nothing to apologize for. *Damn, why is this unnecessarily complicated?*

"It was flashbacks. Sorry if I woke you."

He'd dithered too long. Now Martin had stolen the apology for himself. There was no need for it, though. Liam would be having nightmares if a couple of blokes had grabbed him and held him under water. "I wasn't asleep."

He'd been halfway there, but now he didn't feel tired. His body clock always went haywire after coming off night shift. The daytime nap had been a mistake. Now all of a sudden he was alert and raring to go, without anywhere *to* go. Except to bed. *Great idea.* He started to retreat.

"Wait."

Liam stopped. "Why?"

Martin sat up and switched on the lamp. He drew his knees to his chest. "Did I say anything?"

"When?"

"When I was shouting."

"Nothing I could make out."

"Oh." Silence. "Can you stay?"

"What?" Liam didn't doubt he'd heard right. He just

hadn't expected such a request.

Martin straightened his legs and the duvet slipped to his naked hips. Liam wanted to look away but couldn't. It was enough to battle the uncomfortable heat building in his boxers, combined with trying to figure out what Martin meant about staying. "Why, when, what, why. You ask a lot of questions."

He might, but he still hadn't received any answers. "Why'd you want me to stay?"

"Not to molest you."

Liam chanced a smile. "Already ruled out."

"Good. And like I said, don't matter."

"Tell me." Liam inched forward. "Go on. You might as well."

Martin pulled the duvet to his waist and smoothed out a couple of invisible creases. "The one who shoved me under the water, I've seen him before."

One of his johns, probably, but Liam didn't think that worth mentioning. "Where?"

"This morning. No. Yesterday morning, in the pub. He gave me the extra bruises."

"The same bloke both times?" Liam didn't mean to sound so disbelieving, but if this wasn't some random attack then someone was out to get him.

Martin nodded. "I just wanted to mention it, you know? Just in case."

"In case of what?"

"Why'd you think? In case the next time I go out I don't come back."

The words were cold enough to chill Liam's blood, yet Martin didn't sound bothered by the prospect. He could have meant back here, rather than from the dead. Couldn't blame him, seeing as he hadn't been made to feel welcome. He should have sounded a lot more worried. "Is that likely?"

"Dunno, but I'm beginning to suspect there's a shallow grave out there with my name on it."

"Don't."

"Why not? Unlike most of the soap operas and films out there, it ain't only women who get raped and murdered."

Liam shifted closer, letting his curiosity and perhaps a genuine touch of sympathy get the better of him. "Mind if I sit?"

When no objection was forthcoming, he perched on the side of the mattress. He wished he'd put some clothes on, rather than flashing his out of condition body overhanging a pair of not-exactly-his-finest boxers. He didn't care what Martin thought of him, but he'd have felt more comfortable with another layer or two around him, for decency's sake if nothing else. "Seeing as I'm here, why don't you tell me what happened?"

"Not much to tell. Some bloke cornered me for a blow job in the pub. Only when we get down to it, all he wants is to beat the crap out of me. Least he didn't wreck my face. I got off lightly." He frowned. "Don't look at me like that. How many guys would pay to fuck a face without teeth?"

"You got a certain way with words, Martin. Anyone ever tell you that?"

"Nope. Ain't no fucker interested in what I got to say." He suddenly brightened. "Least I got to keep the hundred for the blow job he didn't get."

Cash was evidently Martin's number one priority in life, and that saddened Liam in more ways than he could understand. "What else happened?"

"Nothing. Except, he was one of them what tried to drown me. I recognized his smell. Cigarettes and some cheap, rank aftershave."

"You sure it was the same guy?"

"I recognized his ugly tan jacket, too. It had a picture of a gun on the back."

Liam thought back to the guy outside the flat. The man he'd assumed was Katie's boyfriend, but wasn't even close to her usual type. He was too rough-looking for one. And too old for two. And he'd been dressed in an ugly tan jacket, complete with gun on the back. "Who've you pissed off?"

"No one." Martin's voice rose a pitch, though Liam hadn't meant to pose the question in the form of an accusation. "Any of the blokes I might've pissed off, which I haven't, wouldn't bother to toy around with me first. They'd take me down one time." He lifted a finger for emphasis. "I'm careful not to piss off those kinds of people."

"Don't you have someone you work for?"

"What, like a pimp?" He laughed, but Liam failed to see anything funny. "Nah. I freelance."

"But you must hang around in some dodgy circles."

"Not really. And I ain't never taken a drug stronger than paracetamol in my life. I also don't drink, so — "

"Occasionally."

"Huh?"

"You told me you drink occasionally. Hence." Liam gestured to where the whiskey sat on the chest of drawers.

"No, that ain't mine."

"Then whose is it?"

"Not important."

Wasn't it? Martin had kicked up too much of a fuss for the bottle to not be. If the whiskey wasn't his, he might've brought people — men — back here who did drink. In which case…

Liam sprung to his feet, straining to control the fire of his sudden rage. "You've had someone else here. How many times? While Katie was home? Does she know?"

Martin recoiled. "Where did this come from? I only had one bloke back."

"So the bottle is his?"

"No!"

"Then whose?"

"I just told you some nutcase might possibly be trying to off me, and all you care about is who a lousy bottle of cheap scotch belongs to? Cheers, big man. It's about as cold in here as the shallow grave that's already been dug for my dismembered body."

"One grave or lots of little graves? Except the one for your gob, that'll be the size of a quarry."

Martin folded his arms. "You ain't funny."

"Then quit with the theatrics." Liam breathed out the embers of his anger. "Start talking properly."

"Define *properly*." Martin lifted his chin. "I didn't make nothing up. I didn't try and drown myself, did I?"

Liam resumed his seat. He decided to take a chance and mention his suspicions. Perhaps between them they might start figuring out what was going on. "I saw him, too."

"Who?"

"The bloke in the jacket. He was hanging about when I came back from the pub."

Martin sat forward. The light from the lamp cut a sharp beam across his face. "You sure?"

"I thought he was Katie's boyfriend, seeing as he called saying he was outside."

"Robbie's tall with dark curly hair. Not bad on the eye, but he's a touch too weedy for my taste."

Weedy? Like Martin was a built hunk. "This guy was in his late thirties. Grubby-looking. And he reeked of stale cigarettes."

Martin dragged the duvet to his chest. "That's him. There was another one, too. I didn't see him, but I heard them talking."

"About what?"

"Not sure. My ears were full of water at the time."

The bitter edge had returned to his tone. Liam didn't blame him. If someone wanted to hurt him, how far would they be prepared to take things? Who might get caught in the crossfire? How was Katie to defend herself if this guy decided to go for Martin's friends in order to get to him?

"You can't just do nothing." Liam watched for his reaction, to see if he was taking any of this in. His life could be in real danger, but all he did was sit there, chin set at a defiant slant, like nothing was exactly what he intended to do. "What happens the next time they corner you?"

"I won't let it happen."

"How are you going to stop it?" For someone who claimed to be streetwise, Martin was doing a great impression of not having a clue. "Especially if there are two of them."

"I'll talk to them. Invite them back for coffee and a freebie while I'm at it."

Liam opened his mouth to inform Martin what could be done with that idea. Then Martin raised his eyebrows. *A joke. His least amusing yet.* "Seriously."

"Seriously?" Martin dropped his grip. The duvet fell away, once again exposing the pale skin of his slender chest. "I will talk to them. Or the tan jacket guy, if he's still hanging around. I got nothing that can't be bought while I'm alive. And they don't want me dead. I heard one of them say something about giving me the kiss of life when they thought they'd gone too far." He frowned. "If they'd tried, I'd have bitten their fucking tongues off."

Why did he have to sound so casual about this whole thing? Liam saw death on a near daily basis and he'd never become immune. He'd seen the shock manifest in Martin's body, and most of this was bravado now. He could deal with fear. Breaking through a front made up of faux arrogance was another matter entirely. "Well, whatever it is going on with you, I don't want Katie involved."

"Neither do I," Martin said with an indignant catch to his tone. "And I'll be out of the way soon enough. The chances are you won't inherit my groupies once I've gone."

"Let's hope." Liam couldn't deny that life was bound to get easier without Martin here with his shady underworld connections, but making him leave now was a touch mercenary. The only way he could appease his conscience was by thinking of Katie. If anything ever happened to her because he'd taken back his demand that Martin leave, he'd never forgive himself. No, he wouldn't put her at risk. Not for anything. He stood and made his way to the door.

"Liam?"

Liam paused in the doorway. "Yeah?"

The bedcovers rustled behind him. "Don't suppose you'd mind sticking around?"

Liam turned around. "Why?"

Martin was lying down in bed with the covers drawn to his neck. "I dunno. Because if I go back to sleep I'll start making a shit load of noise again. I need to take my mind off what happened. That good enough?"

Basic translation — he was scared and he didn't want to be alone. He huddled in bed, the lamp bathing his face with a sickly light. Liam couldn't remember seeing anyone so vulnerable. Whether this was another act or not, he didn't know. But neither could he walk away.

"Ten minutes." He made his way back to the bed and resumed his perch on the edge.

"So it's finally sunk in I ain't after your body?" A suggestive smirk revealed itself in Martin's words, if not his face.

"Almost."

Martin hooked his hands behind his head. His armpits were scattered with a fine dusting of hair the same shade as his eyelashes. He didn't shave everywhere, then. "Sex is overrated, anyway. It's a bit like working in a cake shop and filling your face with cream buns every day. After a while even *you* would go off what's on offer." What was that, a sly dig about weight and Liam's penchant for cream doughnuts? "Then there's me." He lowered his arms and drew the duvet to his shoulders. "Who's never had much of a sweet tooth in the first place."

The comment took longer to translate, but there was nothing to misinterpret. "You're saying you don't like sex?" Liam's mouth dried right up.

Martin wrinkled his nose. "Now you think I'm weirder than before."

"No. I just assumed..." He didn't know what he assumed. Sex with strangers, any stranger with the money, couldn't be much fun. But to actively dislike sex entirely was another matter altogether.

"The blokes I get with pay to get themselves off. None are bothered about how I feel. What I get is the cash."

"Then how do you stand it?"

"I disconnect. In my mind, I go to someplace far away. Somewhere sunny, like Tenerife. I once went there as a kid and it was nice."

"You do that with everyone you're with? Even those guys you like, or who don't have to pay?" This was none of his business. Martin was well within his rights to tell him to lay off such personal questions, but he'd assumed Martin enjoyed his work.

Martin looked at him blankly. "They've always paid."

Then he'd meant it when he said he'd never had a boyfriend? Never made love. Just fucking. For business. He must have to shut himself away every time to stay sane.

Now another question nagged. Something so revelatory, Liam couldn't not ask. "Martin, are you sure you're gay and not—"

"What? Gay for pay?" Again Martin wrinkled his nose. "I've never fancied girls, and I got bored of trying pretty fast."

"It shouldn't be about trying," Liam said quietly. He should know, having tried to find someone he might care about as much as he'd cared about Katie for years without success. He'd also given up on trying.

"I like guys. I like looking at the male form." Martin gestured to the porn wall. "If any one of them stunners wanted to challenge me to feel something in bed, I'd gladly accept. But it's too late for me. I'm getting old and cynical. And I'm so going celibate when I retire."

"When will that be?"

"Dunno. Years probably."

Liam battled to keep his irritation concealed. "I don't understand you. You hate what you do but you want to carry on for years? You have other options."

"I need the cash."

"What for?" They'd had this conversation before. Martin

hadn't given a proper answer then, and Liam didn't hold out much hope of one now.

He shrugged. "Just do."

Pushing for a reply wasn't going to get either of them anywhere. Their conversation dried. It wasn't an easy thing, sitting there half-naked on the bed with a gay rent boy, as opposed to a straight rent boy, if such a title existed, trying to figure out what made him tick. Also, wherever he looked he was confronted by an erect cock. Or a close-up of a smooth, well-muscled arse. Sometimes both together. Those pictures were so out of place considering what he'd recently learned.

"Why all the porn?" he asked the whiskey bottle on the chest of drawers. Just so he couldn't be accused of ogling again.

"There's a method to it. Ain't just gratuitous lechery."

Liam looked back. "How'd you mean?"

Martin raised up on his forearms. "No one wants to be caught having a perv at the gay boy's porn collection, do they? Since mine are on the walls, it's usually enough to keep the straight guys out."

"You get a lot of straight guys sneaking into your room?"

"Some places. Usually after a few drinks and a failed night on the pull. A mouth's a mouth, at the end of the day."

"You let them?" Liam tried to keep any hint of judgment and disgust out of his tone. He didn't think he'd entirely succeeded.

"If they pay up first, why not?"

Liam could think of many reasons, but none Martin would want to hear. "Katie thinks they're hot. Especially the one you used to have on your door."

"Yeah. That's cos he looks like her new bloke."

"Robin's *that* good-looking?"

"His name's Robb—wait." Martin's eyebrows shot up. "You think Poster Guy is hot?"

The heat returned to Liam's cheeks. He leaned back, hoping to catch some shadow. "In a purely visual sense.

He's a model, so one would assume…"

"One would assume?" This time when Martin laughed, Liam almost joined in. "You got the better body."

Liam's desire to laugh dried up. Not so much that he'd never stand a chance against a bloke like that, more because of the clear ridicule in Martin's words. He battled the urge to cover himself with the spare half of the duvet, but that would mean getting into bed with Martin properly. He definitely wasn't about to do that. "No need to take the piss."

"I wasn't. That guy's too skinny. I only picked him because he's got a cracking—"

"Great knob? Like the bloke you had in Katie's bed."

A hint of a smile curved Martin's lips. "Roy's an exception. He's an old guy, but he knows how to make me feel good, too. There's not many who can do that."

"You like him?" Bad enough Martin sold his body to strangers for sex, but there was something extra uncomfortable about the thought of him building relationships with them, too.

"He's all right."

"He's also nearly three times your age, presumably married, and paying what he thinks is a seventeen-year-old boy for sex."

Martin hugged the duvet again. "Don't put your judgmental head back on just yet. We're doing all right here, ain't we?"

Surprisingly, they were. Liam didn't want to spoil things either. "You tired?"

"Nah. Still cold, though."

"Heating's on. You should put on some clothes." He hadn't meant to sound so disapproving, even less so since he himself sat here in a thin pair of boxers.

Martin flipped back the corner of the duvet. "Get in. I see your goosebumps frosting over."

Getting into Martin's bed was not a good idea. He didn't think he was being seduced, but had already knocked the idea of climbing under the covers with Martin on the head.

"You still think I'm after your body? Even after what I said?" He really sounded hurt this time, and Liam didn't want him thinking that.

Liam shooed him across the mattress and climbed under the warm covers. It was a bit tight, but he wouldn't stay for long. Just until he'd proven to them both that he wasn't being lined up as Martin's next paycheck.

Martin lay back down and closed his eyes. With his features relaxed and peaceful, he appeared every inch the teenage innocent he played. Button might con anyone into anything with a face like that. His eyes flickered open again and he flashed a sudden grin. Liam found more familiarity within that self-assured smugness, because this was Martin. Not the work face, which Liam didn't trust.

Martin's grin faded. "Why you looking at me like that?"

"You're different from how I thought. I'm just trying to guess if this is the real you."

"Could say the same about you."

Liam didn't see how. He was always himself, as far as he was aware. "In what way?"

"You've been a total tosser since I got here. But, aside from what I do for a living, I don't understand why."

That was easy. Jealousy. From the moment Martin had moved in, Liam had seen the way Katie had responded to him. Nothing sexual, but something far more meaningful that Liam already shared with her and didn't want to share with anyone else. He didn't feel comfortable enough to confess, even after all that Martin had confided in him.

"It was all about having someone new here. Would've been the same with anyone." A short and inadequate answer. He waited for more questioning. That would give him the excuse he was looking for to leave.

"Good to know it weren't all personal. Thanks for sticking around."

"No problem." He'd already stayed too long. Didn't stop him from sitting there a while longer. Just until Martin had fallen back to sleep. Then he'd go back to his own room. And try to figure out how the fuck he'd ended up in Martin Bailey's bed and almost liked it.

Chapter Eleven

Liam couldn't decide what woke him first. The warm weight across his chest or the loud bang that jerked him back to reality. He opened his eyes to the harsh dazzle of a bulb from the lamp on the bedside table. Beyond the light, half concealed by shadows, naked men frolicked across the walls in a variety of obscene poses. He wished they were the cause of the stiffness in his groin, but they weren't. No, the culprit was the slight weight heating his chest, belly and between his legs. *Especially* between his legs.

When he tried an experimental shift across the mattress, Martin snuffled and whined before stilling again. *What to do? Push him away?* Liam could claim that for his initial urge, but it would be a lie. He'd woken content and now he couldn't summon the energy to feign disgust and horror.

Another bang echoed off the walls, this time accompanied by a less than quiet, "Oh, bugger."

At the sound of Katie's voice, adrenaline blurred his vision. The disgust and horror he hadn't felt before dove on top of him and beat him hard in the chest and gut.

Oh, bugger, indeed.

* * * *

Martin dreamed he was lying on the surface of a warm, calm lake. He drifted along, perfectly content to let the water absorb the many things wrong with his life until he couldn't pinpoint what those troubles were. He let them sink to the bottom, leaving ripples in their wake as he floated free.

Just when he thought he'd be happy lying there forever, the calm water bubbled. A huge clawed hand reared from the depths and grabbed his head. Dragged down into the water, he couldn't breathe. Couldn't move. He opened his mouth, but the monstrous hand kept him under like he was drowning all over again.

"Martin. Shut up." The river monster spoke with Liam's voice.

Martin stopped gurgling and blinked up at a pair of familiar brown eyes. He gripped Liam's wrist and ripped the palm from his mouth. "What the fuck are you doing?"

"Shush," Liam hissed, his hand still hovering threateningly close. "Katie's back."

"So?"

Liam's expression grew more incredulous. "I'm in here with you. What's she going to think?"

"You're not gay. What's the problem?" Even before he finished asking, he realized the problem. It involved the porn pictures and the straight guys and the sad fact that a mouth was simply a mouth. "She wouldn't think that of you." He shoved Liam hard enough that the big guy shifted over on the mattress. "I wouldn't take your cash. You've tested me on that, remember?" He rolled out of bed to the chill of the morning air. Last night he might've made a friend. But in the cold light of day, nothing had changed. "Why are you still here?" He dragged a clean T-shirt from the depths of his drawers.

"I don't know. I must've fallen asleep."

Martin spun with a wicked retort ready to crack the air. When he found Liam fixated on his groin, his retort almost choked him. If he hadn't turned around, that same rampant attention would still be glued to his arse.

Martin didn't suffer from body hang-ups, having stood naked in front of so many men that he'd long ago lost any sense of self-consciousness. But with Liam gawking at him like that, his skin burned from his cock all the way up his torso and roared like a furnace through his face.

He pulled up his jeans but kept his face lowered. "How about I go see if she suspects you and me have been hammering the night away? If she does, I'll be sure to reassure her you won't be seeking no loan from her to settle your debts."

"She's not going to believe I paid you for sex." Liam sounded as though there was about as much chance of Katie believing he'd paraded around the flat in her bra and thong in her absence.

"There you go, exactly my point. There's no reason not to tell her the truth, is there?"

Liam lowered his voice. "I'd rather she didn't know I spent the night here. With you."

At a display of such furtive guilt, Martin realized no one had the right to make him feel so damned insignificant. He'd suffered enough of that the night before with those two goons who'd tried to drown him.

"I won't say nothing if you don't." He grabbed his phone from the bedside table. Two texts awaited him. A reminder from a regular, and an appointment request for later on that morning. He thumbed a quick acceptance to both.

"Can't you do that later?" Liam asked from the bed. "You don't have a lock on your door."

Martin slipped his phone into his pocket. "Katie won't barge in on me. She's got better manners than you."

Liam opened his mouth then closed it again. He'd probably just remembered yesterday morning when he'd barged in with a bin, or last night when he'd barged in with a complaint. "Tell her I got called into work."

"Whatever." Martin slammed the door shut behind him, wanting that lasting sound in his ear rather than Liam's words. Words which served to make him feel one level closer to the gutter than he already was.

Katie was sitting at the table, flicking her way through a pile of twenties. She had on her smart work suit, but her hair stuck out in all directions and she'd not got started on the war paint yet. She was still counting when Martin picked up the kettle.

"This might sound strange, but why was all this cash on the radiator in the lounge?"

Martin contemplated. "Mostly because the radiator in the bathroom's loaded with your knickers."

"Hmm." Katie clearly wasn't anywhere near impressed by that excuse as she was by the money in her hand. "There's two hundred quid here."

Martin grabbed a couple of mugs from the cupboard. "Coffee?"

"Um, no. And it's a bit stiff."

Martin automatically glanced at his cock then winced. *Sex. Obsessed.* "I dropped it." Down the toilet? That would certainly put her off wanting to keep counting those notes. "In the sink."

"The sink?"

"Which was full of water."

"How did you drop so much cash at once?"

"Not sure. Was arguing with Liam at the time."

"Again?"

"Yeah. It's a hobby of mine." He peered through a gap in the blinds. "You see anyone loitering outside this morning?"

"Like who? The postman?"

"No, like a guy in a tan jacket with some stupid gun design on the back."

"Robbie dropped me off and had to go straight to work. Can't say I noticed. Why? Is he one of your admirers?"

Nice way of putting it. Could Liam ever be as tactful? Probably not. "No. And no reason." The car park looked deserted except for cars and a lone, smartly dressed woman with a briefcase heading off to work.

"I was hoping Liam would give me a lift, but he's not in his room. He's not working this morning, is he?"

How much easier would it be to say yes and get Liam off the hook? But then Liam had looked at him exactly how guys looked at him after they'd used his body. With a mix of condescension and contempt. Sod easy. And sod Liam, too. "Liam's off shagging."

"Shagging?" Katie's surprise echoed through the kitchen. "Liam's met someone? When did this happen?"

"Dunno, but he called last night. Said something about staying over. Biscuit?" He offered out the packet.

"No. Who was he with?"

Martin put the biscuits back in the cupboard then set the coffees on the table. "Some racy piece from the hospital." He took a seat. "Nurse, I think."

Katie tapped the pile of notes. "Liam doesn't go for racy."

Martin could believe that. Liam probably wouldn't even cop a feel before he'd asked the girl to marry him.

"He doesn't do one-night stands, either. He has to know a girl a long time before... Oh." She slapped a hand over her mouth.

"What?"

Katie lowered her hand. She picked up her coffee. "Nothing. Forget I said that."

"Forget you said *oh*?"

"Yes." She peered up at the cupboard. "Did you mention a biscuit?"

"Like you'd scoff a chocolate Hobnob for brekkie." Martin shuffled his chair closer. "That 'oh' meant something, didn't it?" The cruel streak running right through him craved the slightest hint of ammunition with which to batter Liam for the way he'd been made to feel this morning. He loathed feeling sordid more than anything.

She sipped her coffee. "It did not."

"Did, too."

She met his eye. "Tell him, and I will kill you."

Oh, wow. This was going to be priceless and Liam was so going to pay for making him feel like trash. "Agreed. Won't say a word." He leaned closer. "Well?"

"If he was having a one-night stand it'll have been with a..." She lowered her voice. "Bloke."

"A bloke?" How did she mean, a bloke? He'd specifically said shagging and she'd repeated the word so she hadn't misunderstood. "Liam's straight." One of the straightest men he'd ever known. But then, he'd caught Liam gawking at his cock. Not once, but twice. "Fuck. Me."

"*You?*"

"No!" He definitely didn't want her thinking that, any more than Liam did. "We can't stand each other." Liam had seen him naked. Liam was straight. "He can't be gay. Not with how he feels about..." He shut his mouth. He couldn't give away that secret, no matter how much he'd like to.

"You mean with how he thinks he feels about me?" Katie laughed. "Liam's not in love with me, hon."

His mind still reeling, he couldn't begin to put his thoughts into words. "How do you know?"

Katie laced her hands together on the table. Suddenly this had gone from a jokey banter to deadly serious. "I'm not saying he is gay. He's had a few girlfriends, but he's never been in a serious relationship. He never looks entirely comfortable when he is with someone. What he is in love with is an idea."

"What idea?" That made no sense. Was she airbrushing over Liam's emotions? Pretending they didn't exist so she didn't have to deal with them? Pretending he was gay so she didn't have to deal with them?

"The idea of being in love. Or getting married and of having kids, the whole settling down routine. He thinks he wants that with me and if not with me then with some other girl. But, and this will sound conceited, I'm like a fantasy for him. What he feels isn't real. Deep down, he knows it, too."

Martin understood about fantasies. He had to become one most nights. But Liam hadn't made a single move on him, not even furtively. Gay blokes found him attractive, and the closeted ones reached for their wallets quicker than anyone else. "Why'd you think he was with a bloke last night?"

"Because he doesn't tend to sleep with a girl until he's known her half a lifetime and even then, it's never spontaneous. He's never as hesitant to jump into bed with a man."

Which was more or less the same thing as being in the closet. Liam fucked men but wanted to settle down with a woman. In five years, when he was married with a couple of kids, he'd be trawling the streets like Chris seeking a Button of his own.

Katie touched his shoulder. Martin fought the twitch working through his muscles to push her away. She'd done nothing wrong. Just told him the truth. A truth he should have worked out by himself already.

"Keep this to yourself, though," Katie said. "He'd be devastated if he knew I know what he thinks he feels for me. Or that I told you he likes the dudes. I shouldn't have said anything."

Martin couldn't remember the last time he'd felt so betrayed. Liam was no better than any of the other blokes out there who looked at him and saw a mouth or a hand or an arse to be used as and when required. No wonder he hadn't wanted Katie to know they'd shared a bed. "I'd rather not have known, either."

Katie pushed her mug across the table. "Could you do me a favor?"

"What?" He wasn't up to favors. He wanted to go back to bed and pretend he hadn't heard any of the last fifteen minutes. But Liam was in his room. And Liam could no longer be trusted.

"A few minutes ago I peed on a stick."

"Huh?"

"In the bathroom." She grasped his hand, fetching him fully back to the present. "Go see if there's one blue line or two. Don't tell me until after I've finished getting ready for work. That way I'll convince myself I can't cry. My mascara isn't waterproof and I'll get fired if I walk in looking like a half-melted wax doll and scare the kids."

She stood and offered out the cash. Martin took it but hardly registered doing so. First Liam was gay or bi or whatever label fit him best, and now Katie was pregnant. The prospect of a baby, he could handle. He liked kids. Or he might like them if he knew any. Liam was different. No. Liam wasn't different at all. That was the issue. Sooner or later Liam would end up being the same as most of the other blokes Martin had shared space with.

Clutching the money, he made a decision. He'd hump his way through the whole day if necessary, but there was no way he could spend another night under the same roof as a closet case.

Chapter Twelve

Once Katie had clattered down the hall and through the front door in her heels, Liam crept from Martin's room. Just like a secret lover, though nothing had happened between them.

No. Not quite true. Something had. Martin had let down some of those barbed defenses and revealed a glimpse of the person beneath. The person Liam might even come to like, given the opportunity, which was a revelation in itself.

After stopping by his room for clean clothes, he made his way through the lounge and into the kitchen. Martin sat with half a mug of coffee at the table, along with the cash from the night before piled in the center.

"What did you tell Katie?"

"Huh?" Martin sounded vague, as though half of him had traveled somewhere else. To Tenerife. Or did he reserve that place only for when he was having sex?

"Katie. Did she notice I wasn't in my room?"

"No."

Liam assumed the answer applied to her not noticing he was in Martin's room either. More relieved, he prepared a cup. "How are you after last night?"

"You care?"

"Weirdly, I do." Liam collected up his coffee and set it down on the table. "You had any more thoughts on going to the police?"

"Nope."

The answer he'd expected, but he'd needed to ask all the same. "Did Katie mention anything about seeing guys hanging around outside?"

"No." Martin gathered up his cash. "And I reckon last night was just a random thing. Could've been different blokes. Hard to tell in the dark." He pushed the money across the table. "Here. Take this as my final month's rent, and tell Katie I'm sorry I couldn't say bye in person." He got up and started toward the door.

"You're leaving?" Last night Martin hadn't had anywhere else to go. Nothing could have changed since then. Liam rose too, and deposited himself between Martin and the door. "Why?"

"Why not?" Martin stepped forward, the top of his head drawing level with Liam's chin. "Don't tell me you'll miss me once I'm gone. Because I know you won't." His eyes flashed sharp as barbed wire. The hard arrogance Liam had come to loathe during the past few weeks in his company had returned, and he didn't have a clue as to why.

"Is this because I didn't want Katie getting the wrong idea about us?"

"You love Katie, right? I'm fine with that. I like straight people. Straight men. Real straight men like you who still won't touch me when there's nothing else available. I told you stuff. I let you share my bed. I wanted…" He shook his head. "No. It's when I start wanting that everything fucks up." He shoved his way past. "Get out of my way, Liam. Let me go."

Liam grabbed hold of his arm. "Not until you tell me what I've done wrong."

Their gazes clashed. The glints in Martin's eyes honed to shining steel tips. "I felt safe here because you were straight. Dead straight." He dragged his arm free and rubbed his biceps. "I let you take my clothes off me. I let you sleep next to me. I woke up on top of you. You didn't once…"

"What?"

Martin bowed his head. "Nothing."

Liam didn't know what to say or where to begin. He'd had no idea Martin was so broken. Or why. Or how. He shouldn't want to know the answers. Shouldn't, but did all the same. "You talk like every bloke you've ever met is a sex offender waiting for his name to be added to the register. You mistrust us all?"

"No. Not all." Martin crossed his arms. "Just them in the closet."

The penny took a while to drop. "You mean me?"

"This morning you looked at me…not like a straight guy."

Yes. Liam had been checking out the compact form of a nicely shaped backside. His focus had naturally been drawn there. It had been only a look, but to Martin a frail trust had shattered.

"Katie told you, didn't she?" He didn't understand why. She knew he definitely hadn't wanted Martin to know. But despite the irrational reaction, Martin deserved an explanation. "So no. I'm not straight. Not one hundred percent. Or even fifty percent. I don't know. I've slept with more men than women. Which isn't many." He could count the number of both genders in single digits. On one hand. "The women, I was seeing at the time. The men, well, they were more based on…"

"Fucking." The word emerged coated in contempt.

"More or less." Liam couldn't argue with the truth. "But I don't touch men who don't want me in return. I would never touch you."

"Why not?" Martin drew himself up. "Am I too soiled?"

"It's not about that." Whether Martin believed him or not was another matter. "Will you do me a favor?"

"No." Martin was quick to put the table between them again. "No more favors."

"Who else you done a favor for lately?" No answer required. Liam could well imagine the favors he got asked to do.

Martin grabbed the back of a chair. "Don't matter."

It probably did matter, but Liam wouldn't push. "My favor doesn't involve anything more than you thinking about finding a real job. I can put a word in at the hospital in the canteen. It'll probably only be part-time for now, but—"

Caustic laughter grated the air. "What, twenty hours a week on minimum wage? A lot of good that'll do me."

Liam braced against the insult. He did well enough to pay his rent every month and had bought his car outright. He wasn't in debt and he could afford a few pints once a week. He certainly didn't hate himself, which, he suspected, was more than Martin could say. "It's got to be better than what you're doing now."

"You think? Do you know how much I make a week?" Martin moved around the table, suddenly challenging in his swaggering gait. "Fifteen hundred quid, tax free. And that's only an average. How much do you take home? A fifth of that if you're lucky."

Liam tried not to react to the sum of fifteen hundred pounds a week, or the total sum of six grand a month, or to put it another way, seventy-two thousand pounds a year. If that was true, where did it all go? Certainly not to his hole-ridden trainers or his charity shop jeans.

"Why'd you need the money so desperately?"

Martin looked away. "Will you shift out the way? I got two appointments today and I don't intend to miss neither of them."

Liam puffed out his chest and blocked the doorway entirely. Appointments. Was that the official term for selling himself? He was still carrying out his everyday routine even though someone out there was trying to get him.

"I'll pay your fee if you stay here."

Martin once again retreated behind the table. "What?"

Yeah, he was asking himself the same thing. The answer being nothing more than attempting to keep a potential friend safe. That was a good thing, wasn't it? "Four hundred pounds. Keep the two hundred on the table. And the two hundred I took out of the ATM last night. Stay." He forced a smile. "Then we can talk."

"Just talk?" Martin's expression hardened. "After the way you looked at me this morning? Yeah, right."

"I am not going to touch you." He raised his palms. "I'll

swear on whoever's life you want. Katie's—"

"No." Martin barked the word. When Liam frowned, he shrugged stiffly. "Just not her."

"My parents, then?" It didn't much make a difference, since Liam would never break the promise. "I care about them, too."

Martin looked unconvinced. "I still need to keep those appointments. I can't be unreliable or I'll lose business."

"Then I'll drive you." What was he saying? Play chauffeur for a prostitute. Way to step up in the world. But he had offered and, since he'd offered, he couldn't take it back.

Martin gaped at him. "Why would you do that?"

"Because I want to." This was the right thing to do, and he was doing it. "Will you let me?"

Martin stared at him. Probably weighing up the pros and cons. Getting chauffeur-driven to work safely, or take his chances by walking and risk running into the goons again. No option, really. No choice to be made. "If I do, you can't come in. You'll get mistaken for a trainee."

A trainee rent boy? Now there was a thought. "I'll wait in the car."

"Promise?"

As if he'd invite himself in to watch. No. This was about keeping Martin safe because there was no one else to take the challenge on. Everyone deserved one other person who cared if they lived or died. Even Martin. "Promise."

Chapter Thirteen

Much to Martin's relief, Liam did what he said he would, and drove. Apart from asking the address, no other words were exchanged. Martin was grateful for that, at least. He didn't know what to make of Liam now. Didn't know what to make of himself, either, seeing as he'd been completely oblivious to the fact that the guy he'd innocently shared his bed with was attracted to men as well as women.

Plenty of men were gay in private, but to the world played the heterosexual to perfection. That was fine, because pleasing them was what he'd been paid to do. He purposely avoided gay men outside of work because he couldn't allow his life to get weighed down by the vaguest possibility of sexual attraction. He made sure he flat-shared with women or straight men, in the same way he lived with Liam and Katie. Sure, sometimes those straight men wanted more out of him. Mostly that didn't bother him too much, because he didn't care about those guys. But he liked Liam. Liam was safe. Or had been. Now, he was possibly the most dangerous man Martin had ever met.

Graham lived alone in a two-bed semi in the suburbs. Martin had known him about a year. He'd lived alone since his mother had died about six months before he'd first contacted Button through a subtle personal ad in the local paper. They met about once a month. Although Martin rarely made calls in private homes, Graham was a safe exception. Their time together was about as predictable as a brown nylon cardigan. The same could not be said of his time with Liam.

"This one," he said as they passed along a street full of

small, modern houses on an expanding estate.

"The one with the gnomes?" Liam spoke as if people who decorated their lawns with colorful plaster statues were a totally different species from the men who paid for sex.

"Yeah." Martin snapped free of the seatbelt. "You can go now. I'll make my own way back."

Liam pulled up at the side of the road. "Two appointments, you said."

"I can walk to the other one from here." The second one he'd agreed to this morning had been from Charlie, the owner of a small hotel off the high street in town. Charlie arranged hook-ups for a cut of the profit, and was as close to a pimp as Martin would get.

Liam switched off the engine. "I'll wait."

Martin considered arguing. There hadn't been anyone hanging outside the flat. No one had followed them here. He knew because his paranoia had kept him glued to the wing mirror all the way. In the end he stayed silent and opened the door instead.

"Martin?" Liam leaned across the passenger seat. Gold embers flared bright in the depths of his brown eyes. Martin had never noticed before. Come to think of it, he'd never seen Liam under natural outdoor light before. "You don't have to—"

"I'll be about half an hour." Martin slammed the door, trying to tune out those gold flecks and how pretty they were, even shimmering with disapproval.

He made his way up the immaculate garden to the front door. A couple of baskets hung either side, loaded with pink and purple blooms as neatly trimmed as the lawn. Inside, the house was just as pristine. Graham wouldn't have things any other way.

After ringing the bell, he forced his back straight and his shoulders completely still. He would not check if Liam was watching with that steady, condescending and downright judgmental stare.

The door opened. Graham ushered him inside so quickly

he might as well have had 'rent boy delivery service' printed on the back of his jacket. When he turned around, Graham's thin, somewhat crooked body pressed to the closed door.

"Young Master Button." His watery eyes shimmered from behind his thick-framed glasses. "My curiosity demands to be sated. Who is that rather large brooding beauty situated beyond my driveway?"

Brooding beauty? Liam was beautiful, true, but in a way totally incompatible with Martin's idea of beauty, which would be a desert island full of twenty-one-year-old asexuals. People lacking the complication of desire. Then he could retire in peace.

"He's straight," Martin said before Graham could get the wrong idea. It wasn't exactly a lie. Liam had been straight until this morning, but Graham didn't need those details.

"What a pity. My glands were beginning to salivate at the prospect of tasting such a full-bodied aperitif."

"Huh?" Martin didn't always understand everything Graham said. The man had, at one time or other, been a teacher. Or a college professor. From the bits and pieces Graham had confessed, his contract had been terminated as a result of 'a dalliance with one or two select prodigies'. Martin read that as fired for touching up lads in exchange for improved grades.

"Never mind, sweet boy." When Graham smiled, his teeth protruded over his lower lip. He looked like a rodent but was harmless enough. "Would your friend like to come in? Would he enjoy a cup of tea?"

Martin raised his palm. "Forget it. He's just my driver. And he'd knock your teeth out long before he let your lips anywhere near his—" When Graham's eyes flashed, Martin winced. He'd sliced a jagged hole in Button's shiny veneer. Graham didn't like him to use dirty words. The last time he'd said 'cock' in Graham's company, he'd had his mouth washed out with a couple of squirts of anti-bacterial handwash. Not something he'd want to try again in a hurry, not for a lousy twenty extra. "His body."

"Ah." Graham's shoulders slumped under his beige cardigan. "Such is life. Take off your shoes. I'll make some tea." He picked up an envelope from the side table and offered it out. "You have shaved?"

Graham wasn't talking about his face. He rarely shaved there, though he was expected to remain hairless everywhere Graham's mouth was likely to make contact. Most of his clientele liked him bare down there too, so he kept himself hair-free as a matter of course.

"I'm extra smooth today, just for you." Martin took the envelope then produced his sweetest smile. The one that made his cheeks ache.

"Excellent." Graham shuffled back through the door into the lounge in his brown plaid slippers.

Martin took off his recently washed, still squidgy trainers and set them neatly on the doormat. He trod up the cream-carpeted stairs in his damp socks and entered the bathroom at the end of the hall.

Everything inside this house had been scrubbed until it sparkled, but the bathroom was exceptionally bright and spotless. Not a stain or stray hair to mar the sterility, yet the only place in Graham's house where he felt remotely clean was the shower.

After counting out the one hundred pounds Graham paid for a home visit, he pushed the envelope into his back pocket and took off his clothes. He folded them neatly into a pile on the padded chair in the corner of the bathroom. The usual foul-smelling antibacterial gel awaited him inside the shower cubicle.

He spent a minute or two more than necessary luxuriating in the strength and power of the water buzzing hard over his skin and warming him from the outside in. Graham never minded how long he took. Perhaps the reasoning behind such patience was the longer he remained under the jets, the cleaner he'd emerge.

With wrinkled fingertips and toes, he stepped from the shower, careful to keep his dripping confined to the spongy bathmat outside the cubicle door. He grabbed a towel from the free-standing heated towel rack and briskly dried off, keeping his mind focused on rubbing the water from his skin rather than wandering beyond the front door to the end of the drive. If he were to walk to the frosted glass and open the window wide enough to peer through, he might catch a glimpse of the car. Or of Liam, sitting with arms folded in that disapproving stance. Awaiting his return.

A gentle knock drew him back inside the bathroom and to the slight chill wafting over his moist skin. "Button? Is everything all right?"

Martin discarded the towel in a damp heap. Water droplets shimmered on his shoulders and chest. His hair was still wet, but his balls were smoothly shaven and that would be all that mattered to the man waiting beyond the door. And that the towel was dropped in the dirty laundry basket under the window.

He wrapped himself up in the folds of his disguise and fixed on the mask made up of Button's smile.

"Yes. Sorry. I was making myself extra clean for you."

"Your tea's getting cold," Graham replied, still not sounding irritated or impatient. More like a servant offering a gentle reminder.

He never drank Graham's tea. Or anyone else's when working. He trusted Graham as much as he trusted most of his regulars, but the risk of spiking was too high to chance.

Button dumped the towel in the laundry bin then swept open the bathroom door with an eagerness Martin didn't feel. Button adored being touched and devoured by all kinds of strangers in his quest for affection. To Button, the money was a formality and Graham was his extra special favorite man in the world. Later, when he moved on to his next appointment, Button's extra special affection would shift right along with him.

"Come along." Graham sidestepped from the door and once again gestured for him to go ahead.

Their appointments always took place in Graham's

second bedroom, which contained a wardrobe and a chest of drawers. On top of the drawers sat a tray loaded with two cups of tea, a small tube of lube and a pair of latex gloves. Floral curtains were drawn across the windows and a matching rug sat on the floor by the bed. The bedding was always fresh, crisp and white, alive with the fresh scent of laundered sheets. Martin climbed onto the mattress and lay flat on his back, deepening his breath to help him relax.

Graham wisped a hand over the air above his discolored ribs. "What happened here?"

His skin tightened, though no physical contact had been made. Graham never went near him without the gloves. He didn't have to think too hard on his answer. "I fell off my bike on the way to college."

College, not school. He'd considered playing younger, as Graham liked youth very much. But since he couldn't get his conscience to allow such a thing, college it was.

"Didn't hurt too badly, I hope?"

"No. Hardly bothers me now."

"Good. Good." Graham moved back to the drawers and slurped tea. His avid gaze cast a lingering chill along Martin's body from head to toes then back again. He set down his cup and unbuttoned his cardigan. The rest of his clothing soon followed, each piece removed and hung from a hook on the back of the door.

Graham's pasty skin, stick-thin arms and distended middle-aged belly stirred not so much as a spark of passion from Martin's depleting reserves. But what killed him stone dead inside every damn time was the latex gloves Graham took from the tray and put on like a doctor preparing for a prostate examination.

Martin relied on his body to summon the correct amount of desire to ensure everything worked as and when it should. After last night and the possibility that someone wanted him scared or dead for reasons he couldn't imagine, arousal had become more difficult to trigger.

The end of the bed dipped and Graham crawled toward

him. Cold latex probed between his knees. He hadn't realized he'd been clenching his thighs so close together until Graham tutted when they refused to be moved.

Martin let out a slow breath and forced his muscles to soften.

When his limp cock sank into the narrow hollow of an eager and endless throat, something severed inside him. He disengaged, leaving Button to take over while he returned to the car to Liam and those gold-flecked eyes.

"How's it going in there?" Liam asked, peering at the house.

"Same as usual."

"What's he doing?"

"Sucking me off. He ain't half bad at it, neither. I just wish…" Martin clamped his mouth shut. Don't finish that sentence.

"What?"

Then again, since this wasn't the real Liam, there was no reason not to be honest. *"I just wish he was someone else."*

"Anyone in particular?"

"You, I guess." It was okay to say so. This was just a fantasy, after all.

"Me?" A broad grin spread across Liam's face. *"I bet I'd do it better than him."*

In reality, Liam was nowhere near as confident as this. If he were, and Martin didn't have so many hang-ups, their conversation might go along these lines.

"You'd make me feel something. You already do. That's half the reason I got so pissed off when Katie told me you liked guys. That and the whole closet thing." He paused, uncertain whether it would be wise to continue. He never got the chance to talk about his feelings to anyone. No one cared enough to want to know about them, but it was safe to talk to Liam this way. Just to the fantasy version. The real version would run a mile. *"I know you wouldn't touch me. I'm just scared that if you did, I'd like it. That's why I can't stay."*

Liam's scent wafted an enticing spice as he stroked the vertical line of Martin's fly. *"And there's nothing I could do to get you to change your mind?"*

The question reminded him that this conversation was only taking place within his deluded head. Liam wanted the flat to be about him and Katie. No third wheel getting in the way.

"No. But this is fantasyland." Martin wriggled back in the seat, giving Liam all the access he required. "You might give it a go, whatever."

Liam flashed a sexy grin. "I might." He drew the zip of Martin's fly all the way down. When his warm hand reached inside, Martin swelled to attention with a speed that both shocked and excited him at the same time.

He thrust up with his hips, desperate to bury himself between Liam's lips. A warm mouth hugging his shaft made him groan out loud with tangible thanks. He clutched the seat either side of his thighs, focused on the mouth pleasuring him. Liam lapped the underside of his cock, before lavishing the head with a generous swathe of tongue.

Martin arched, lost in the decadence of Liam's eager mouth. A glow rippled over him. When the rough column of an insistent finger breached the ring of muscle at his entrance, he opened his legs and marveled at how far his thighs spread, considering the confines of the car. The finger twisted up inside him, accompanied by a flicker of pain which he chose to ignore. He wasn't about to let a shade of discomfort ruin this moment.

Bringing his hands down to stroke the lush fullness of Liam's thick hair, he paused. Couldn't touch. If he did, he'd know he'd only be clutching at the thinning, lank strands of an aging, disgraced teacher.

Although he wasn't ready to return, the rhythmic waves of orgasm pulsed through him far too soon. He jolted back into his body and to the thickening sounds of Graham swallowing his climax in greedy gulps.

Having feasted on the final trickle, Graham released him to the cool air. He lay there trying to process reality again as a grunting, red-faced Graham proceeded to jerk off between his thighs until a gushing stream exploded over his belly.

"Young Master Button." Graham licked a fat dribble of cum from his lips. "We both tapped the motherlode this morning."

Martin stifled a sound he refused to call a sob. Wet warmth coated his skin from belly to chest. Revulsion slithered through him. "Please could I take another shower before I go?" The words escaped in a rush. He couldn't bear the prospect of being denied permission to leave here with a clean body.

Graham snapped off the latex gloves. He discarded them alongside his tea on the tray. "Under one condition."

Martin sat, and the cooling ribbons of Graham's spunk dribbled toward his groin. He resisted the urge to wipe himself clean with the sheet. Graham didn't like him to do that, and he didn't want to piss Graham off, seeing as he hadn't yet been given permission to shower. "What condition?"

Graham kept his back turned as he put on his shirt and cardigan. "You tell me who Liam is."

The name jolted him alert. "What? Who?"

Graham fastened a couple of buttons on his shirt. "You cried his name precisely upon orgasm. Is he the young man in the car?"

"No." He spoke a little too sharply. "Uh, he's from college."

Graham's eyes sparkled from behind his glasses. "Ah. A budding romance?"

"Not that, either. He's straight."

"Just like your driver. That is a shame."

No, it wasn't. If Liam had been straight, they might have become friends. That couldn't happen now. Even if Liam didn't want him for sex, guys like him didn't queue to date a whore. Especially guys like Liam who would always choose a nice girl to take home to their mother. The best thing all round was to move on before any of that awkwardness had a chance to happen.

"Can I shower?"

Graham looked at him. "May I."

"May I shower?"

A nod. "You may. On the condition I observe. I'd like to ensure you clean yourself. Thoroughly."

Another condition? Graham had said there would only be the one. Still, he didn't much mind being watched. He'd just pretend he was alone.

"Thank you," Martin said after he'd caught Graham waiting for Button's manners to catch up.

Chapter Fourteen

Liam shifted in his seat to ease the pressure against his backside. He tried not to think about the goings-on inside the house, with the old bloke who had opened the door. The images in his head were nauseating to say the least. Even the radio failed to obliterate them completely.

He considered a stroll up the front path and tapping on the door, but ruled that out for obvious reasons. He had nothing to do but sit here and ponder why he'd made the offer to play chauffeur. The bloke in the tan jacket being the main topic of consideration.

Less than twelve hours ago, he'd have shaken the guy by the hand. Twelve hours ago, Martin hadn't yet faced a potential drowning. Something had changed between them overnight. He'd taken the opportunity to talk with Martin properly, not just grunts and complaints and insults. They'd shared a bed, if unintentionally, which admittedly wasn't the wisest move he'd ever made. Not that any move had been made in that sense, but he regretted nothing. Even if he should.

As he returned his attention to the house, the front door opened and Martin stepped onto the path. The punter huddled in the doorway behind him. Frail and stooped, mouse-like in appearance. Liam shuddered at the thought of Martin being touched by that. Even in exchange for cash.

Martin trotted down the path as relaxed as if he'd just dropped off a newspaper, then slipped back inside the car. "I've got to go to the Albion Hotel next. You know it?"

Liam had heard of the place. A veritable flea pit by all accounts. Martin probably thrived in such a dive. "Yeah."

Martin had washed his hair in the house. Now he wore it scooped back off his face. His cheeks were a ripe pink. *From the shower, or the sex?* Now that was something he definitely wasn't about to ask. "So, uh, how did it go?"

Martin fastened his seatbelt with graceful ease. "All right, I suppose."

"What did you have to...?" He couldn't—wouldn't—finish.

"Blow job."

"What?"

"He sucked me off. He's..." A strange light sparked in the depths of Martin's eyes. "Wow. Another déjà vu moment."

"How'd you mean?"

Martin grinned. A real smile, not one of those fake arrogant ones Liam had grown to despise. "This one's a good one. Now I say he's not half bad at it, and that I wish—"

"Enough." Liam clapped his hands over his ears. "No sordid details."

When Martin didn't say anything else, Liam chanced a look at him. He was staring hard out of the windscreen. His cheeks bloomed redder than before.

Liam lowered his hands. "What's the matter?"

"Nothing." Martin shook out of whatever half-trance he'd sunk into and unclipped his seatbelt. "Thanks for the offer of a lift, but I reckon I can walk from here." He made to open the door.

Liam grabbed his arm. "I said I'd take you, and I will. It's safer if I do."

Martin stared at the restraining hand on his biceps. "What, are you my bodyguard now?"

"No." Liam released him. "I'm trying to help."

"Fine. Take me to the hotel. I'll walk back, pack my shit and get out of your way. Agreed?"

Liam didn't want to agree, not with all this going on, yet if he didn't Martin would walk and get into more trouble along the way. The next word stuck in his throat. "Agreed."

Martin clipped his seatbelt in place again. "Can we go

now? I'll be late otherwise, and that's not professional."

What did Martin know about professionalism? Had he ever worked a proper job in his life? "Is this whole thing about you leaving because I happened to glance at your backside this morning?"

Martin looked incredulous. "What, you got no memory of trying to bribe me to leave? No memory of making it clear how much you didn't want my slack, maggoty arse infesting yours and Katie's precious home? Fuck knows why you want me around now. Or why you're ferrying me about town. You're not on the payroll, big man, so don't be getting no ideas on a wage packet."

Caustic Martin had made a sudden and vicious return. Liam couldn't talk to him when he was in this mood. He started the engine instead.

The Albion was a dump of the lowest order. The doors opened straight out into the narrow street. Paint peeled from the wooden window frames and the glass itself didn't look as though it had seen a cloth since Dickensian times. The nets at the windows could've hailed from Miss Havisham's bridal gown.

If he voiced the comparison aloud, Martin probably wouldn't understand. He only knew himself because he had to help Katie with exam questions for her degree. He steered his mind away from Katie. What would she say if she discovered he'd driven Martin to his clients? Here he was, practically condoning Martin's occupation. She'd never believe it possible. A day ago, a few hours ago, neither would he.

"Another regular?" Liam asked, pulling up in the town car park across the road.

"No, but the appointment was made through someone I trust."

"How'd you know it's safe?"

Martin gave him a weird look. "The world ain't out to get me, Liam. Just one scummy bloke. Or two." He surveyed the hotel through the car window. "You can go. I don't know how long I'll be."

"I'll drive you home, you can collect your things and then I'll take you to where you're staying tonight."

"That's not what we agreed. Yesterday, you wouldn't piss on me if I was on fire. Now it's like you, I dunno, like me."

Like him? Not so far from the truth that Liam couldn't offer a smile. "My conscience wouldn't let me sleep tonight if anything happened to you. It's nothing personal. Just the burden of morals and principles."

"Then I'm glad I got none." Martin opened the door. "You must have a ton of better things to be doing than waiting for the likes of me."

"Nope." Liam rummaged in his jacket pocket, seeking change for the parking meter. "How long you think you'll be? An hour?"

"An hour?" Horror etched across Martin's face. "Not bloody likely. Thirty minutes, at most."

Liam didn't understand the emotion. He'd been gone longer with the old guy.

"If on the off chance I'm not, could you come looking? Ask Charlie at the desk." He fixed Liam with his big blue eyes. "Please?"

Liam wasn't fooled by the alter-ego, but he understood that the risks Martin faced were real.

"I can do that. We should swap numbers, too."

When they were done, Martin climbed out of the car. "Thirty minutes." He peered back through the door, his expression grave. "Don't forget."

"I won't."

Seemed like Martin wasn't quite as nonchalant about his appointments as he'd like Liam to think.

"Thanks." Martin almost managed a smile.

"Oh, and Martin?"

"Yeah?"

Liam swallowed. He didn't want to sound like some sort of over-cautious parent, but it needed to be said. "You will be careful, won't you?"

Martin frowned. "I always play safe. Well, for the past few years at least."

That wasn't what Liam had meant. Not safety as far as protection went, although of course that was equally as important. And got him thinking. "What do you mean for the past few years? How long have you—?"

"Got to go, I'm running late." Martin slammed the door shut then jogged across the road to the hotel.

Liam clung to the steering wheel to stop himself from dragging Martin back to the car and demanding his last question be answered. *Past few years?* The more he thought on that, the more he realized he didn't want the answer. And here he was, just sitting here letting an increasingly vulnerable Martin get on with whatever he'd been paid to do.

* * * *

Liam slotted a few coins into the meter then wandered into town. He bought beer, snacks and a copy of the local newspaper. Such a shame most of Martin's stay had involved them bitching at or ignoring each other. Now he was leaving and Liam couldn't get rid of the guilt. The trouble was he didn't have a clue what to do about it, except get Martin safely to his various hook-ups and try to make out like they were mates.

He flicked through the paper and munched on a Mars bar while circling flats for later viewing. Since he was most of the way responsible for Martin leaving, the least he could do was help find a suitable new place. As time passed, he started reading the rest of the paper to keep distracted. Fifteen minutes ticked by. Then twenty-two. Twenty-nine. At thirty-two minutes past the hour, Martin still hadn't returned. Not even at thirty-five minutes past.

Liam hadn't noticed anyone enter or leave the hotel, probably because he'd had his face stuck in a newspaper in the hope of distracting himself from listening to the voice inside his head that informed him, rather snottily, how Martin's problems were more than likely of his own making. Even so, the guy in the tan jacket lurked like a pantomime villain at the back of Liam's mind, creeping closer with each fresh minute.

Having set aside his newspaper, his watch took up most of his attention now. Martin had specifically asked for a check after half an hour.

Bloody morals and principles.

Liam threw open the car door.

The hotel reception matched the neglected exterior. Walls the color of a red wine stain, complete with a cheap desk situated at the far end of the room. A variety of keys hung on hooks from a numbered board. Adjacent to the reception stood a small bar area dotted with rickety chairs and scarred table tops. A set of carpeted stairs opposite the entrance led to the upper level. The air stirred with dust and the raw odor of illicit sex as Liam made his way to the reception.

A big, bald guy materialized from a door behind the desk. Charlie, presumably. "Help you?"

"Yes. I'm looking for a…" He was inclined to say guest, but Martin wasn't a guest. What was he here? An employee? He wouldn't go by the name Martin, though. He'd be an entirely different persona. "Button."

"Button?" Charlie's bushy eyebrows leaped to the center of his forehead.

Liam blushed like he'd skipped back ten years and his mother had caught him ogling porn on the family computer. "Yes. I've got an appointment."

"Another one?"

Liam stood straighter. Did he give the impression of being a regular? "No. This is my first time."

Charlie gave him a once-over. "You don't say."

Did it matter what this creep thought of him? He was never setting foot inside this place again. Once again Martin's big, pleading blue eyes flashed into his mind. Accompanied by one word. *Please.* "Where is he?"

"Room twelve." Charlie nodded toward the stairs and Liam started in that direction. "Go gentle. Button's already had a busy afternoon."

How busy could a thirty-minute session be? He didn't ask. Didn't want to know. Room twelve sat at the end of a narrow corridor laid with a moth-eaten red carpet that puffed dust with each step.

One knock received no answer. A second knock fetched a sob. A quiet noise, almost like a sex sound. He pressed his ear to the door. "Button? You in there? Let me know you're okay and I'll go, like we agreed."

The cry sounded again. Louder this time, like no sex sound he'd ever heard. Not that he'd had a ton of experience that way.

"Martin? Answer me." He tried the handle. It wouldn't budge.

Another cry passed through the door. Muffled, but with more urgency.

"Open up! Now. Or I'm calling the police." Liam shoved his shoulder hard to the wood. A jarring pain vibrated through to the bone, but the door remained upright and locked. "Hold on. I'll go and get another key."

He hurried back to reception to find Charlie on the phone.

Liam stared hard at the board behind the desk. The key hung on the hook beneath the number twelve. Whoever had taken that room had returned it, and left Martin in enough of a state he couldn't talk. An icy dread bled under his skin. "I need the key to room twelve."

Charlie lowered his arm. "What are you babbling about?"

"The key to room twelve." Liam punched a fist down on the counter. "Hand it over. Now."

"All right, fella." Charlie returned the phone to his ear. "Call you back, buddy. I got some business to attend to here." He rang off. "Now where's the bloody fire?"

"Mar—Button—he's stuck in the room. Don't you check them?"

"Those blokes haven't been gone ten minutes."

"Blokes?" *Dear God, there was more than one?* "Could you unlock the door?" Liam dredged up a pleasantry because it beat the alternative of mashing this numpty's face into the desk.

"All right, all right." Charlie unhooked the key and lumbered around the counter. They took an age to reach the room, with Liam uselessly ushering him on from behind.

As soon as the lock clicked, Liam bulldozed the man out of the way and forged inside. He came to a dead stop two paces in.

Martin lay spread out on the double bed, naked and tied with what looked like stockings to the wooden bars of the head and footboards. He'd been gagged. His mouth was full with what looked like a sock. He was conscious, but his eyes kept sliding half closed. That wasn't all. There were words written across his chest. Words crudely scrawled in thick black marker.

Anytime

Anyplace

Anywhere

A pile of bank notes sat on the bedside table. Liam breathed through his mouth. He didn't want to catch the barest scent of what had gone on here.

Charlie chuckled. "Told you'd he'd been busy."

Busy? This wasn't a part of any thirty-minute sex session. Couldn't the guy see the fear and the anguish in Martin's face?

"Out." He shoved at Charlie's solid but sweaty chest. "Get *out*." He slammed the door in the odious man's face before turning back to the bed.

Martin raised his head. His eyes were wide, glassy with fear and the bleary focus of someone waking from anesthetic.

Liam hurried over to the bed and dragged the makeshift gag from his lips. The sock was damp with saliva. As soon as it was out, Martin gasped for air. He could have choked to death if he'd been left much longer.

"What happened?"

Redness stained the skin around his lips and under his cheekbones. A tear tracked down the side of his face and soaked into the pillowcase.

"Don't know," he said, his voice rough and faint.

"You must know something." Liam examined the knots in the stockings. Martin had struggled to free himself but all he'd succeeded in doing was drawing the knots tighter.

"There were two of them." Martin sank back into the pillows. "One must've been standing behind the door. The other one answered. Soon as I stepped inside, he put something over my mouth. They held me down. I tried to fight them off, but it all got weird." He turned his face aside. "Feel sick."

"Try to hold it in. I'll have you free in a minute." Liam abandoned the knots at Martin's wrist and resumed working at where the stocking had been secured to the headboard. "Did you get a good look at them? Was one of them Tan Jacket Guy?"

When he met Martin's gaze, the blueness was vivid enough to sweep away this whole sordid situation. He couldn't think, couldn't recall where he was or what he was doing while those breathtakingly beautiful eyes were fixed on him, watching him. Trusting him. But that wasn't Martin looking at him. Couldn't be. Martin was tough and irritating and would never stay silent for so long without a biting remark to cut the air.

"Was it?"

"I think so."

"Did they do anything else?" He scanned the length of Martin's body, seeking signs of injury.

"They didn't touch me. My hands are numb, and I'm about to puke, but they didn't..." He turned away and retched into the pillow.

Liam worked harder on the knots. The nylon had cut into his wrists, leaving thick red marks biting into the delicate skin. "I'm going to need scissors."

117

Martin lifted his head from mattress. "No. Don't leave me."

"I won't be long." He headed for the door at a jog.

"Liam." Martin released such a pitiful wail that Liam stopped and checked back over his shoulder. "Please," Martin said, straining at his bonds.

"Two minutes." Liam forced himself away before he could be caught under the powerfully seductive blue of Martin's gaze again.

Charlie lounged on a chair behind the desk this time, glued to the monitor.

Liam scanned the smaller ledge behind him. A pair of scissors sat next to a stack of unopened brown envelopes. "There. Hand them over."

Charlie patted along the desk, his eyes stilled glued to the screen. He found the scissors then held them out blades first. He wasn't even watching porn, as one might expect in a place like this, but some tacky soap opera.

Liam weighed the scissors in his hand. "The people who paid for the room, describe them."

Charlie grabbed the mouse and the volume increased.

Liam raised his voice. "Was one of them wearing a jacket with an image of a smoking pistol on the back?"

Charlie's focus remained fixed on the screen. "Can't say I noticed."

"You noticed enough to take their money, I bet. Did they pay by card?" If so, he might get a name.

"Cash." Charlie's gaze flickered his way. "Detective."

"Have you seen them here before? Are they regulars?" He kept his words strong, refusing to be intimidated. He knew the answer he'd get.

"Never seen 'em before in my life. I don't know why you're so twisted up. Button's done far worse than engage in a spot of mild bondage with a couple of overexcited fellas before. Now do you mind? I'm trying to watch this show."

Never mind about what Button had or had not done in the past. What had happened to him today hadn't been

118

consensual. This fat bastard didn't care, and all the while Martin was still lying in that bed tied up and alone.

On returning to the room, he found Martin staring blankly at the ceiling. When Liam started hacking into the restraints, Martin barely responded until the last of the stockings had been severed. Then he sat and rubbed at his wrists while Liam set about gathering his clothes from the floor.

"I had a word with the reception guy, about the men who...who paid for this room." 'This room' sounded much better than 'paid for you'. "He was cagey, but I reckon if we push we might get a decent description out of him, if nothing else."

"Charlie takes money, not names. He don't know shit. Even if he did, he wouldn't say nothing. It's, like, client confidentiality or something. Just pass me my clothes and let me get dressed in peace."

Client confidentiality? Who did this Charlie think he was? He wouldn't ask and risk another biting reply. But equally as worrying as the men was Martin's apparent nonchalance. Like this had all been a part of his day, now consigned to the past.

Liam dumped the clothing on the bed then made his way to the door. "I'll wait outside."

He paced the grubby hallway for minutes before the door opened again. Martin stood there, head down, arms wrapped around himself in shamed defeat. Behind him, Liam noted the money had disappeared from the bedside table drawer. Safely tucked inside Martin's back pocket, he'd bet.

Chapter Fifteen

Martin trailed after a stomping Liam, determined not to take his fear beyond the Albion's door. The goons hadn't touched him on the inside. They'd done less to him than most had when he was conscious. He clung to that certainty and focused on Liam's retreating back.

"*Oi*, Button," Charlie called from reception. "You owe me."

"Give him the lot." Liam paused in the doorway to the street. "It's as filthy as this place."

"I can't. I need it." Martin made his way to the desk. Twenty-five percent of each trick through the door. He counted out one hundred pounds in a mix of tens and twenties and placed the notes on the desk.

Charlie snatched them up in one fat, freckled hand. "Same time tomorrow?"

"No. I'm taking a break." Not for long, just until his nerves had settled. "I'll call you when I'm ready to come back. And when I do, just give me regulars for a while. Yeah?"

"Whatever you say." Charlie's expression softened. He gestured toward the door to where Liam had been standing a moment before. "Tell that friend of yours one of them was wearing a light-brown leather jacket. They paid in cash so no contact details. But they won't get through the door again. I promise you that."

"Thanks." No great revelation. He'd already worked out they were the same blokes. They kept paying him for his time, too. Now all he needed to do was find out what they wanted. If not his living body or his corpse, what else did he have to offer?

Liam was waiting out on the street. He gestured to the cash in Martin's hand. "You going to enjoy spending that?"

The contempt cracked Martin's shield. Cold air rippled under his clothes. He drew his jacket closer. Shame wasn't an emotion he indulged anymore. Shame did not pay the bills.

"Why not?" He tucked the notes into his pocket. "I earned it."

"Yeah." Liam's upper lip curled. "So you did." He stalked across the road to the car without another word.

"It's for a deposit, arsehole," Martin called after him. "Don't look down your nose at me. I need someplace to live, don't I?" He was shouting. His throat burned with the effects. A woman passing by eyed him like he was some half-crazed drunk. She crossed the road to avoid him.

Martin leaned against the hotel wall. An image blistered through his closed eyelids and scoured his retinas. Lying on the bed with voices to-ing and fro-ing around him. One voice in particular kept echoing inside his skull. *"Tempted? Even if I wasn't a billion percent straight, I wouldn't poke that communal cesspool with yours."*

"I'm not pissed off with you."

He opened his eyes. Liam stood before him wielding a tissue.

"I'm pissed off with the scum you have to deal with. I don't understand you and I never will. But you've been through enough shit today, so I won't dump any more on your doorstep."

Only when the tissue wafted across his face did Martin sense the wetness on his cheeks. He'd been bawling. Big fat girly tears. He swiped at them with the back of his hand. "I don't need you and your judgments. I don't need your fucking snot rags, neither." He shoved an arm into Liam's chest, but Liam didn't budge. Fixed as a bollard, he was. "Get lost."

Martin started up the road with a determined stride and got as far as the corner. When a car horn blared behind him, he checked over his shoulder just to confirm it was a shabby estate tailing him before increasing his speed.

"Would you get in the car?" Liam called from the open window.

He kept walking.

"Martin."

He lifted his middle finger and showcased his reply. Only when he heard a familiar bleep did he lower his hand and pull the phone from his pocket. One new text. He opened up the message. Three words.

Anytime. Anyplace. Anywhere.

His stomach lurched. The phone bleeped again. A video this time. He opened that up, too. The screen filled with a close up of the same words scrawled on a pale chest. His chest. The camera panned out. He wasn't tied to the bed at this point. They could have done anything and he wouldn't have known. He watched with a macabre fascination until a large, tan hand pried the phone from his grip. The same hand also guided him to the car. He slid into the passenger seat without a fuss.

Liam climbed in the other side then pressed the phone to his ear. "Put your seatbelt on."

"Who're you calling?" Martin asked vaguely, trapped as he was in a padded bubble of dumbness.

"Them."

Martin lunged for his phone. "Give it back. It's my problem and I'll deal with it. What makes you think you could sort it out any better than me?"

Liam pushed a palm into his chest and held him back. "I'm not trying to pretend the problem doesn't exist."

"Neither am I. I'm prepared." Martin slumped back into his seat. "I got life insurance."

"Life insurance? You?"

He couldn't work out if Liam sounded more surprised or amused. "Why not? My life is one big fat risk, in case you hadn't noticed."

Liam lowered the phone. "You think you'll get a pay out if you get murdered? What do you think would happen when the insurance investigators find out what you do for a living?"

"What's that got to do with anything?"

"I'm no expert, but isn't the occupation of rent boy classed under criminal activity, and therefore exempt?"

"Therefore exempt? You're a hospital porter, Liam, not a lawyer." He hadn't thought about the small print. They'd have a hard job proving what he did for a living. He only advertised anonymously in the local newspapers and certain sites online, but he never used apps or posted his picture. He didn't want to risk his past coming back to haunt him years later. He did plan to live a respectable life. One day.

"Who'd get the money?" Liam asked. "Not you, since you'd be dead."

"Maybe I want to be buried with a pile of treasure." Martin snatched his phone from Liam's hand. "Like one of them pharaohs."

Liam's lowered brow indicated that he remained royally unimpressed. "You said you had no family. Who's it for?"

"No one." He clutched his phone and stared out of the side window. A crow pecked at a half-eaten sandwich on the pavement. If Liam knew the truth, would he be more understanding or accepting? No. No one in the world could accept what he'd done. "Just make sure I get RIP carved on my gravestone, since I ain't getting none in life."

"You are one cold fuck. Anyone ever tell you that?"

"No." Martin turned to Liam with a rigid grin. "Been told I'm pretty hot, actually." When Liam didn't look away, he let the grin drop. "Can we go now? You're parked on yellow lines."

"It's a reference to an old advert."

"What is?"

"The 'anytime, anyplace, anywhere' line. Martini. It's my

mum's favorite drink. She used to sing the song a lot when I was a kid."

"So what?" He'd assumed the phrase referred to his availability. He was glad he hadn't voiced that idea. He didn't like to show his ignorance. "Means nothing."

"It means if the phrase wasn't a random coincidence, then whoever's behind this knows your real name. Martin. Martini. What do you reckon?"

Martin didn't know what he reckoned. He scrolled through his phone and brought up the video again. They definitely hadn't fucked him. But as for anything else, he couldn't be sure. Didn't want to know, either. He hit delete before he could change his mind.

"Nice one." Liam swiped the phone from his hand. "Now you've got rid of any evidence."

"Evidence of what?" Martin grabbed the phone and slipped it into his jacket pocket. Liam's somber stare weighed hard on his body. "Yeah, I know. You don't get me. That's just as well. Cos if you did, you'd wish you didn't."

Liam twisted the key in the ignition. The engine spluttered then revved. "Put your seatbelt on," he said, a lot more quietly than before.

Chapter Sixteen

Apparently, Martin wanted the world to think he wasn't bothered by any threat to his safety. He hadn't done such a good job in the hotel room when fear had shimmered below the surface of his eyeballs, but had recovered enough to take the cash from the bedside table. Now he stared out of the window as if nothing out of the ordinary had happened. There really was no figuring him out. Perhaps that was just as well—he'd soon become someone else's gateway to the underworld anyway.

Halfway home, Martin's phone tinged again. A slither of dark and unpleasantly cold dread slicked its way from Liam's chest to his belly. He could only hope they hadn't sent another video. The next one could show them going further than taking off Martin's clothes, tying him up and drawing on him. Liam was trying not to care, because that seemed to be what Martin wanted. But he couldn't help himself, and, right now, Martin had no one else to fight his corner.

Eventually, Martin took out his phone and stared at the screen. Relief smoothed the dread from his face. He thumbed a text. Liam didn't dare take his attention from the busy road long enough to read the contents.

"Someone you know?"

Martin returned his phone to his pocket. "Yeah."

"Friend? Or client?" Nope. Liam wasn't doing too well at this whole 'giving up caring what happened to Martin' thing.

"Right, cos I got a contact list brimming with mates."

Client, then. Martin had never mentioned friends or family before. No one but men who wanted to fuck him. Or, if these latest adventures were anything to go by, torture him. What a pleasant and fulfilling life he must lead.

"You don't think you should take a few days or nights off, considering?"

Martin looked at him. "Considering what?"

"This afternoon." Funny how Martin had no problem going on the attack if he felt unfairly judged. But with actual physical threats, he preferred blanking them out like they never happened. "You could've been stuck there for a lot longer if I hadn't been around."

"Charlie would have found me."

Liam got the impression that if Charlie had found Martin dying in one of his rooms he'd lock the door and wait for the body to rot rather than call the authorities. "Then why ask me to come looking for you? Why not him?"

"Because I didn't tell him how long I'd be. He didn't ask. *Unlike you.*"

That sounded distinctly like an accusation. But then Martin evidently didn't appreciate being cared about anyway. "Sorry for caring," Liam muttered. He had no desire to start another argument. The air in the car was spoiled enough already.

They stewed in smoldering silence until they reached home. Once they'd parked, Martin stormed out of the car and into their building.

He was lounging against the door to the flat when Liam caught up with him, arms folded, a scowl burning up the opposite wall. Once the door was open, he rushed straight to the bathroom. The thump of the lock echoed down the hall, followed by the shower thundering to life. Evidently not quite as unaffected by his ordeal as he'd like Liam to believe.

Liam wandered through to the lounge, his attention snagged by the computer desk. Not so much the desk as what sat upon it. A key. A key attached to a rubber chimp. Martin's key. The one he'd supposedly lost last night.

As Liam made to pick it up, he became distracted by the green light on the printer. No one had used that thing today, unless Katie had popped back in her lunch hour. But why would she, when she had plenty of printers at work? He switched off the power then wandered into the hall.

Martin emerged from the bathroom, a towel wrapped around his waist. The bottom of the towel skimmed his ankles so that it resembled more of a skirt. Made a change from the handkerchief-sized towels he usually swanned around in.

Liam dangled the key between them. "Thought you'd lost this."

Martin peered closer. "I did. It's in the river."

"Can't be, since it's here. Are you...?" Liam dropped his gaze to the inflamed skin of Martin's chest. The lettering remained underneath, the words fractured like a half-lazered tattoo. "What have you done to yourself?"

"Nothing." Martin wrapped both arms over his damaged skin. "They used permanent marker and I had to scrub it off." He stared at the key still dangling between them. "I had it when I went out last night."

"Obviously you couldn't have. Here." Liam pushed the key closer. "Try not to lose it again."

"Keep it." Martin turned away. "I'm shifting out in the morning."

He was still insisting on going, then? Nothing Liam had said, nothing that had happened to him today, had gone partway to change his mind? "You don't have to do that."

"I said I would." He padded barefoot to his door. "You can stop pretending like you give a shit now." He turned to head inside. "I don't need no—" His breath caught. He staggered back. "No. This is not happening."

"What isn't?" Liam moved into the doorway. Then he saw it. A new picture on Martin's door, replacing the oiled-up Robin lookalike.

An image of Martin laid out on the bed at that flea-pit of a hotel. Naked and tied, eyes closed like he was sleeping.

The writing over his chest was clearly readable. Liam just reached the 'anyplace' scrawled at the top of Martin's belly before a hand swiped in and ripped the picture from the door.

Liam made a grab for him. This was all the evidence they had left. "Slow down. Just wait a minute."

"Why?" Martin spun around. "You want to look? Here." He pressed the image to Liam's chest. "Does it get you off? You want to decorate your room with that? Go ahead, see if I give a sh—"

"No." Liam grabbed his wrists, instantly stilling him. "I won't, if you don't want me to. Just breathe. Let's calm things down a bit here."

Liam held on until the panic faded from Martin's eyes. When it did, the mask slipped. The hard-as-nails façade Liam had assumed was Martin Bailey fell away. The man left in his place looked completely lost as to what to do next.

A powerful protective streak flowed through Liam. He had to fight the desire to wrap Martin up in his arms. He wouldn't be thanked for it and would more than likely end up with a bruised something or other for his trouble.

Instead he loosened his grip and let Martin pull free. "This involves more than you now. This guy, or guys, broke into mine and Katie's home. They printed this out on our printer."

Martin stared at the crumpled image still balled in his clenched fist. "You don't have to tell me." Before Liam could stop him he opened the door and stepped inside.

Nothing else had been disturbed. No new additions to the walls. Martin surveyed every picture before dragging his bag out from under the bed.

"I don't want you to leave." Liam stopped just shy of stepping on the bag. "There are other ways of dealing with this."

"Yeah, and it's my problem." Martin dropped the bag on the mattress and opened the zip. "I don't want you two involved, either. So it's best I go."

"But we're already involved. These blokes invaded our home. We need to call the police."

"What for? Nothing's missing. No locks broke. All they did was stick up a new poster." He got up and moved to the chest of drawers. "Ain't nothing to report."

When Martin turned with an armful of clothing, Liam was on the bed. Head bowed, hands in his lap. He looked defeated, though he was getting exactly what he wanted. The flat. For himself and Katie so he could delude himself they had a future together.

Martin returned to the bed and dropped his clothing into the bag. As he made to make a return journey for the rest, Liam caught his wrist.

"You've got evidence enough here," he said, stroking a thumb across the red marks etched into his skin. "And your chest."

The light caress of Liam's thumb made Martin shiver. Not with pain — though his grazed skin was irritating enough — but something more closely related to pleasure. He let Liam's touch linger a little too long before pulling free.

Liam let him go easily enough but didn't look particularly happy about doing so. What Liam needed was a lesson in reality. What life was for someone who made their living selling their body. He shoved his bag to one side and took a seat on the bed.

"You don't get how many guys like kink," he said, thinking perhaps Liam never ventured beyond the missionary position. "That's all the bruises will prove once the cops find out what I am. What I've always been."

"You really haven't ever had a boyfriend, or slept with someone you liked? I mean *like*, and not for money or favors or whatever other motive you'd have?"

Martin didn't know why he'd given Liam such personal information in the first place. He hadn't been under any obligation. The confession had just slipped out. It wasn't as if he could take it back now either, not convincingly. "I never met the right person."

Liam's heavy gaze dropped to Martin's mouth. "Do you kiss them, your clients?"

Where did that come from? "Kissing's for people who care about each other. Not for the likes of me." The truth was, he wouldn't let any of them near his mouth with theirs. Kissing was an intimacy he'd never shared. Not willingly. "I'm way too jaded for that."

Liam's smile lifted the shadows from his face. "You reckon?"

"Yeah, I reckon." Martin smiled, too. *Easiest way out of an awkward situation and the danger of sharing too much. Just make a joke out of it.* "Can prove it if you want."

Liam stared at him.

Fuck. It was meant as a casual remark, something to laugh about. But Liam wasn't laughing and, come to think of it, neither was he.

He used the ensuing silence to retrieve the rest of his things from the drawers.

"Yeah, go on then."

Liam moved in front of him, broad and tall and braced like he was making a challenge instead of accepting one. But, since Liam had filled his quota of good deeds for one day, Martin offered one of his own by way of return. "Forget it. My mouth's been in some grotty places."

Liam shrugged. "I like your mouth, for what it's worth."

"About fifty quid." Which was about all the good that had ever come out of guys saying how much they liked his mouth.

Liam moved toward him. "You wouldn't be kissing me as a client."

"No?" Martin backed up until his rump hit an open drawer.

Liam pressed his big hands to the drawer, either side of Martin's upper arms, and pushed it shut. His ocean-scented aftershave swirled in the air between them. Too close. Way too close. "You're not jaded. You're the opposite of jaded.

But that's for you to prove me wrong."

"Is it?" As Martin leaned back, his hips jutted forward. The proximity warmed the space under the towel until there was no space left.

Liam pushed closer. "You *did* offer."

He had, but he hadn't intended to be taken seriously. "You can't really want a snog off a whore."

"Don't I?" Liam cocked an eyebrow. "It'd be a new experience for us both."

The light sparking in Liam's eyes indicated he wasn't being altogether serious. Martin didn't know why the nerves were coiling in his gut. All he had to do was prove he was immune to a kiss from someone who didn't even like him. That couldn't be too much of a chore, could it?

When he thought about it like that, the whole process wasn't quite so intimidating. He rose on his toes and pressed his mouth to Liam's in the briefest graze. He'd planned to draw back just as quickly, only Liam's lips were warmer than he'd expected. Softer, too. The kiss tingled all the way through his jaw and flurried through his chest. Just as he moved closer to explore in finer detail, Liam broke away.

"Was that good?" he asked, slightly breathy, as if there had been any doubt.

"It...wasn't bad." Martin pulled away and sidled toward the bed. He couldn't show Liam just how bad the kiss wasn't, and the towel didn't disguise much of anything, even being a bath sheet. "You proved me wrong."

He really hadn't wanted to be wrong. He'd wanted to prove how dead he was inside, that was all. Yet the kiss had ignited some dormant emotion he couldn't begin to understand.

"Right." Liam sounded proud of himself. Why? There were no life points to be won in kissing a whore. "While you come to terms with that, I'll go get the new lock."

"Huh?" Liam cared about him? Since when? That kiss wasn't anywhere near enough to change Liam's opinion of him.

"After I've gone, put the chain on. They left your key, but we don't know if they made a copy." Liam moved to the door then scratched a hand through his hair. "On second thoughts, it'd be safer if you came with me."

"The goons won't come back." He wished he sounded more confident than he felt. "They did what they wanted."

"Still. Just to be on the safe side, you should come with me."

"Nope." Martin sat back on the bed. "I'm staying."

Liam didn't look so certain. "Just put the chain on now before you forget."

"I will. Now go. The sooner you're out of here the sooner you get back."

"Ten minutes. Then you and me are going to talk some more."

"Sure." He tried to rustle up some enthusiasm. "Can't wait."

Liam eyed him, seeking the sarcasm Martin tried desperately hard to keep off his face, then headed down the hall without finding it.

Martin went to the kitchen window and peered through the blinds. Only after Liam had got into his car and pulled into the road did he return to the bedroom to finish packing. Once that was done, he took out his phone and made a call.

Chapter Seventeen

The kiss lingered on Liam's lips all the way to town, even though, technically, what they'd shared could hardly be described as an actual kiss. It had been more like a tentative exploration between the school stud and a shy virgin. Except Liam was no stud and Martin no... On second thoughts, Martin had never had a relationship. Never shared his body with someone who wanted him for him and not just as a means of getting off.

Martin couldn't have faked the nervous anxiety that had kept him rigid as a mannequin most of the way through that brief kiss, to the point where Liam had wondered if he'd done the right thing. He'd had to back off or risk breaking his promise not to touch. And get accused of all those things Martin had feared him doing.

At least they now had the rest of the afternoon, the evening and all night, if necessary, to talk things through. The first thing Liam had to do was convince Martin to go to the police. Then see about talking him into another line of work.

Although he had no right to impose his morals on others, that afternoon he'd witnessed how deeply Martin's occupation affected him. Liam had clashed against the hard-faced barrier of Martin Bailey, fleetingly glimpsed the faux innocence of Button, and now he'd met this third person. The real Martin. The Martin he liked. The Martin he'd kissed. He hoped to spend the evening with this latest Martin, too.

Buying the new lock was easy. Fitting it might pose a problem, but with Martin's help they'd get it done in no time. Once back at the flat, he checked the car park for loiterers. He'd been gone twenty minutes. Long enough. But if anyone was keeping an eye on the building, they were doing so well out of sight.

He knocked on the door rather than use his key. Partly because he wanted to give due warning he wasn't a goon. Also because the chain would still be connected the other side. "Hey. It's me."

No answer.

He knocked harder. "Martin? Can you let me in?"

Still nothing.

Martin wouldn't not answer the door. Not unless he was physically incapable. Had they got to him again, those goons? What would they have done to him this time?

Liam fumbled for his key. The door opened smoothly. Too smoothly. *What happened to the chain?* He stood still and listened to nothing but the sound of his own heartbeat thudding away in both ears.

"Martin?" he called.

The name bounced off the hall and fetched back nothing but silence. Last time the goons had tied him up and written on him. This time…would they have hurt him? Really hurt him? Sickness roiled in Liam's belly, but still he forced himself down the hall.

Both the lounge and the kitchen were empty, but then the lounge and the kitchen didn't have a bed that someone could be tied to. What about Martin's room? That was where he'd been the last time Liam had spoken to him. Sitting on the bed and impatient for Liam to go. And come back again.

Liam tentatively pushed open Martin's bedroom door, half expecting to find his bloodied corpse displayed on the bed. He almost cried out his relief when he found nothing on the mattress but a heap of blankets. And on top of them, a note.

Soz L. Desided 2 move on. U dont need my hassels. Say bi 2 K

4 me. M xx.

Liam picked up the piece of paper. Martin hadn't been murdered or even kidnapped. He'd done a runner. All the fear and sickness in Liam's belly faded to a cold numbness that took all the strength from his legs. He slumped down on the bed. Across the room the drawers in the chest stood open and empty. Even the bottle of whiskey Martin was so precious about had gone. All that was left was the furniture and porn stills. And this note that spelled out, however badly, that Martin wasn't coming back. And Liam didn't have the first clue as to go about finding him.

* * * *

Martin took the train to Chichester and, from there, a taxi to his destination. The large, modern hotel was located on the outskirts of the city and was way fancier than he'd expected. A place packed with clean beds and decent facilities rather than the bug-infested charge-by-the-hour places he was used to.

His room was better than he'd expected, too. A double bed, naturally, took up most of the room and there was a table under the window with two padded wicker chairs either side. Plenty of wardrobe space, a TV and a full bathroom with a heated towel rail.

He made a coffee from the courtesy tray on a set of drawers next to the bed then stretched out in one of the chairs by the window. After taking a moment to revel in the luxury of having a whole hotel room to himself, he took out his phone and switched it on. Four missed calls from Liam. He wasn't in the mood to start explaining, but he did owe the confirmation that he was safe.

"Where the hell are you?" Liam bellowed so loudly, he had to angle the phone away from his ear.

"In a hotel. I just wanted to let you know you can stop making out like you care whether I'm dead or alive now. I'm not your problem anymore."

"But I do care. You should know that by now." The hurt in his voice automatically made Martin want to apologize, but he quickly quashed the urge. "Which hotel?"

Martin peered between the slats of the blinds at the car park below. "A good one. Four stars. It's got a swimming pool and a sauna and—"

"Room for a pony?"

A white Rolls-Royce glided into a space at the front of the hotel. He was early. Or just keen. "What?"

"Never mind. Quit showing off and tell me where you are?"

"Why? You want to come join me?" A nice thought, but an invitation offered too late. A broad, suited figure got out of the rear of the car and made his way toward the reception doors. Roy had a chauffeur. *Just how loaded is he?*

"What are you doing holed up in some posh hotel?"

"What do you think?"

"You're with a punter? Who?"

Martin released the blinds and moved to the bed. "I just wanted you to know I'm still alive. And now that I have, I've got to go. It's been good, getting to know you and finding out you're not such a pompous twat as I thought. You're the best kisser I ever knew. Which don't say much, I know. But still, it's true."

"Just shut up a minute. I need you to—"

"Delete my number, 'kay? I'll do the same with yours."

"No chance. I'm going to call you again. You'd better answer. And tell me exactly where—"

Martin ended the call. His thumb hovered over 'delete contact', but refused to lower. He just couldn't bring himself to sever the final connection. He'd do it later, when he'd had time to rationalize things.

He took off his clothes, shoved them into the wardrobe along with his bag then lay out on the bed. Belly down, as chest up wasn't the most attractive of positions for him right now. Shame it wasn't darker so he could disguise the fact he was damaged goods and not worth the price he was about to charge for his soul.

Pushing his cheek into the pillow, he gathered up the frayed edges that made up Martin Bailey and bound them down deep inside, knotting the strands under the weight of his guilt. Martin was easy to hide, but Button never as easy to find. He waited for the vacuous innocence of his alter ego to take shape.

The door clicked. Heavy footsteps crossed to the bed. A cool touch brushed over the base of his spine. Martin cringed. Button sighed. A breath puffed over the same patch of skin, and a pungent spicy aftershave swirled the air.

"Now this, I'd happily greet every afternoon of the year." Damp lips kissed skin an inch above his arse crack. "Utterly beautiful."

Martin wriggled under another kiss. "Hi, Roy." He half-rolled over before remembering he couldn't do that. Perhaps he should have kept his T-shirt on. Not that it would make much of a difference. Roy would have that whipped off him in no time. "You want to play?"

He looked at the man gazing longingly down at his body, still oblivious to what it was about him that captivated Roy so much. His body was adequate. Nothing special, but Roy didn't mind his size or his lack of muscle definition. Neither did any of his other clients, come to that. But none of them explored him as keenly as Roy. None of them looked at him with such blatant hunger, either.

"In time." Roy stroked his arse.

He wriggled, rubbing the smooth cotton, trying to encourage an erection.

"These bruises match my prints," Roy said absently, with neither pride nor regret. "The marks on your ankles are new. What are they?"

Martin hadn't thought them so noticeable. As usual, he'd been wrong.

"Just a guy who likes to tie me up." When Roy fixed him with a hard stare, he laid his head on the pillow. "It's nothing. I'm getting cold lying here."

The same hand that had circled his ankle scooted up his calf and thigh and came to rest, palm down, on his arse again. "Turn over."

He couldn't. He'd be considered more trouble than he was worth. Roy was a husband, father and grandfather. He wouldn't want the complication of an employee's problems. But when Roy issued a command, he had no choice but to obey. That would be his role in life now. He wasn't hard, so his dick was unlikely to distract from the redness smothering his chest.

Roy hissed out a low breath. He stroked the bruises before transferring his touch to the faded lettering etched across Martin's chest. "What does this say?"

Martin turned his head aside. All of sudden, he'd rather be anywhere else than here. Anywhere except semi-conscious in a one-star hotel with two strangers who had it in for him. Which was the whole reason he was here in the first place, wasn't it? "I don't know. It was a joke."

"Look at me when you speak."

Martin forced himself to meet Roy's darkly curious gaze. "I don't know who he was. Not a regular. Just someone I never plan to see again."

"When were you with this person?"

"Today. I didn't understand what it meant."

"The words, or the phrase?"

"I don't know." *Damn, why the interrogation?* "Both. The words were stupid, anyway." He rose up on his elbows. "You do still want me, don't you? I'm not scarred for life."

"Show me your wrists." He grabbed an arm, causing Martin to fall back into the pillows. "What were you tied with?"

"Ladies' stockings." *God, how embarrassing.*

Roy examined one wrist before reaching for the other. *Best not mention the drugged part.* He wasn't sure how Roy would react.

The way he was acting was scary enough. Martin held

no real feelings for the man beyond his wallet, and had assumed Roy felt the same way about his body. But here he was being examined so carefully, so thoroughly, and with concern rather than lust, that he wondered if there was more to it. Did Roy care for him, and for more than just the obvious? He didn't want to think about that. It would complicate matters and his life was complicated enough.

"What else happened? Who was he?"

Martin considered denying all knowledge, but Roy was going to be spending a great deal of money to get him so honesty was the least he owed. "There was two of them. They've been following me. I don't know who they are. I didn't get a good look at them." Was there such a thing as being too honest? Roy might be put off if he knew exactly what they'd done.

"What happened?" Roy insisted.

"They tried to drown me." He closed his eyes so he didn't have to gauge the expression on Roy's face, or whether he was about to be dropped like a soiled pair of pants. "Not to kill me," he added quickly, "to scare me."

"For what reason?"

"Don't know. They didn't give one."

"And when did this happen?"

"Last night." *Was it so recent?* Last night might as well have been a hundred years ago. "In the river near where I live."

Roy's voice softened. "Why would they do such a thing?"

Fucked if I know. Not Button's words, and Martin refused to let the mask slip. "Don't know." He opened his eyes. "Might've been a jealous wife. She could've hired a couple of guys to scare me off her husband."

"That's your theory?"

It made sense, now that he came to think about it. Someone like Chris' wife, who already suspected her husband was having an affair. She'd have to be a callous bitch to do that. "I guess so. Is it off now?"

"Is what off?" Roy flipped back the edge of the sheet.

"Come along, get underneath."

He complied, though Roy made no move to join him under the covers. "You and me. Me working for you full-time."

"Why should it be off?" Roy took out his phone and scrolled the screen. "You do understand you won't be working for me, don't you? You'll be owned by me. Entirely. Willing to obey my every request."

"Um." He'd guessed he'd have to be free as and when Roy wanted him. The word 'owned' put a whole new perspective on things. What would happen to Martin if Button was to be made available twenty-four-seven? "What would I be expected to do?"

Roy put his phone away and took a seat on the edge of the bed. "Your duties wouldn't include overseeing the company accounts." He smiled. A joke.

"That's just as well. I can't carry off the whole designer suit look as well as you." Martin raised an arm free of the covers and smoothed the mauve silk of Roy's tie. "Plus, I'd need help putting one of these on, and taking it off." When he reached up with his other hand to start doing precisely that, Roy gathered his fingers and kissed the tips.

"The flat I have in mind for you is close to the city itself. It's only temporary, until I can arrange something better, but it won't be ready until the morning. You caught me on such short notice. Not that I'm complaining." A smile was poised on his lips. "I'll take you there in the morning, right after we have you tested."

"Tested?"

"Indeed. For disease."

Martin hadn't expected a maths exam, but he wasn't a damn farm animal. "I'm not diseased." He tried to sit up, but Roy pressed a hand to his chest and pushed until he sank into the pillows.

"Then the test will only be a formality. A necessary formality, at that."

Whatever. A blood test was nothing, especially since he

knew he was clean. What he should focus on now was the money side of things. And Roy was going to have to dig deep if he wanted Button's company for any real length of time. "What about...?" Heat warmed his cheeks. He had more luck sending blood there than to his dick. "Payment?"

Roy smiled, almost warmly this time. "You'll be well cared for, with an allowance to suit." He checked his watch. "But as of now, I have to go and deal with some business."

"You're leaving?" They hadn't discussed figures yet, and he couldn't force the issue. Martin could, but not Button. But to Roy, Martin didn't even exist.

"I'm afraid so." Roy leaned closer. "I have several places to be this evening, most of them simultaneously."

When a pair of wet, pursed lips loomed over him, Martin snapped his head to one side. He might have signed his soul away but he wasn't letting Roy's mouth anywhere near his. Liam was the first and last person to kiss him, and that wasn't ever going to change.

Instead of the wet press of lips, a low sigh swept over his cheek. "I'll see you in the morning. Be ready to leave at ten."

* * * *

Alone again, Martin stretched out and luxuriated in the coolness of fresh clean sheets. While it was self-indulgent to laze about in bed in the early evening, this was his last night of freedom. After tonight, there wouldn't be any other men but Roy in his life. While the news pleased him in one way, in another he wanted only to pull the covers over his head and hide here forever. Since that wasn't possible, he got out of bed and retrieved the whiskey bottle from his bag. He placed it next to the TV and in full view of the room. One look soon subdued every last one of his frequent and numerous doubts.

He ordered a three-course meal courtesy of room service, then lamented the fact that he didn't have a pair of swimming shorts so he could make use of the pool and work some of that chocolate fudge cake off. The gym didn't appeal, and he'd always considered saunas rather sordid places. Despite this hotel being family-friendly and unlikely to catch the clientele he'd taken saunas with in the past, he'd rather avoid anything seedy. *Right. Like seedy doesn't run through my blood.*

From tomorrow, he'd belong to someone. Physically belong, not emotionally, as Roy would never mean more than a paying punter. He'd have to earn his money. What was the going rate for owning someone body and soul?

The TV wasn't enough of a distraction to quiet such questions, so he jabbed his hair with a comb before changing into his best sweater and jeans.

He found the bar off reception and ordered a Coke. As he checked out his surroundings, he registered someone standing beside him.

"Stick another half a lager in there."

Martin set down his drink and studied the guy's profile. Squat, chunky. Mid-thirties. Black eye. He didn't recognize the eye, or the face. What he did recognize, though, was the voice. He'd heard it before. Just earlier that same day.

"Tempted? Even if I wasn't a billion percent straight, I wouldn't poke that communal cesspool with yours."

Chapter Eighteen

The goon paid for his drink rather than billing it to his room. He probably didn't even have a room. Martin waited until he'd taken a seat at a table before daring to give some thought as to what happened next.

He couldn't have been followed here, not after two taxis and a train. And if scaring him into running had been the intention, job done. What more could they possibly want?

The goon had cadged a newspaper from somewhere and raised it between them like a shield. Martin took out his phone. More missed calls and texts from Liam. Ignoring those, he redialed the number the message and video had been sent from.

On the fourth or fifth ring, the goon set down the newspaper and drew a phone from his pocket. Confirmation of what he already knew.

The goon checked the screen then looked up. Or as much as he could look with one eye swollen half-shut.

Martin ended the call, set down his Coke and made his way over.

He took a seat across the table. "What do you want?"

"Excuse me?"

"Let's not do that." He wouldn't allow a single shred of fear or doubt to interrupt the moment. He wanted this over and, for it to be over, he had to know this loser's intentions. "Don't pretend you don't know who I am. You've seen me naked." He kept his voice low. He wasn't ready to make this conversation public, but would if he had to.

"Don't know what you're talking about, kid." The goon picked up his drink. His hand trembled so much that the froth cascaded down the side of the glass to pool on the mat beneath.

"One last chance to tell me who you are and what you're doing following my arse. Or you'll regret it."

The goon let out an uneven laugh. "Are you drunk or deluded?" He scanned the bar. "Where's hotel security when you need them?"

Martin had expected this reaction. Standing up to the goon now would more than likely end in a fight which would get the pair of them ejected from the hotel altogether. And he'd be left with nowhere to sleep tonight.

Mart dredged up a fraction of the fear he'd felt while being held under the water by this man. The anger resulting from the humiliation of lying comatose and trussed up on a bed in the Albion and being found by Liam, possibly the one bloke who could have meant something to him. Once he had the adrenaline flowing like lighter fluid through his veins, the rest came easy.

"What do you mean, too old?" He raised his voice, imagining himself on a stage auditioning for a lead role in some West End play. The director sat before him. The audience surrounded him, already their attention migrating his way. "When I was ten, I was too young. It didn't matter then, so why does it matter now? You've had me and used me for all these years. You—"

The goon leaped to his feet, his bad eye puffy, swollen and twitchy. "Shut up. You sick twisted dirty fuck." He turned to his audience. "I never met this kid before in my life."

"No? Then who tied me to the bed all afternoon?" Martin stood too and thrust back his sleeve. The livid redness encircling his wrist was visible to anyone who wanted to look, and he reckoned every eye in the place had already tuned in. "You brought me here so we can be together and have sex all day, and now it's the evening and I'm too old for you? On my sixteenth birthday? Thanks a lot, *Uncle Ian*."

His next breath caught in his throat. Why out of all the

names in existence had he chosen that one? Because he was wound up and desperate, that was why. And Ian was the ugliest name in his vocabulary. "Oh, and don't think about following me to our room, because you won't be welcome." He spun on his heels, aware of the rapt audience's attention accompanying him all the way from bar to lobby to lift.

When he shut the door on his room, the pit of fear and doubt and, most of all, the real sense of isolation opened inside him. What if these guys tracked him to the end of the earth and shoved him off? Who'd notice? Roy? Only in so much as he'd have lost his potential purchase. Liam might, but he'd soon have other worries on his mind. Such as Katie's condition and a baby that should have been his.

When Martin's phone vibrated in his hand and Liam's name lit the screen, all the reasons for not answering disintegrated. It wasn't so often any of his wishes came true that he could afford to ignore one now. "All right."

"You answered?" Liam sounded surprised. "You still at the hotel?"

"Yeah."

"What's wrong? You sound weird."

Martin opened his mouth. Nothing. That was what he needed to say. Had to say. But what came out was, "They're here."

A beat of silence. "How?"

At least Liam didn't have to ask who 'they' were. He didn't feel so alone now, hearing his voice was enough. "Dunno. The one I spoke to wouldn't tell me nothing."

"You spoke to one? Where are you?"

"Why'd you want to know?"

"Because you answered the phone, dipshit."

"All right." No point in making out like he wanted anything other than Liam with him. Safe company, that was what he needed right now. And only Liam could provide that. He gave the name of the hotel, expecting nothing, but hoping all the same.

"Where's the guy paying for the room?"

145

"He's coming for me. Tomorrow. To pick me up, I mean, not—"

"I got what you meant. Room number?"

"Two-twenty," he said, before he could talk himself out of it. "If you're coming, wear an emergency moustache or something."

"A what?" Another pause. "You mean a disguise?"

"I don't want no one to know you're here." Including Roy, who wouldn't be best pleased if he discovered his new toy had another man in the room he'd paid for. As platonic as things were between him and Liam, Roy wouldn't see the innocence in their relationship. That didn't matter so much, as Roy wasn't the problem. The goons were. They'd seen Liam. They knew what he looked like. Or at least, one of them did. He didn't want to put Liam in danger. Then again, neither did he want to spend his last night of freedom alone.

"I'll think of something." Liam lowered his voice, probably so Katie didn't overhear if she was home. "No one will know I'm there except you."

Chapter Nineteen

Liam arrived at the hotel following a forty-five-minute car journey that felt ten times as long. A moustache was a disguise too far, but he had ferreted a black beanie from the depths of his wardrobe.

A quick scan of the lobby didn't reveal any skulkers or loiterers, in tan jackets or otherwise. While the reception desk was being kept busy by a couple and four young kids with excess energy, Liam headed toward the lift.

He found the room and knocked with two light taps.

"Who's there?" A cautious voice enquired from the other side.

Liam tried to conjure a witty reply, but two things stopped him. One, he couldn't think of anything and, two, bad timing on the humor front.

He went with the safest option. "Liam."

The door drew back a couple of inches. A blue eye peered through the gap. "You're right." A hint of full, rosy lips joined the eye. "You are Liam. Is the hat new?"

Liam dragged the beanie from his head. The musty scent of mildew puffed the air. "You going to let me in? Or do I stand here in the hall while you take the piss?"

"You'd do that for me?" The eye widened. "That beats an evening of reality TV."

Tired of the banter, Liam pressed his palm to the door and pushed.

Martin stumbled to the bed. He threw himself on the mattress and laughed. "Man, you get wound up way too easily." He sat back up and squinted. "What're you doing here? Did I invite you?"

The invitation hadn't been subtle, even remaining unsaid. Liam shut the door behind him. He tossed the beanie, aiming for the center of Martin's smug face. "You were pissing your pants on the phone. I took that as invitation enough."

The grin melted. "I'm not scared of them. I put the one downstairs back in his hole."

"How?" Liam couldn't imagine Martin confronting one of them head-on. He wasn't built for attack, unless he was hiding a black-belted karate suit under his clothing.

Martin touched his fingertips to his lips. "With these."

Liam's stomach shriveled. "Please tell me you didn't."

"Like fuck I did." Martin grabbed a pillow and tossed it at Liam's head.

Liam took a swift step back and the pillow thudded at his feet. "How, then?"

"I convinced everyone in the bar he's some raving pedo. Damn funny, too." Martin gestured to a couple of chairs under the window. "Sit down. You make the place look like a prison cell."

Prison cell wasn't so far off, considering the reason Martin was here, but Liam wouldn't voice his thoughts. He felt uncomfortable enough with Martin's mood. *Too chirpy by far.*

He took a seat and studied the whiskey bottle next to the TV. Still half empty. Whatever else Martin might be, drunk wasn't it. "You any the wiser on what they want?"

"Nope." Martin swung his bare feet up onto the bed. He might have the mouth of a sewer, but his body held a dainty charm Liam found more than appealing. He wouldn't dare share such observations, which would almost certainly be taken as more insult than compliment.

"Does the guy who's paying for this room know anything?"

Martin pulled a face. "He was pissed off when he saw my wrists and what they did to my chest. That's why he went, I reckon. To let me get some rest. Said he'd come back in the

148

morning."

"To take you where?"

Martin stroked the vague abstract pattern on the quilt. He'd calmed considerably now. He might, with a bit of time, even start listening to reason. And come home. There was no way this evening was going to end anyway else.

"He's letting me have one of his flats to live in."

"This the bloke you had in Katie's bed? The one who wanted...exclusive use?"

Martin leaned against the headboard. "His name's Roy and I like him, so why not? I get a free flat and a good allowance. The easy life. Don't know why I was so reluctant to accept his offer before."

Probably because before those heavies had shown up, Martin had no intention of becoming anyone's full-time sex toy. "He's your get out of jail free card?"

Martin shrugged. "What else can I do? The goons won't leave me alone. They're everywhere I am. It's like they implanted some sort of a tracker on me." He paled. "They couldn't have, could they?"

Liam stifled a laugh. "Not unless it's up your arse. Which I doubt, seeing as you're doing most of your talking from there."

Martin's face darkened. "I still don't know why you're here."

"Yes, you do. But tell me to go, and I will." Chances were, he wouldn't. But still, he was curious to see how much he was wanted here.

"Nah, it's pointless you driving all that way again at this hour." A sudden grin lit Martin's face. "Want to share the bed? There's plenty room enough for two."

Liam leaned back in his chair. "And what would your new owner say about that?"

"He ain't my owner." The smile faded. "And I'm not talking about fucking, am I? Just sharing space, like last night." He moved to the wardrobe and rummaged in his bag. Wielding a toothbrush, he disappeared into the

149

bathroom. "Hey, Liam?" His surprised tone drifted from the open door. "There's complementary toothpaste. Told you this place had class."

He emerged from the bathroom in a super-snug pair of pastel-striped underpants, dumped his clothing in the bottom of the wardrobe, then climbed on top of the bed and lay down. The bruises remained livid against his otherwise flawless skin, but showing them off didn't appear to be too much of an issue. He tucked one hand behind his head and grabbed the remote from the bedside table.

"What do you want to watch? Porn? That's extra, but since Roy's paying I reckon we can afford it." He aimed the remote at the TV. A channel list popped up.

"No."

"Not even straight porn?"

"No porn." For someone who didn't like sex, Martin was obsessed. "I'll take a drink, though. Does this place have a mini bar, or can I finish up the bottle you got there?" He grabbed the whiskey.

"Leave it alone." Martin dropped the remote. He launched himself off the bed then snatched the bottle from Liam's hand. "I told you before, this ain't for drinking."

"Why not? What other uses does it have? Because I'll tell you now it makes for a lousy ornament. And don't give me bullshit about occasionally drinking. No one but an alcoholic would react that way to a half empty bottle of whiskey."

"What would you know about alcoholics?" Martin hugged the bottle close and returned to his spot on the bed. He drew his legs to his chest as if to give the bottle extra protection. From what, Liam hadn't a clue. "There's a mini bar under the TV. Go for your life. Just leave this one alone. 'Kay?"

Not a chance. The story behind the bottle intrigued Liam as strongly as ever, only secondary in importance to talking Martin out of letting this Roy character buy him like a slave. For now, though, he opened the small fridge and peered inside. "You want anything, occasional drinker?"

"No."

He took out a miniature Southern Comfort and a small can of lemonade. He usually stuck to lager, but tonight something stronger was called for. He found a glass in the cupboard next to the mini bar and made his drink. "Is there a film we can watch? The kind with actual dialogue? Where the actors mostly get to keep their clothes on?"

"Probably." Martin offered the remote. "You choose."

Liam sat on the end of the bed and flicked through the channels. He found a random action film neither of them would have to think too deeply on.

"I've seen this before," Martin complained. "A ton of times." The mattress rippled as he wriggled. "Plus, I can't see because of your massive head."

Liam took a big gulp of his drink. "I'll get a chair."

"Why? You may as well sit next to me." Martin still held the bottle between his thighs, but didn't look so defensive anymore.

The bed would be a more comfortable option, and Liam didn't want to make an issue by playing the martyr on a chair that would cease to be comfortable half an hour down the line.

He kicked off his shoes and climbed onto the bed. Although he tried his best to focus on the TV, he couldn't help but be consumed by the warm, almost naked body barely more than a breath away. It might have been less distracting if Martin could have found his way back into his clothes. Or at least covered up with the blankets. Holding the bottle between his thighs looked rather suggestive as well.

"You going to cling to that thing all night?"

"What?"

Liam nodded at the bottle. "The whiskey."

Martin shifted a hand to the neck. Even more suggestive now, and he apparently didn't have a clue. "You won't touch?"

"No, I won't touch." Liam raised his palms. Won't touch the bottle, and won't touch Martin. That would be his mantra from now on.

Martin got off the bed and carried the bottle to the wardrobe. When he opened the door and bent from the waist to ferret in the bottom, his snug underpants defined his small but perfectly formed backside. God, what an arse he had.

As much as Liam didn't want to look, and he wasn't so much looking as ogling, he couldn't pry his attention away. Not until Martin straightened, and only then because he didn't want to get labeled a pervert. No better than the men who used Martin's peachy body for their own sordid sense of gratification.

"You not watching the film?" Martin asked as he returned to the bed.

"Seen it before."

"That's what I said. And you picked it."

Yes, precisely because it wasn't to either of their taste, and made things easier to talk with no distractions. "Can I ask you something?"

Martin resettled on the bed. "No."

"Why not?"

"Because it'll be about Roy, and I don't want to talk about him."

Liam picked up his glass and downed the rest of the contents. The sweet blaze of the Southern Comfort reignited the fire in his belly. But the temperature in the room had dropped several degrees. There was no point in making out like he'd been about to mention something completely unrelated. "I wanted to ask—"

"I said no, didn't I?"

Yes, but real friends told the truth even if the truth wasn't wanted. "I reckon he knows about those blokes. The goons."

"Because I told him about them."

"No, I reckon he already knew. Before you told him. I reckon he was the one who sent them after you."

Martin stared at him. "Why would he do that?"

"Because he knew you'd run to him. Think about those pictures over your walls. Roy would have known about them. He saw the one on your door."

"Your door. He thinks mine is Katie's, remember?"

Why did he so badly want Roy to be the innocent in all this? Was he really so dense? "What if Roy never believed Katie's room was yours?"

"He did. He believes everything I tell him." He looked away. Probably embarrassed about how vehemently he'd just defended his new owner. "It weren't Roy." He glared at the film he wasn't watching. "Just drop it."

Drop the truth? Drop what had been staring him in the face? Roy could send him a video confession and he still wouldn't think the man capable of the crime. If he asked Martin to leave with him, what answer would he get? A big fat no, which was why he hadn't bothered to ask. He couldn't work out why he was bothering to stay.

"I've got a better idea." Liam climbed off the bed and pushed his feet back into his shoes.

"What idea?"

"The idea where I get to say enough's enough, and go home."

"Go?" Martin flew off the bed and deposited himself between Liam and the door. "I don't want you to go."

"Then what do you want me to do? Wish you all the best while you go and sell your body to some old perv who could only get you by having his mates or his henchmen terrorize you into it?"

"Henchmen?" Martin forced a laugh. "Roy's no gangster."

"He might be."

"Well, if he is I'm flattered. That he'd go to them lengths just to get me."

"You mean the lengths that led to you getting beaten up, drugged, tied up, humiliated, written on, half drowned?" Liam didn't need to add the stuff about breaking into their home to get his point across.

153

"So when you put it like that…"

Liam moved closer. "If you want to come back with me, you can. We can go home now. Katie's out again so she need never know you'd gone."

Martin raised his face. "Us sharing space never worked out too well, did it? You couldn't wait to get rid."

"That was before."

"Before what?"

"Before I started to care about you."

"You care about me?"

Liam would have thought it was a given, since he'd high-tailed it down the motorway to be here. But evidently, nothing could be taken for granted. "It's crazy, but there it is. I care about you too much to let you sell yourself to that arsehole. Or any arsehole. What do I have to do to stop it?" Liam stepped so close that the mint of Martin's toothpaste freshened the air between them. "Tell me and I'll do it."

Martin melted back against the door. His hard outer shell disintegrated. All Liam could see in him now was uncertainty and shock. That anyone should dare care about him and want to help him.

"Don't leave. That's all. My life is going to change tomorrow. I'm going to be paid not to have a mind of my own. That's okay because I—"

"It's not," Liam said. "Not by a long shot. But there's nothing I can do here. Those goons can't get to you long as you keep the door closed. And you clearly think you've made the right decision so I just don't know what I'm doing here. Do you?"

A spark flared to life in Martin's eyes. Not the defensive barbs this time. Something bright rather than glinting. "I want you here. If I didn't I'd soon tell you to fuck off, no worries."

"Is it my turn to feel flattered?"

"I don't know. I don't know what to say to you, except, you're like one of those guys on my wall."

"A porn star?" *How was he supposed to take that?* He didn't feel too flattered. Then again, he wasn't exactly insulted, either.

"No. I don't mean like all oiled up and ready for action. I mean…" Martin's brow creased. "Remember what I told you about wanting one of those guys to teach me what it was to fuck because it's like an expression of feelings and shit, not just cos it's the quickest way to make money fast?"

"You mean the thing two people do when they have feelings for one another. Where money isn't involved, except a meal and a bottle of wine beforehand?"

Martin's lashes dipped. He gave a slight nod. "I was thinking I might want you to teach me what it's like. Just something I can keep with me, cos I won't… I don't want to regret I didn't ask."

Wow. A single drop of raw emotion and Liam suddenly didn't know what to say either. He focused on the last word. "Ask me what?"

Martin squirmed some more. "You going to make me say it?"

Liam shifted back a step. He couldn't quite believe Martin would say it. Much less know just how he was supposed to react. "Just look at me and ask."

Martin raised his face, catching Liam's gaze before darting away again. "You can touch me if you want."

"If *I* want?"

"Yeah. I've seen you looking. You like what I got. Most guys don't even wait for permission for a grope of my ars—"

"Martin, stop." Liam raised a palm. Way to a sour a mood with a few simple words. "Please. Just stop."

"Fuck." Martin shut his eyes. "I don't mean to be like this. It just comes out. I can't stop it. Half the time it ain't even what I mean to say."

"You don't need to be defensive with me. I'm not one of your punters. I'll stay with you tonight, even if it's to try and talk you out of your plans for tomorrow. You don't have to convince me with sex. I'd rather we went back to bickering over what to watch on the TV."

Martin smiled. "No one's ever chosen the telly over me before. Hardly confidence building."

"You have more than enough confidence for the both of us."

His smile faded. "Not when it comes to asking for what I want. And that is you, in case you was still wondering."

Liam sighed. "I'm not sure it is. Not really." It didn't feel right like this, especially as there wouldn't be anything more than sex to satisfy a curiosity. "I don't want to…take advantage."

"Are you serious?" Martin's jaw dropped. "I'm a fucking whore. I got nothing left to take advantage of. If anything it'd be me taking advantage of you."

"Don't. Don't ever say that." Liam curled his fingers around Martin's bare shoulders and pulled him close. He smelled clean. He wore none of his lifestyle on his skin. Only the temporary bruises and the pen marks offered a clue as to what he was, but it didn't matter how many men he'd been with. It wasn't about that.

"Will you do it? Like when I kissed you and that was good." Martin's palms pressed against his back. "I just want to do it once with someone I like. And not for money, but because it's something we want to do. Together. If you want to as well."

This definitely wasn't about money. It was about Martin, who, for reasons of his own, wanted to be with him tonight. Everything else, even the rights and the wrongs, could be dealt with later.

Chapter Twenty

"Do you, then? Want to, I mean?" Was this a bad idea? What would happen if they did tumble into bed together, and all this intensity between them dissolved? Sex would become what it always did. A basic function he, for the most part, found tedious and vaguely degrading. "Liam?" Martin wriggled his hips in an effort to rouse Liam from the awkward stupor he'd fallen into. "Say something."

Liam blinked. His pupils contracted. "What? You changed your mind?"

"About this? No way." When Liam's gaze continued to scour his body, he had to fight the urge to curl up in a corner. "What are you doing?"

Liam's lashes lifted. "You don't like to be looked at?"

Martin swallowed the comment Button would have made about loving the attention. Button wasn't here. This was just him. And he wouldn't lie. Not to Liam. "Not the way you are, no."

"Why not?"

He wasn't sure. He'd never much liked being the center of attention, which made things difficult when his job depended on getting himself noticed.

"Because it gives me delusions," he said, because Liam was still waiting for an answer. "Makes me think you got the better deal when I know it's the other way around."

"I just want to spend time with at the real you. Not the brash, hard-faced shit you are most of time."

"Hey, what the –?"

Liam's finger brushed under his chin, killing his objection stone dead. Their eyes met. "I get now it's a barrier you put up to stop anyone getting to see the real you. The you I'll keep looking at until you're ready to take things further."

No one said nice shit like that to him. Ever. Even though there were only two versions of him. Martin and Button. There was no third, hard-faced shit. That was just him all along. Any more characters in his head and he'd worry he was becoming schizophrenic.

"I am," he said, trying to keep calm and reasoned and not give way to the turmoil of emotions coursing through him. "I'm ready if you are."

Liam leaned in, seeking a kiss. The rich tang of whiskey heated his breath and flicked a switch in Martin's head. An image flared to life. Liam's dark hair drained to the color of a sandy beach. His body, usually so big and warm, contracted to hard, angular bones. All the while his breath kept getting hotter and more toxic until Martin's lungs locked in protest.

"Stop." His chest heaved. He hadn't realized he'd thrown out a palm until it slammed into Liam's chest.

"But I thought you wanted — "

"I do," he said quickly. "It's just, you reckon you could clean your teeth first?"

Liam touched his lips as though he'd only discovered they were there. "My breath stink?"

"It's not you. It's..." He didn't get a chance to finish.

Liam took off toward the bathroom and slammed the door shut.

Martin stood there a moment longer, backed right up against the door. He'd ruined things. There were no words to fix what he'd done. To attempt an explanation would lead to more questions he couldn't answer.

He pushed himself off the door and made his way back to bed. That was the only thing left to do now. Hide under the covers and hope Liam would assume he'd fallen asleep and wouldn't wake until morning.

* * * *

In the bathroom, Liam took Martin's toothbrush from the sink and smothered the bristles with paste. He scrubbed until the enamel on his teeth screamed in surrender and his tongue had reached the texture of a threadbare rug. Only then did he lay the toothbrush down and spit a mouthful of blood into the sink. All this, just because he'd had a drink.

Being around Martin was like standing in a fine china shop with a dozen toddlers to control. Liam wasn't the one smashing the valuables up but, ultimately, he was responsible. Or felt responsible. That was the whole reason he was here, wasn't it? To keep Martin safe. Definitely not to fuck him.

That same morning Martin had been afraid Liam would touch him. How could things have changed between them so quickly? Obviously, they hadn't. Martin claimed he wanted to be touched, but his body had other ideas.

The attraction between them hadn't all been one-sided. Martin wanted him. Wanted this. He'd been the one to make the first move. Move as in asking. Despite that, though, come morning, Martin would leave for a man he was planning on selling his body to until his age caught up with him. Or Roy got bored of him, whichever came first.

Trying to talk some sense into Martin did in no way translate to actually sleeping with him. At least in theory it didn't. But all those things Martin had said about wanting to be with someone by choice and not for monetary gain, had hit Liam hard. And Liam wanted this, too. He wanted Martin more than he'd wanted anyone in a long time. Wanting Martin had probably been the whole reason for wanting him out of the flat in the first place.

Martin had the most perfectly attuned body to spark his libido. Petite, and thin enough that shadows haunted his ribs. Big, overwhelmingly blue eyes and fluffy hair that rarely saw a comb. *Damn.* A frisson of arousal seared to his cock. He might have lost his erection back in the bedroom, but it didn't take much more than an image of Martin's body for the heat to flash back.

Just what was going on here? Was he actually falling for the guy? How could that have possibly happened? Martin didn't make himself easy to love. Button was supposedly the one they all fell for. In as much as their wallets would allow. Liam loathed Button. But Martin was the person he really wanted to get to know.

When Liam cracked open the door, the light was off. Weak moonlight filtered in through the partially closed blinds, revealing a slim ridge under the covers.

Liam undressed in the dark then climbed under sheets as cool as the back lying next to him. He rolled on his side and gently brushed his fingers across Martin's spine. "Hey, you still awake?"

The warm skin twitched under his touch, but Liam didn't get an answer. Martin wasn't sleeping. No heavy breaths weighted the air and his muscles were way too tensed up on the other side of the mattress.

"I'll just lie here next to you, then." Liam stretched out, seeking somewhere close to comfortable. "I'm too tired to drive home." He didn't add that the two goons might still be lurking downstairs. "I'll leave before you wake. I've got to be home early, since I'm meeting this Robbie." He wasn't sure yet how he was going to cope with hiding what he knew. That didn't matter. Martin was his priority. And morning remained a long way off.

The far side of the mattress dipped slightly. "Robbie?"

"Katie's bloke." One day he might get used to those words, but they didn't slide easily from his lips, that was for sure.

"I know who he is. It's just, you usually call him Robin."

"Do I?" Liam didn't particularly care what the guy was called. He was bound to be a prick all the same.

"I'm sorry," Martin said softly.

"For what?"

"For what I said about your breath. It ain't you. It's me. Me and alcohol. I wanted to kiss you and not the booze. Sorry, man."

What was the deal with the alcohol? He could ask until he was blue in the face and never get an answer. Still, had to be better than the alternative. That his breath had reeked so much it had turned Martin completely off him. "Probably wasn't a great idea. You and me. Us."

The mattress shifted again. "Why?"

"Because twenty-four hours ago we both admitted we couldn't stand the sight of one another. And if not that, you don't fuck people you like. And I'm still fighting hard to keep that closet door wedged shut."

Silence tightened the air between them. "But I would've made an exception for you."

"Me, too. But we…"

When Martin climbed on top of him, the rest of what he'd been about to say tumbled right out of his head. Tight fingers embedded in his hair. A too-eager tongue raked over his, probing and thrusting and stifling. Gripping Martin's ribs, he rolled them both over and instantly broke the kiss.

"What are you trying to do?" Liam sucked in some air. "Suffocate me, or pull out all my hair?"

"What?"

Liam pried the claws from his scalp. "There's no rush."

"But I…" Martin gulped. "I got no clue what I'm doing."

No, because he was only experienced in fucking. He didn't know how to make love and Liam wasn't so sure he himself was in any way qualified to teach. But one thing Liam was certain of, he'd do everything he could to try.

Chapter Twenty-One

Martin smoothed a hand through Liam's hair, flattening the strands he'd practically yanked from his scalp just moments before. "Can I get the condoms? I really want you in me."

Liam tensed above him. "Are you sure?"

Hadn't they already agreed they were going to fuck? "Why wouldn't I be?"

"Because I thought..."

"What?"

A nervous swallow rippled the air. Liam's eyes glittered down at him in the darkness. "That you'd like it the other way around."

The other way around? It hadn't occurred to him. He'd assumed Liam would make for a natural top. To cover the awkwardness of the silence, Martin laughed a lot more manically than intended. "Ain't no one ever assumed I'm a top before."

"I didn't assume," Liam said, kind of haughtily. "I just thought you might prefer a change from what it is you usually do."

"So you assume I always bottom?"

"I didn't assume that, either." Liam rolled away, onto his back. "Why don't you tell me what you want?"

The loss of their closeness left Martin cold in more ways than physically. Still, no one had bothered to ask what he wanted in bed before, though he'd find it easier to explain what he didn't want.

He snuggled closer. "You were right the first time. I don't top. I don't get hard that easily, and most punters don't give a shit what I'm feeling anyway. If I had to top all the damn time I wouldn't make much of a living." He hitched in a breath. "Sorry."

"What for?"

"For talking about them. It's what I do. What I am. Guess it's off-putting."

"No." Liam's fingers tickled across his spine. "It's off-putting because I know you hate what you do. I reckon you'd rather be anyone else than Button, but still you keep going."

Because there was no other option. Liam skimmed too close to a truth that could never be told without risking their new closeness. He couldn't bear being hated again, and for things to finish between them that way.

"We don't have to do anything you're not comfortable with," Liam said when he didn't answer. "It was just a thought. Something different for us both, so that we'd be in the same boat."

Martin lifted his head. "You mean you've never…?"

"No." Liam's teeth flashed through the darkness. "Which is why I suggested it."

"But, you'd want to do that? Give your virginity to someone like me?"

Liam's laughter breezed between them. "I'm not a sixteen-year-old girl, Martin. And I don't think there is anyone else quite like you, is there?"

Martin couldn't answer, he was too numb to speak. No one had ever offered to give him something so precious before. His own virginity had been lost far too soon and it definitely hadn't been special. Liam deserved special with someone much better than him, that was for sure.

"What's this? Have I rendered you speechless for the first time ever?" Liam rolled on top of him, pressing him down into the mattress. "You're not intrigued? Not even a little bit?"

He hadn't been. But now Liam's tone had lightened and there was even a bit of excitement in that question. Even more in the hard ridge prodding his lower belly. He slicked a hand to the base of Liam's shaft. The thick column jumped and swelled under his touch.

"Does the thought of getting buggered by a twink boy like me *really* turn you on?"

Liam's hesitation only added weight to the answer that was still swelling in Martin's hand. Maybe all Liam had been waiting for was the right opportunity. And the right twink boy.

"I'll do whatever you want."

At that, an unexpected spark of something very intense flamed through Martin's body. Out of all the men he'd been with, he couldn't recall one of them ever offering to give up control to him. Whatever *he* wanted? He didn't know what he wanted. But it was enough to know what Liam wanted.

He wriggled out from under Liam then switched on the lamp. Squinting against the glare of the bulb, he pulled open the bedside table drawer and plucked out a couple of condoms. After tossing them in the vague direction of Liam's chest, he delved back in for the lube. When he turned back to the bed, Liam was examining the condoms as if he'd never seen them before.

"You put them on your dick. They keep you safe."

Liam looked up. His face was hard as stone. Hard as his cock tenting the sheet, even. "Were you expecting to be with him tonight?"

The answer was obvious, wasn't it? Roy had paid for this room.

"I'm glad it's you."

"Are you?"

"Do you hear me complaining?" Martin pushed the drawer shut. He didn't want to get into an argument, especially an argument about Roy. For tonight, he'd rather just forget Roy existed at all. Fortunately Liam was proving an expert distraction.

He swept his gaze from the hair-dusted expanse of chest to the solid girth of Liam's erect cock. The thick curve of his thighs pressed together and trembling betrayed his nervousness. "Roll over for me."

"What for?"

"For something good." Martin grinned. "At least, I hope it'll be good."

Liam didn't look overly convinced. Still, he did as he'd been asked and presented his beautifully broad arse to the ceiling.

Martin settled between Liam's open legs then slipped his thumbs into the narrow crack. He dipped close to the tight knot of Liam's opening, then flicked out his tongue.

Liam's head reared off the pillow. "What're you doing?"

"Just loosening you up. It'll hurt otherwise." Martin smoothed a hand down the furrow of Liam's spine. "Try to relax."

Relaxing didn't seem to be something Liam was good at. His head remained up. Alert. His arse remained tightly clenched. "You don't have to do...well. *That.*"

"Don't worry, big man. You ain't forcing me." Martin pushed his thumbs a little deeper into the furnace that was Liam's crack. "You reckon you could be a bit less tense? I promise to make this good if you let me in."

Liam pushed his face back into the pillow. His arse flattened a little, allowing Martin to tug both cheeks apart with his thumbs and once again glimpse the ripe pink pucker within. He'd never taken the time to really look at another guy's arsehole before. He'd rimmed a few in his time, but not without a hefty cash incentive. This was the first time he'd ever done this because he wanted to. Because he knew if he could get Liam into this, it would go a long way to relaxing him for the next step.

He leaned in and lapped at the clean musk of Liam's scent. When Liam's muscles started to soften, he angled the tip of his tongue over the molten opening. The heat seared through his taste buds, setting them aflame. He slicked the softening entrance with saliva then pulled back just enough to ease a thumb inside. With a firm bit of pressure, the tip broke through.

"M...Martin?" Liam grunted above him.

Martin looked up. "Hmm?"

"It, uh" —he grunted—"burns a bit."

"It does?" Martin frowned at the one thumb tip he had barely inched inside. "I guess saliva's no substitute for lube."

He fumbled for the lube, which he found hidden in the sheets. "I wasn't kidding when I said I haven't done this before."

"What you did before with your tongue. That felt really good."

"We can do that some more if you like. We don't have to do nothing else if—"

"No," Liam said quickly. "I'm ready for more."

Martin wasn't so sure about that. But he focused on slicking his index finger with a generous helping of lube. "I'll go slow. We can stop at any time. I won't... I won't hurt you."

"I know you won't." Liam smiled over his shoulder. "Just don't go booking that trip to Tenerife."

"Huh?"

"That's where you go, isn't it? When you leave your body behind."

Oh. That Tenerife. "If I'm going to make it good for you, I need to be right here." He pushed a fingertip to Liam's hole and broke through to the first knuckle.

Liam flopped back into the pillow.

"Are you okay with this?" Martin focused on the back of Liam's head. When he got a nod, he pushed in a little farther.

Liam groaned. But it didn't sound like he was in pain. Martin tilted the tip of his index finger, seeking the spongy bud of Liam's prostate. If there was pain it would be gone in a moment. He knew he'd hit jackpot when Liam's arse lurched in the air.

"Fuck!"

"Good?"

"Understatement." Liam lifted his head. "Can you do that again?"

"I reckon." Martin grazed over that same spot. "How's that?"

Liam wheezed out a breath. When he looked back over his shoulder, his cheeks were practically pulsing with heat. "Can we do it now? *Please.*"

"But I only got one finger in you yet. My cock is —"

"I can take it."

No, he couldn't. Not yet. His arse clamped around that one finger. There was no chance of a cock fitting into that tensed-up space.

"Let's see if you can take this first." Martin pulled out and lubed up another finger. He wiggled the tips around Liam's clenched hole. Soon that velvet sheath would be gripping his cock. *What would that be like? Better than a mouth? Tighter, most definitely.* And it would be Liam's body. He couldn't imagine anything more pleasurable than that. Except, perhaps, for Liam being inside him.

Liam's breath sounded sharp through his nose and harsh through his mouth. His body yielded just enough that both Martin's fingers disappeared to the second knuckle.

"How does that feel?" he asked, sliding his fingers in and out, beginning to build a rhythm.

"Like I want more." This time when Liam looked back at him, his gaze was darker than before. "Like I need to feel you inside me. I can take it, Martin. Just watch me."

Martin pictured exactly that, Liam taking his cock. Now there was an image that sent a shock of unexpected fire through him. And if it was what Liam wanted, then maybe they should just give it a go.

Martin slowly withdrew his fingers.

As soon as they were out, Liam scrambled up off his belly. Surprisingly, he was still hard. His cock stood fat and heavy and glistening with pre-cum. He settled back on the mattress, raised his knees to his chest and gazed out expectantly from between them. "Well? What are you waiting for?"

Chapter Twenty-Two

This was it. He could have won an award for drawing this moment out, but now Liam was ready. Eager, even. Lying on the bed, legs drawn up, and one hand clamped around each meaty thigh to hold them up and open. Hot as fuck. Or would be, if the responsibility of satisfying him wasn't down to a used-up virgin. *A virgin.* He'd almost laughed in Liam's face at the mere suggestion. But Liam had been so serious, so sincere…and so right. Because, technically, Martin had never been the one to do the fucking.

"Martin." Liam's brown eyes were hazy and soft, and in direct contrast to his very hard cock between his raised knees.

Martin reached forward and lightly touched Liam's shaft. The silky skin was ridged with thick veins. He rubbed what was left of the lube on his palms along the broad length. "You got that condom?"

Liam pushed his hand between his knees and opened his fingers. There it sat on his palm. "You want me to put it on you?"

"No. I can do it." Martin wasn't sure how much longer he'd last, anyway, but having Liam's hands on him might be a step too far.

He slipped off his pants then took the offered condom from Liam's hand. The latex gripped him like a second skin. His cock tingled. With eagerness or just with the effects of the latex, he didn't yet know.

He eased a hand under each of Liam's hair-dusted thighs and pushed them up and back. Liam's arsehole glistened, freshly stretched and waiting. He swallowed, still unsure he could actually pleasure someone by fucking them. It was a pleasure he had never really received. Only from Roy and he didn't want to compare the experience. He certainly wasn't going to try to match Roy now, no matter how successful the technique had been on his traitorous body.

Liam peered up at him with dark, glittering eyes. "Just do it."

"Get it over with, you mean?" He was stalling. He didn't know why. He wanted this, he really did. It was just... "If I'm lousy, I can suck you off. I mean I won't — "

"Martin," Liam said, more firmly.

"I *know*." He couldn't help but think about his first time, though there was no real comparison. But it was still going to hurt. Best to concentrate instead on making Liam's first time a positive experience. Because this would never happen between them again.

"Put it in me. It's what I want." Liam's voice was breathy, but not hesitant. This had to happen soon or there wouldn't be anything left to put in him.

"I know *that*, too." Martin held an even pressure until the head of his cock breached the tight ring of muscle at Liam's entrance. The extra lube helped, immersing him in that increasingly familiar earthy scent.

"Yeah." Liam gritted his teeth. "I can feel you."

"Don't sound so fucking surprised. I ain't *that* small." Martin let out a breath. A rush of overwhelming pleasure surged through him, bringing with it the familiar tingle in his balls. This was about to be over before it had started. He tried to concentrate on his breathing. Anything other than the head-on tumble of approaching bliss.

Liam hissed in a sharp breath. His lips drew back from his teeth in a pained grimace. Shit. This wasn't supposed to be about hurting. "Liam. Push back against me."

Liam's eyes were red and shimmering, but focused. "Don't stop 'til you're in all the way in. I can take it." The words tumbled free without a pause for breath.

Being locked half in, half out made his brain itch with

indecision. He could pull out now. The urge to come had wilted somewhat, his cock would do the same. But he was right about one thing. Being inside another person, the tightness was so much more intense than the soft, wet pull of the most eager mouth.

"Come up here and kiss me."

Martin shuddered. His cock sank in another inch or so. "Wait. I'm not sure how this feels."

"It's supposed to feel good. Doesn't it?"

"Yeah. I mean I think…" He didn't know. The sensations cascading through him made him twitch to pull out. He needed time to process what this was. His cock actually throbbed as fast as his heartbeat and he had no idea what that meant. Or whether Liam could feel the throb inside him.

Liam's hot palm clasped his arse and he lurched forward. His cock forged all the way inside. Something inside him detonated.

"Fuck!" He dropped forward, catching himself on his hands either side of Liam's torso on the mattress. "Gonna come." The words were more grunts uttered through a rush of red-hot adrenaline. Liam's hard cock pulsed against his lower belly.

"You're not." Liam's calmness broke though the roar in his head.

He couldn't breathe. Liam gripped his arse, holding him locked tight. Their bodies slicked together, slippery sweat and the constant throb of approaching orgasm.

"Look at me," Liam commanded. Martin raised his gaze from the fur of Liam's chest. "You're not going to come."

No, but he needed to do something. He couldn't just lie here, his cock like a raging ember threatening to explode.

"Now do what I asked before and kiss me."

Kiss him. If he moved at all he would come, he knew it. His body was never predictable, and control over what it did had always been impossible. But Liam grasped his head and yanked him down. The hot salty softness of Liam's lips invited him in and their tongues melded together.

A muffled whimper sounded low in Liam's throat.

Martin panted down at him. "All the way in, big man. Does this mean you ain't a virgin no more?"

"I think it's safe to assume." Liam's face remained tense, though his cheeks glowed through the shadows.

"Am I doing it right?" He was halfway to withdrawing before a full throttle rush of pleasure powered over him. This time, though, he managed to control himself. "I need to do that again. Can I?"

"Since there's no way I'm letting you pull out." Liam's legs closed around his hips, ankles hooked in the small of his back. Holding him, but not so tightly he couldn't move. "Kiss me again."

Martin slid back into the hot depths, and this time it was so damn easy. The same tingling thrills speared over him, centering deep in his balls like no kind of sex had ever given him before. What had he been so afraid of? He wouldn't attempt to compare all those guys who'd had him to this.

He caught Liam's lips between his own. Liam's tongue roved into his mouth and he tasted pure passion. He reached down, determined to clasp Liam's erection. When his fingers closed around a softening cock, he drew back. "Liam?"

"It's all right."

"But you—"

"Please." A note of desperation lifted Liam's tone. "Just fuck me."

Martin hesitated, flashing back to the pain of his first time. But with his cock held snug, and Liam telling him to continue, he couldn't quite connect that this was the same thing.

He rocked his hips and again reveled in the delicious kick of heat. "Like this?"

Liam grunted. "Like that. Just go easy."

He'd assumed he was going easy, but as another quickly stifled flare of pain flitted across Liam's face he realized he wasn't going easy enough. He slowed his thrusts. "Tell me when it starts getting good, then I know I'm doing it right."

"It is good," Liam said in the same strained tone.

Martin squeezed Liam's softening shaft. "No, it ain't. Not yet. Give me your hand." Unquestioningly, Liam did so. Martin caught his wrist and guided the hand down between their bodies. "Jerk yourself off. It'll help, like a distraction."

"From what?"

From the pain, Martin wanted to say, but Liam would assure him he wasn't in any. "Just do it."

He pushed back into Liam's heat. The same rush of arousal rippled over him with each thrust, so fucking addictive. He barely registered the rhythm of his hips moving to the pump of Liam's fist until he wasn't easing anymore. He was slamming. Grunting with each forceful snap of his hips.

"Yeah." Liam's teeth were bared, his expression tight, but this time something was different. Light, not shadows, danced in the depths of his eyes. His lips formed curves, not harsh, thin lines. "Don't stop now." He shuddered, his shivering muscles vibrating through Martin's body, hand working hard and beating against Martin's belly. "You're hitting me just right. It's good. So fucking good." The last 'good' emerged through a groan so intense his eyes near rolled back into his head.

Martin drew a breath to reply, then another. He wasn't so much breathing as panting. Sweat glistened across Liam's brow and chest. The solid thwack of their bodies connecting flavored the air with a carnal urgency that drove him on with an overwhelming desire to crash headlong into an ecstasy he'd barely been able to imagine before.

Liam furiously jacked off with one hand, the other clenched the headboard.

"Liam, I need to…"

Liam stared up at him with barely focused eyes. "Do it," he said, his voice little more than a breath.

All the permission required.

Martin's release roared through his ears as the summit

gushed through him, filling the condom harder with each fresh buck of his hips. When the final dribble seeped away he collapsed, so exhausted it took him a moment to register that the regular pulse against his belly was Liam jerking off between them.

"Oh, man." Forcing his remaining strength into his muscles, he gripped Liam's cock. "Let me." This wasn't entirely for Liam's benefit. He'd heard being inside someone when they reached orgasm was something special, and he wanted to experience this with Liam. There wouldn't be any other opportunity than right now.

Supporting himself with one palm flat to the mattress, he slid his fist the length of Liam's shaft and used the thick drops of pre-cum he found there as lubrication. Five firm strokes had Liam rocking his hips fast into Martin's fist. Another two and he froze mid thrust. His cock twitched. His arse twitched harder. Semen fountained between their bellies in a warm, rhythmic wash of pleasure.

At the same time, Liam's arse pulsed around him, filling him with a fresh, tingling heat. Less intense than the sex, but no less fulfilling. Or would have been if a certain unwelcome thought didn't once again creep into his head. That this was as close as they could ever be, and would never be again.

With a sigh, Martin dropped against Liam's chest. Their bodies melded in a sweet, earthy mix of sweat and cum. The ripe scent wisped around his nostrils, lulling him toward a well-sated doze.

"Hmm. I reckon I understand the drama of it all now" he said, resting his cheek against Liam's shoulder.

"Drama?" Liam also sounded wearily content, like he'd enjoyed this just as much, and that was enough to warm Martin all over again.

Martin swallowed, taking a moment to assemble a coherent sentence. "I mean, if this is the way I make my punters feel, I reckon I'm underselling myself. By about six thousand percent."

Martin sat up long enough to discard the condom on the bedside table, then he quickly settled back in the bed. His warm arm slid across Liam's belly and his cheek pressed to Liam's chest, just like real lovers in the aftermath of passion. Liam could almost believe they were lovers too, if Martin hadn't dropped in that line about his punters. A reminder that Button wasn't going anywhere.

For now, though, they were together. That would have to be enough. Liam wrapped an arm around Martin's shoulder and placed a kiss on his fluffy head. Fine hair tickled his nose and the scent of his own body swirled up his nostrils.

Martin slid a hand down to Liam's shaft. "You're still half-hard, you randy fuck."

"Yeah, well, it's been a few months." Liam sighed. "I'm just showing my appreciation."

"Either that or I didn't give you what you wanted. I did try to warn you I wasn't much of a top."

Liam stared at the ceiling. He wouldn't bite. This was just Martin seeking reassurance. It had been good between them. As good as a first time could be. "You're the best I ever had."

"Only cos you ain't had no one else." Martin lifted his head. Peered down into Liam's face. "Next time you can do me. *Then* I'll show you how good I can be."

"Is there going to be a next time?" Liam would like nothing more. And he'd equally like to show Martin how good he could be. But they'd have to go home together first. And Martin's fading smile told him that wasn't going to happen.

"Probably not." Martin resettled his cheek on Liam's chest. "And anyway, it'll be morning soon."

Would it? Not a sliver of light penetrated the blinds. It was late rather than early. No more than one a.m.

"You want me to go?" Liam held his breath. Going was the last thing he wanted, but he didn't have a clue what Martin wanted and that was all he cared about.

"No. I want you to stay."

"You sure?"

"Yeah." Martin's arm tightened across Liam's belly. "Positive."

And right there seemed to be the last word on the subject. How was he supposed to sleep with what was about to happen in the morning? Even basking in the tail end of orgasm, Liam remained alert and awake with the one question echoing through his head.

"Why'd you need the money?" He didn't expect a reply but needed to ask, anyway. "You don't get a penny yourself, do you, aside from rent and food. You wear old clothes. You got holes in your shoes. You—"

"I don't need much to live on. I'm just being responsible and saving for my future."

Liam sighed. "I'm never going to get the truth out of you, am I?"

Another long silence stretched between them. "If you knew the truth, you'd wish you didn't. So don't ask again, cos I can't tell you."

In other words, all the questioning in the world wouldn't yield any kind of result. Except Martin choosing to shift positions and move farther away, possibly leaving the bed altogether. He wanted that even less than he wanted to remain in the dark about Martin's financial situation. So he stayed quiet and clasped his hands together at the base of Martin's spine.

After a while, Martin's breath slowed and deepened. Liam closed his eyes and his mind started running away with all the reasons Martin would need to earn so much money and never get to spend it. None of those reasons involved anything legal. He didn't care about that. Well, he cared that Martin had obviously gotten himself into some kind of trouble, and he had increasing cause to wonder if those goons chasing him were a part of it.

Liam had never been in any kind of trouble. His parents had brought him up right, and he'd wanted to make his own way in life with law-abiding honesty. Martin was exactly the kind of person he'd never involve himself with. Now he'd gone and slept with the guy. He'd enjoyed every moment. He enjoyed Martin's company, too, underneath all the bitterness and bravado. That was as much of an act as Button. In many ways, Martin was as vulnerable as his alter-ego.

Liam didn't have a clue what was going to happen in the morning, but he'd make sure Martin was absolutely certain about going anywhere with Roy. The man Martin was using as a means to escape the two goons intent on terrorizing him. This wasn't escape — why couldn't Martin see that as clearly as he could? Liam was certain now that this Roy was behind everything that had happened, and had paid people to scare Martin into changing his mind. If that was true — even if it wasn't — Liam would do everything in his power to change Martin's mind back again.

Chapter Twenty-Three

Martin woke surrounded by a thick cushion of warm, sweaty skin. The cold reality of falling asleep in the arms of a punter made him twitch with the urge to escape. Just as he braced to pull away, he took a breath loaded with an honest, earthy scent that could belong to no one else but Liam. As the tension lifted from his muscles, he burrowed closer.

The glaze of early morning shimmered through the closed curtains and bathed the room in a natural golden glow. That was no guarantee the sun would continue to shine on his day. Soon the other hotel guests would wake, doors would bang and voices would carry down the hall, bursting this perfect bubble of contentment. He liked this peacefulness, where he could almost believe he and Liam were alone.

He and Liam. He'd have to stop thinking in those terms. Even if their situation allowed them to be together, a future relationship wouldn't get any further than Liam introducing an ex-whore to his parents. And he couldn't even class himself as an ex yet. One day, maybe. When his looks had faded and no one wanted his body for sex anymore. He wasn't sure Liam would be prepared to wait so long for him, or want what was left.

Now his sour thoughts had ruined the moment. He hadn't even needed to hear the other guests in the hallway. After untangling himself from Liam's sleeping body, he headed for the bathroom. His body ached from last night's sex, but in a completely different way from how sex usually affected him the following day. He didn't feel grimy, either. His dick felt a little sore and his lower back burned, but they were good aches. With good memories attached to them.

He used the toilet, cleaned his teeth then stepped under a warm shower. Time to wash away all traces of last night, but not for the usual reasons. Last night was a one-off and it was no use fantasizing things could be any different. He just had to accept what they'd shared over the past couple of days as a respite against what was to come.

When a firm weight dropped across both shoulders, he barely stopped himself from flinching. It wasn't Roy. Not yet.

Liam's touch tickled over his shoulders, washing his body with slow, careful strokes, fingers frothy with lather. They never strayed below waist level, despite the solid erection brushing his arse and lower spine.

"Why'd you need the money?"

Martin opened his eyes. *Not this again.*

"If you won't tell me that, at least tell me how much you owe. Because I'm right about that, aren't I? You do owe someone."

Oh, yeah, he owed someone. Way more than any amount of money could pay back. But hard cash was all he could get. Was all he knew how to get. He didn't need to think too hard about the figure. "Two million, four hundred and ninety-six thousand pounds."

"No. Seriously. I'd like to help."

Liam's arms clamped around his waist, warming him in places he couldn't allow himself to be warmed. Next week's fee would make the overall total thirteen hundred pounds less, but then his calculations could only ever be guesstimated. "It doesn't matter how much cos I won't take nothing off you. Wouldn't even when you were a particular hate figure of mine and drove me up the wall." He turned and pressed his cheek to Liam's chest. "I'd take this all day if I could, though."

"It's only you stopping you." Liam placed a kiss to the top of his head. "I don't want this to be a one-night thing."

"Don't." There was no point in discussing this anymore. All they'd do was argue their final few moments away, and he didn't want that. Not with the first man he'd slept with properly. As in, because he'd wanted to, not because he'd had to. He placed his palms to Liam's sides and pushed. "I'm going to live with Roy and there's nothing else to be said." He shoved back the shower curtain, stepped out of the bath and grabbed a towel off the rail.

"Live with?" The rush of water stopped, leaving behind a ringing silence. "Since when did this become *live with*?"

No. 'Live with' was wrong. Roy wouldn't be living with him. Just fucking him as and when. Did he subconsciously imagine 'living with' was a better term than 'whoring for'? Or 'owned by?' "He ain't going to be living with me. I didn't mean to say that."

"You still did, though." Liam climbed out of the bath, sopping wet and half-hard. "You got feelings for this guy?"

Feelings? No. He didn't hate Roy, but their relationship was based on business. Nothing more. The anger on Liam's face suggested he believed otherwise. As did his clenched fists and his tense abs, and ever-so-cute slightly wobbly bits that served as padding to a *very* solid body Martin considered pushing backward to the bed and —

"Hey." Liam shouldered him aside. "Don't look at me like you want to screw me when you already belong to another bloke." He marched from the bathroom and slammed the bathroom door shut behind him. "Oh, fuck."

Martin peeled himself off the tiles. Was that an 'oh, fuck, I'm sorry I pitched you through the wall?' Or just a general 'oh, fuck you'?

"I don't belong to him," Martin shouted to the closed door. Whether Liam was listening or not didn't matter — he'd have his say if he was talking to an empty room. "I'm just going to be working for him. And I like him. He's good in bed." He opened the door ready to finish defending himself. The first thing he did was collide with Liam's naked back. There he stayed, partially hidden, partially protected from the figure sitting in the chair by the window.

"Oh, *fuck*."

"Good morning, boys. I'm early, I'm afraid." Roy ran a slate-gray eye over Liam's body. "I hope that doesn't pose too much of a problem."

Just how much of their conversation had Roy overheard? Everything bellowed through the open door, for sure. Including all that bragging about how skilled he was in bed.

"No." Martin struggled to find his voice through the nerves clogging his throat. "I was just spending time with a..." What was Liam to him? Someone more than a friend, yet not a lover either. He'd had neither before, but given the chance he might have found both in Liam. But people like him didn't get those kinds of chances and he didn't want to agitate Roy any more than he already had. "A friend."

"So I see." Roy's attention meandered to the unmade bed, and from there to the used condom resting on the bedside table. "Do you work together? Or was this more of a social occasion?"

"We don't work together," Martin said quickly, stepping in front of a naked Liam. "He's not like me."

"I was talking to your friend."

"Why?" Liam asked in a strangely husky tone. "You interested in doing a bit of business yourself?"

Doing a bit of business? What did that even mean?

"I'd pay well for the privilege." Roy's voice carried the same throaty catch.

"Fine. Name your price."

Martin spun around, light-headed with the shock of what he'd just heard.

Liam stood there, tall and proud. His shaft might be soft and withdrawn, but his eyes gleamed in challenge.

"Button?" Roy asked, behind him. "How much do you think would be a reasonable fee for this young man's services?"

Martin didn't know, or care. All he could think about was if he didn't do something, Roy would fuck Liam, and

Liam might well let him just to prove some ridiculous and unnecessary point he probably wasn't aware of.

"Nothing." Martin drew himself up and yanked the towel from his hips. "He's not for sale." He refastened the towel at Liam's waist and dropped his voice. "Don't play games you don't understand."

Liam's glare burned right through him. "I'm playing your game, *Button*. I reckon I understand all I need to." He whipped the towel away then strode over to the bed and lay down. "Two hundred. Each."

"Done." Roy rose and pulled a wad of notes from his wallet. He discarded the cash on the table, not even bothering to count it. His jacket was next, dropped on the floor without a second thought. This was new. Roy never discarded his fancy clothes so casually.

Liam lay on the bed, hands behind his head, top teeth set over bottom lip. His chest punched up and down too fast. His impressive cock remained in retreat, along with his withered scrotum.

"Turn over." Roy opened his shirt to reveal a thick strip of tanned paunch. "I'll take you on all fours. Button, you'll watch from the chair."

Martin's stomach lurched. He felt sick. He needed to hide in a corner. No. He needed not to be here. Why was he still here? The door was unlocked. He could leave. Naked, if there was no other way. But then who would protect Liam? There wasn't anyone else.

"Liam, you need to get dressed." Martin lurched to the bed and grabbed Liam's arm. "Don't think he won't have you, because he will. And I'm not letting it happen. So you can just f —"

"Button!"

Martin froze. He stopped pulling on Liam's arm. Liam hadn't shifted an inch, anyway.

Roy was steadily watching him from across the room. An overweight balding businessman carrying every one of his sixty years of his shoulders. Except for when he smiled. Then he revealed a glimpse of the darkly handsome charmer he must once have been.

But Roy wasn't smiling. He didn't appear the slightest bit aroused either. No, Roy's menacing expression suggested he'd much rather slit Liam's throat. Or Button's.

"Please, Roy," Martin said softly, because Button was still right here. Letting him take charge was going to be the simplest way out of this. The most spineless, too. But pride was something Martin had lost years ago. He wasn't even sure he'd had any to begin with. "I'll do whatever else you want. Just tell him to go. You don't want him. He ain't... *isn't*...even your type." Liam was as big as Roy. And dark. Not small and fair like Button.

"Button, calm down," Roy said in a low voice. He held out his arms. "Come here."

He didn't want to. Not to go anywhere near Roy. But this had already been agreed, and those goons weren't going anywhere. He was the one who had to go. For Katie's sake, even if not for Liam's. But the journey toward those outstretched arms was far too short, yet he had to force his feet to carry his body forward, inch by slow inch.

As he dropped into Roy's embrace, he gulped his last breath of clean air. The next he took filled his lungs with the overpowering scent of Roy's poncy aftershave.

Chapter Twenty-Four

Liam sat up. His pelvis and lower back burned from last night, but that was nothing when compared to the sting of this fresh humiliation. From here he had a prime, if unwanted, view of Martin's naked, still-bruised arse as Roy's thick slab-like hands covered both cheeks. When he raised his head, he met eyes as cold as a tombstone and a smile as dead as any seasoned gangster's.

It had been a test, lying down for Roy. He was pretty sure the same applied to Roy. Liam had hoped Martin would come to his senses before any bluff would have to be called. Now it appeared he'd just proven to himself that Martin didn't have any sense. Roy, Roy's wallet — and cock, for all Liam knew — had won.

He dressed as fast as he comfortably could without appearing in a hurry, painfully aware that two sets of eyes were scanning him all the while. He wasn't proud of his body. It functioned well enough but he didn't take as much care of his physical appearance as he might. None of that had mattered when he'd been confident he could win Martin over to his way of thinking. He'd made the assumption that what they'd shared had been something worth more than money. He'd been wrong. Now he'd lost a dignity he hadn't known he had.

"I'm sorry," a soft voice said.

Liam met the glazed blue of Button's too big, too wide eyes. "Why? You said you wouldn't change anything for me, so it's not like I wasn't warned."

Button took a step closer to him. "I would have, though. If things were different."

"You mean if I was as loaded as your new owner here?" Liam threw out a hand toward Roy. "Or do you mean if I was as good as him in the sack?"

"It's not about that. I just meant..." When Roy's hand came down on his shoulder, Martin sucked in a breath. "I don't know what I meant. Just...forget it."

Forget it. And there was a command Liam couldn't refuse. He stalked to the door and threw it open. The air was already a hell of a lot cleaner in the corridor.

"Liam...wait!"

Liam stopped. Against his better judgment, he checked back over his shoulder.

Martin stood even closer. Perhaps just a couple of steps away. A hair's breadth behind lurked his new owner. Martin didn't speak. He just stared with that same pleading desperation.

"Say the word, Martin. We can still go home."

Martin swallowed. His eyes shimmered with unshed tears. Tears that couldn't be his because Martin never cried in front of anyone. These tears belonged to Button. And Liam was more than done with him.

"I can't." Martin lowered his head. He might as well be apologizing to the carpet for all that 'sorry' meant.

"Well, *Liam*. I think your answer is fairly conclusive, don't you?"

Liam switched his focus to a victorious Roy. "Yeah. I do." He forced a smile of his own. "Enjoy your purchase, mate. I know I did." Liam turned away. Strode out into the hall before he could catch Martin's reaction. The heavy door swept shut behind him. He took a couple of deep breaths then strode down the corridor with no other thought in his head than getting into his car and driving home as fast as legally permitted. Faster, if he could get away with it.

Chapter Twenty-Five

Liam didn't get any further than a turn of the key in the ignition. Even before the engine sparked to life, he already knew he wasn't going anywhere. He didn't know what exactly he was going to do yet, since offering himself up on a plate to Roy hadn't exactly seen much success. He wouldn't have touched that slimy fuck for a million quid, but Martin had believed he'd been serious.

The pressure of Martin's fingers still branded his arm. And checking the depth of the red marks alone was enough to keep him in the car park, not yet ready to desert the naïve little idiot still inside the hotel.

Martin stepped out about fifteen minutes later, bag over his shoulder, head bowed, hands shoved deep into his pockets. He stopped outside the main doors and studied what appeared to be a particularly fascinating crack in the paving.

Liam willed him to look up, to realize his mistake and come running. They could go home together. There didn't have to be anything more to their relationship than friendship, always assuming they had made it as far as friends.

Not that it mattered too much, because Martin didn't even glance in Liam's direction. He wasn't even left alone for more than a few moments before Roy emerged from the hotel, fastening a long, woolen coat. When he spoke, Martin smiled. Too wide. Too fake. Too Button. *Are you okay?* Was that what he'd been asked?

Roy hooked an arm across his shoulders and led him to a car. Not just any car. A sparkling white Rolls-Royce parked not far from the lobby. As Roy gestured for him to climb inside, Martin surveyed the car park. Maybe seeking a way out, or just scanning for goons. Either way, his eye didn't catch the battered estate car several rows down. And even if he had, he'd already made himself more than clear. Martin Bailey didn't need rescuing.

Liam remained in his car, engine idling, until the Roller glided toward the exit. Only then did he ease the Vauxhall's gear stick into first and chug along behind.

It wasn't long before the Roller turned off the bypass and meandered through residential streets lined with eighties-style red-brick houses. Liam tagged along far enough behind that he almost lost them a couple of times. But a white Rolls-Royce wasn't exactly going to blend with the Fords and Citroëns for long.

Eventually the car pulled up in a parking bay next to a small block of flats at the end of a cul-de-sac, far enough away that other parked cars blocked him from view.

The block was a fairly modern building, divided into four separate apartments, each supplied with a wooden balcony and a parking space. There were no cars, though. Except for the pristine Rolls-Royce.

From where he sat across the road, Liam could make out Roy ushering Martin up the steps to the farthest flat from the road. That narrowed things down. He now knew which flat Martin was going to be living in. Roy's den of iniquity. He didn't want to think too much on what they were going to get up to in there, or how long he was prepared to wait out here while they were doing it. Or even why it made a difference. Nothing would change. Martin had already assured him of that.

When his phone chirped in his pocket, Liam was almost grateful for the intrusion. It prevented him from following the worst of his thoughts to their logical conclusion.

"Where are you?" Katie's irate voice shot down the line.

"Out." What was her problem? She'd barely been home for days herself.

"Oh. This is your latest plan, is it? Let's pretend we forgot all about the lunch you insisted on so you could meet Robbie, and that way you can really show him who's boss."

Robbie? Damn. Liam slumped back in his seat. Midday lunch for three. He checked his watch. Ten past. She'd even reminded him when he'd called the night before. How could his absence not look contrived now?

"I don't know what to say. I forgot. I've been busy."

"Doing. What?"

"Helping Martin move."

"Move? Where to?" Curiosity softened her voice. "Martin has a home with us. Oh, unless…" The sharpness returned. "What did you say to him?"

"Nothing." Why should the fault automatically be his? Because he was the one always complaining about Martin's presence. "He's decided to live with some bloke."

"What bloke?"

"A boyfriend bloke." Why not? A simple explanation far better than the truth.

"I didn't even know he had a… Does this boyfriend know what he does for a living?"

"How should I know?" He felt his own temper rise. She was always so bloody concerned about Martin, who didn't give a shit about her because he'd even left without saying goodbye. He could walk out on his life and start another without looking back on the old one. Only emotion-free zones could do that. "It's done. He's moved and I'm about to make the drive back."

"Where are you?"

"Chichester."

"Wow. He really has moved. He won't get his deposit back. He does know that?"

"I think he does." Martin probably didn't need to worry about money anymore, anyway. "Are we done talking about Martin now?" Every mention of that name forced him a little deeper into the murk of his own inadequacies. He'd lost. He'd been thrown over for a married grandfather with money to burn. He'd get over it. As long as Katie stopped slicing at the wound with her razor blade questions.

"Yes. I suppose so." Her accompanying sigh was wistful. "Listen, love, sorry for biting your head off earlier, only I thought… You know what I thought. Anyway, you'll love Robbie. He's bought beer. Give him a chance, okay?"

That was exactly what he'd do. It seemed everyone he knew would rather be with someone else. Maybe it wasn't Roy and Robbie who were the arseholes. Maybe the arsehole had been him all along. "I'll do my best."

"You mean it?"

Did she honestly believe he'd become some hyper-jealous moron? Considering the boyfriends she'd introduced him to in the past, she probably had reason to.

The weird thing was what he'd begun to feel for Martin wasn't like he felt about Katie. When he looked at Katie he wanted to hold her, cuddle up with her on the couch at night, the two of them together like a married couple. When he looked at Martin…*well*. Last night had been the accumulation of looking at Martin.

"Liam, you still there?"

"Yeah. I'm just preparing my 'meet the best mate's new boyfriend' speech. Best behavior. Promise."

She laughed. "There's no need for a speech. Just be your best friend's boyfriend's newest friend. That might take time, but Robbie's not going anywhere." There was a warning there. A 'don't force me to choose' warning. Would she pick Robbie if he did? Would he choose Martin? Right there was the difference between them. He already knew that Katie would never ask.

"I'll do my best." He ended the call, then Liam started the car. If Martin wanted him, he'd call. Otherwise, there was nothing more to be done. Staking the place out was doing him no good whatsoever. Martin wasn't his problem and had made himself perfectly clear. With that thought squarely at the forefront of his mind, Liam turned the car and headed in the opposite direction. Toward home.

Chapter Twenty-Six

That evening, Martin stretched out on a new king-sized bed which was too big for the room. This, Roy had proclaimed whilst showing him around, would be the space where they spent the majority of their time together.

He tried not to think too much about the implications of what that actually meant. Right now he was alone here and he'd savor the time. Roy was in the lounge. If he listened hard he could hear the soft murmur of voices. His body might be simultaneously aching and melting, but his mind buzzed with activity. With regrets, mostly, at the way he and Liam had parted. He'd had the morning all set out in his mind. They'd shower and dress together, share a coffee. All very civilized, like friends. Perhaps they might even have shared a parting kiss. Not like friends, but like the lovers they could never be.

Why Liam had offered himself to Roy, Martin didn't understand. Didn't want to, either. Didn't dare contemplate how far things might have gone. He'd rather have dropped dead than let Roy have sex with Liam. Either that or die preventing it from happening. Somehow, thinking about Liam giving himself away like that was even worse than the immediate future. As in, being chained to this bed more or less as and when Roy demanded. But until those goons had finally learned to leave him alone, what other choice did he have?

All the way back from the hotel he'd itched to check behind him, yet he hadn't dared for fear Roy would notice and want to know why. He didn't want to explain the extent of his goon issue until absolutely necessary. Hopefully, he wouldn't have to. A month, two max, and he'd disappear.

The voices continued to murmur on in the lounge. Why Roy had to bring one of his business acquaintances here, Martin had no idea. This wasn't an office. It was supposed to be a home. He couldn't make out what they were saying, no matter how hard he strained his ears. Not that he was even interested in Roy's business dealings. But he still pushed back the covers and swung his legs out of bed. As he did so, a surge of heat exploded through his lower body. No bruises on the outside this time, but he had a whole host of them on the inside. Roy was going to have to calm things down. A weird thing for a twenty-one year old to say to a sixty year old, even if that twenty-one year old was supposed to be seventeen.

Martin grabbed his jeans off the floor and stepped gingerly into them before heading into the hall. This was his flat now, so he had a right to know who Roy had invited in. The living room door was open a crack. He stepped closer. Roy's voice rang out loud and clear.

"Sometimes I wonder why I pay you such an exorbitant salary, Shaun."

"You pay me to drive you. Not ferry street trash to the clap clinic." Shaun, whoever he might be, sounded vaguely familiar.

"I didn't pay you to terrorize the boy to within an inch of his life, either, but you seemed to take great joy in doing so."

"It worked, didn't it? You got your toy." The cigarette-roughened chuckle that followed was definitely way too familiar.

"After a fashion. I'll talk to him. Button's a simple soul. Once he knows my reasons, he'll accept them."

"You think?" A snort. "I wouldn't accept them."

No. They could agree on something. Martin had had enough of skulking in the shadows. He pushed open the door. Roy sat on the couch, looking casual with a glass of some amber liquid in his tumbler. Whiskey, probably.

Roy's surprise quickly hardened to his usual impassive expression. The other guy, he'd already recognized. The goon lounged in the armchair, a can of beer resting on his thigh. He had his hideous jacket unzipped to reveal a tatty gray T-shirt beneath.

"You?" Martin said softly, barely squeezing out the word through his tight throat. "What the fuck are you doing here?"

"Ah, Button. I was wondering when you'd wake up." Roy set his glass on the coffee table. "Come sit." He patted the couch beside him.

Martin remained in the doorway. The goon quietly sipped his beer. Where had the alcohol come from? This was supposed to be his flat and yet the last thing he wanted here was alcohol. No. Alcohol was second to last. The goon was the very last. "Why the fuck did you try to drown me?"

"Calm the language." Roy's palm hit the couch again. "Come. I won't make the request a third time."

The request sounded far more like a demand. Martin did, however, want to know what the hell was going on. So he inched over to the couch and perched his throbbing arse right on the edge of the leather. As far from Roy as he could get. Acutely aware of his state of undress, clad only in his underpants, he clenched his hands in his lap and tried to keep his embarrassment below simmering, along with the rage Button was barely managing to keep in check. He could hide behind his alter ego for a little longer. Then when it was safe, no matter what excuse Roy had to explain this all away, he was getting the fuck out.

Roy slipped an arm along the back edge of the couch. He gestured with his fingers. "Closer."

Martin switched from the beckoning finger to Roy's face. "Don't push it."

Rather than the flash of anger he'd expected, a flicker of amusement glittered in Roy's eyes. "I believe you're owed an apology."

"You think? You got any idea what it feels like to have

your head held under water by a couple of blokes, who for all I knew, were out to kill me?"

The goon snorted. "It was a little dip in the river."

Martin powered to his feet. "You fucking liar!"

"Button. Sit *down*."

Well, there was that third time. Martin clenched his fists. But he did as he'd been told. Because Button always did.

"Now. Apologize."

"What?" Like fuck he would. Hell wouldn't so much as have frozen over but be built over with motorways and housing estates, the lot, before that happened. But Roy wasn't looking at him. Roy was very much focused on his sulking goon.

"Not you." Roy rubbed a hand across his forehead. "Shaun."

"*Me?*" This time it was the goon who practically leaped out of his chair in shock.

"You'll apologize for your over-exuberance, and what's more, you'll be Button's personal chauffeur until further notice. Starting tomorrow when you take him to the clinic for his tests. Is that clear?"

"You're kidding me." The goon found his boss's firm gaze. "There is no way I'm sharing car space with that gobby little —"

"You won't have to." Martin rose from the sofa. He'd already listened for far longer than he needed to, and it was getting late. He didn't fancy wandering through an unfamiliar town looking for a cheap place to stay at midnight. "I don't need no apology. What good would it do me?" He turned toward the door. Two minutes to pack and get out. No problem. His bag sat in the bottom of the wardrobe, and all his things were still in it.

"Button," Roy said, his tone as demanding, as certain as ever. "Sit down and listen."

Fourth time of asking. It would be the last. Martin stalked into the hall. He returned to his room, threw on the clothes he plucked from the floor, then collected his bag from the bottom of the wardrobe.

Liam had known the truth all along. Why hadn't Martin listened? Because he never did. Because he always assumed he knew what was best. Why wouldn't it have been Roy? No one else had offered to pay for his exclusive use. No one else wanted him that much. Fuck, he'd told Liam he thought it was flattering. But it wasn't. Right now, after what Shaun had done to him in the past on the order of a man who wanted to own him, it was pretty much terrifying. Enough to make his hands shake as he sealed up his bag after checking that his whiskey bottle was safely cushioned inside. There was nothing else he needed.

He made for the door, passing the lounge and not pausing to check inside. Roy and Shaun were still in there. They hadn't come looking. He still didn't quite understand why. Not until he got to the front door anyway. Grabbing his jacket off the hook with one hand, he pushed down on the handle with the other.

Locked.

He wasn't even surprised. Or particularly bothered. There was more than one door out of here. They were only two floors up here. He could jump the balcony. *Easy.*

Martin presented himself back in the lounge. Roy didn't bother to even look up. He was too busy flicking through some papers he must've pulled from his open briefcase on the coffee table.

Shaun the goon watched him though, wearing an odd little smirk Martin wanted to knock right off. But no one said a word. There was no sound apart from the rustle of paper, the creak of an old leather jacket and the sound of Martin's own heartbeat thudding in his ears.

The balcony doors were covered by a set of vertical blinds, but the doors didn't require a key. They locked from the inside.

"Button?"

Martin slid back the blinds. His hands shook as he reached for the catch and twisted. The door clicked open. Cold air rushed in, instantly whacking him with full awareness. If he didn't get out of here right now, whatever the risk, there was every chance he'd never get out.

"I forgot to ask. Did your mother enjoy those roses?"

Martin froze. One foot in the cool fresh air, the other trapped in the stifling closeness of the flat. He looked back, not certain that he'd heard right and hoping with every atom of his body he'd definitely heard wrong. "What?"

"Yes." Roy scanned the papers on his lap, all the while tapping his lower lip with a pen. "I wasn't too certain what she'd prefer. Roses or lilies. Both are her favorites, so I've heard." Roy stopped tapping. "Shut the door, would you? There's quite a chill in here. Don't you agree, Shaun?"

Shaun slipped a palm down to his fly and squeezed. "Nuts like ice." He flashed a crude grin. "Fancy blowing some of your hot air on 'em?"

"Not on my time." Roy set his paperwork down on the coffee table. "The door, Button. Soon as you like."

Martin turned back to the window. His reflection stared back at him, cold and gray as a ghost. Carefully as he was able, he drew the door to.

"Lock it, please. You can never be too careful."

Martin twisted the lock then drew the blinds across.

"Good boy." Roy patted the sofa cushion once again. "Sit down."

"How did you know?" Martin asked, stepping away from both his bag and his jacket. "About…" He couldn't say her name. Not here. Not in front of Roy or the goon. "About the roses."

"Shaun can be very discreet when he wants to be. Can't you, Shaun?"

Shaun indulged a stretch, his skinny denim-clad legs stretching halfway across the room. "Invisible man, me."

Shaun had followed him, then. To the home. For how long? *Fuck.* What did it even mean? Was this a threat? *Of course it's a fucking threat.* What would Roy do to Sandra? What could he do?

This time when Roy gestured to the seat next to him, Martin hesitated only a moment before taking it.

Chapter Twenty-Seven

Two weeks later

Liam sat in his car in the same place he'd parked two weeks before, and watched the flats ahead of him. He'd also parked here the previous week, but there'd been a white Rolls-Royce in a bay outside the building. He'd waited a good couple of hours, but in the end he had left before the Rolls. Today there were no cars at the building.

The goons had disappeared as soon as Roy had got what he wanted. Button. Too much of a coincidence, perhaps. Liam just hoped Roy was being good to him. Which was why he was here. To find out.

After a further few minutes of idling, he got out of the car and started toward the building. The wooden stairs creaked under his footfalls, but held steady as he made his way to the top.

To the left of the door, a wall bricked off entry to the balcony. It also prevented any view through the glass doors. There was no doorbell to ring or letterbox to rattle on the solid door. So he raised his fist and knocked.

Of course, Martin might not be there. Roy could have taken him out for the day. Or Roy had gotten here by other means and they were in bed. Fucking. Now there was a thought to spark a flood of unwanted images. He knocked the door again. Harder.

No answer.

Just as he raised his fist to try a third time, a floorboard creaked on the other side of the door. "Shaun? What you knocking for?"

He thought Martin sounded okay, but he didn't have a clue who this Shaun was. He opened his mouth to ask, but Martin's voice filled the void.

"Roy? That you?"

Liam leaned closer to the door. "Guess again."

"Liam?" Martin practically screeched.

"Third time lucky. Can you let me in? I'd like to talk to you."

The air stilled on the other side of the door. "How'd you find me?"

"I followed you back from the hotel." Perhaps admitting such a thing should make him feel like a creepy stalker himself, but he didn't. He didn't feel like anything other than a concerned friend who'd done the right thing. "Can you let me in? I won't stay long. Just 'til I know you're all right."

"I am. I'm fine."

He sounded way too insistent for that to be true. "I'd like to see for myself."

The floorboard creaked again. "I can't let you in."

"Why not? He hasn't locked you in, has he?" Although he was only half joking, the silence from the other side of the door spoke volumes. "What, he has?"

"No. I've got a key." An indignant catch lifted Martin's tone. "But Roy would do his nut if he found you here."

Liam wasn't interested in what Roy thought. "I'm going nowhere until I've seen you." He focused on the front door. This determination had been building all week. He knew how stubborn Martin could be, but he was prepared to wait.

"You're a stubborn fuck." After a moment, the lock clicked. The door opened. A small pale hand shot out, grabbed him by the sweater and yanked him inside.

Liam stumbled forward, shocked by Martin's unexpected strength. He turned to find Martin leaning back against the closed door. Blond hair frizzy and uncombed, though his eyes were big and blue as ever. He wore a pair of dark jeans and a thin white long-sleeved shirt. New clothes Liam hadn't seen before, courtesy of Roy, most probably.

"Five minutes." Martin relocked the door. "You can't stay any longer. I never know when he's going to show up."

"Who? Roy? Or Shaun?"

"Shaun?" Martin spun. The key somersaulted to the wooden floor. "How'd you know about Shaun?"

"You thought I was him, remember?"

"Oh. Right. I did." Martin scratched a hand through his unruly hair. "Roy always calls first, but Shaun just turns up whenever."

"Who is he? Not another punter?" Liam's heart sank at the possibility. Did Roy have him entertaining all sorts in here? Like in those sordid docudramas full of drug-addicted prostitutes and the monsters who made millions from their suffering.

"He's my personal slave."

"*Slave?*"

A sly smile tilted Martin's mouth. "Yeah. It's his punishment. Roy says he has to do whatever I want, within reason. Which means I can't get him to sunbathe on the fast lane, but I can get him to drive me into town."

"Punishment for what?"

Martin pushed out his bottom lip. "We don't have to talk 'bout him, do we?"

"No," Liam said. Not yet, anyway. He'd rather not have been presented with the Button face, though. "How've you been?"

"Does it matter?" Martin frowned. "I threw you over for Roy, didn't I?"

Wasn't as if he was likely to forget. But there was far more to it than Martin was willing to say. And that was the other reason he was here. To uncover some secrets. "It's for purely selfish reasons, mostly."

"How'd you mean?"

"Well." Liam shrugged. He'd been honest so far. Might as well continue along that same vein. "If you must know, I can't sleep for thinking about you. I can't concentrate at work, either, because there you are taking up headspace. And I won't be able to get on with my life until I know for sure that you're okay and that he's treating you right. Then I'll go, and you don't have to see me again."

Confusion clouded Martin's gaze. "I don't get why you'd still give a shit after what I did. Man, you were better off mooning after Katie than me."

Mooning? Is that what Martin thought this was about? Liam tried not to grit his teeth. This was just Martin's hard-faced persona on the defensive again because he didn't know how to handle someone actually caring about him. That was okay. Liam could deal with his defenses. "Maybe I was. But I'm here now. And you're not about to send me away without a proper answer, are you?"

He'd given Martin no bait. Nothing to argue against, even if all he got by way of return at first was another harsh stare. "Fine." Martin crossed his arms. "I suppose you want me to show you around."

"This place?" This hovel, more like. Peeling wallpaper. An odd stench of damp in the air. Roy hadn't exactly pushed the boat out to accommodate his new plaything.

"Yeah. You want to see that I'm doing okay, don't you?"

A guided tour wasn't exactly what he'd had in mind. A deep conversation was more like it. But if Martin needed time to ease into a more serious chat, then Liam had that time to give, even if Martin didn't. "Yeah. Okay. Why not?"

"Okay. Let's start in here." Martin led the way into a small lounge.

The two leather sofas and large TV looked expensive and proved a stark contrast to the drab wallpaper and scratched laminate flooring. The doors leading to the balcony were covered by a set of dark vertical blinds.

Black as prison bars.

Liam shuddered.

"How's Katie?"

The question cut the air, dragging Liam's attention away from the open blinds. "Good." He perched on one of the sofas. "And pregnant." The word wasn't any easier to say out loud, but he was finally accepting the reality, at least.

"Are you dealing with that okay?" Not a spark of surprise lit Martin's tone.

Which could only mean one thing. "You *knew?*"

Martin lowered his gaze. "A little bit."

"A *little* bit? You either did or you didn't, and I'm fairly certain now that you did."

"Yes, then. I did." Instead of taking the other sofa directly across the room, Martin came and perched next to Liam. "She told me that morning you were hiding under my bed terrified she'd think we'd shagged. She swore me to secrecy. Even if she hadn't, it weren't my place to say. I had issues of my own to deal with at the time."

Martin's issues. A never-ending list of them. But he hadn't come here to talk about Katie. "Can we talk about you?"

"It's only been a couple of weeks. I'm doing okay."

"Are you, though?" Liam raised his hand to brush Martin's cheek.

Martin was quick to bat the hand away, but, as he did so the loose cuff of his shirt rode up to expose an inch or so of discolored skin.

Liam caught the wrist and pushed back the sleeve. Oval-shaped bruises marked the pale skin in an almost perfect circle. "What has he done to you?"

"Nothing." Martin tugged free. He sprung off the couch and went to stand at the 'bars' shielding the doors. "It's just sex, and he pays me stupid money for it. Did you know I get my own balcony? I'll show you."

Liam crossed the small distance to where Martin stood facing the doors. "I've got no interest in the balcony."

"Well, you should. It's a good view." He drew back the blinds, stopping only when Liam's hands pressed to either side of his hips. "Liam..."

Liam pushed his nose to the back of Martin's blond hair. He breathed the sweet scent of fragrant shampoo. "You smell good."

Martin stood stiff and rigid, one hand on the door now and the other at his side. "Uh, thanks."

"I keep thinking back to that night. Our night." Liam tightened his grip, enjoying the feel of the bony arcs under his palms. "It wasn't just sex, was it? It didn't feel like that to me."

Martin bowed his head. "You know it wasn't."

"Then why are you here instead of at home with me? Your room's still right where you left it. We could leave—"

"Liam, please." Martin unlocked the door and slid the glass panel back just enough to step over the threshold. "Come see the view." He disappeared outside, leaving Liam no choice but to follow.

The balcony overlooked the postage stamp gardens from the houses across the car park. The nearest garden contained a child's trampoline and a brightly painted summer house. *Not exactly a view to die for.*

"Is this where you and Roy sit for afternoon tea?" Liam gestured to a set of cheap plastic patio furniture by the rail. Somehow he couldn't see the man parading around with his male lover, even out here. Not in view of the houses across the way.

"No. I sit out here by myself a lot, though. Just to think." Martin went to the rail and stared out over the gardens.

Liam joined him. "Think about what?"

Martin lifted a shoulder. "Just stuff."

He was clamming up again. Time for a change of subject. "How are the neighbors?"

"There ain't none. Not in this block."

"None at all?" That had Liam's alarm bells ringing yet again. No immediate neighbors. No one to run to if things got out of hand with Roy. In whatever capacity.

"This is just temporary. Roy's getting the whole building refurbished in a few weeks. He's freeing up a house for me from his portfolio."

"Good old Roy." Liam swallowed the bile of pure jealousy. No use trying to pretend otherwise. This was exactly how he'd felt when Katie had a boyfriend. And he wasn't going back there again.

"I'll show you the kitchen next," Martin said with a fake brightness that set Liam's teeth on edge. He retreated across the lounge and through another door.

The kitchen was old and unimpressive. Aged brown base and wall units, and a small table with two chairs under a bare window at the end of the room.

"So this must be the place where you enjoy your cozy breakfasts together of a morning?" Liam asked, picking up a box of cornflakes from the counter.

"Don't be a bitch, Liam." Martin swiped the box from his hand and set it back down. "Come see the bathroom." Already he was leaving the room.

This must be the express tour. Designed to last no longer than the five minutes Martin had said they could have.

The bathroom was filled with an avocado-colored bath, toilet and sink. Blue tiles lined in moldy grout. On this room, Liam passed no comment. He'd learned his lesson from before. Being called a bitch was a first for him and he held no desire at all to hear it again.

Martin returned to the lounge then glanced back as though he expected Liam to follow him. But Liam wasn't quite done exploring yet. There was one more door through which he had yet to venture.

"What about the bedroom?" He placed his fingers on the handle. "You haven't showed me that yet."

"Go in," Martin said with a nonchalant wave of his hand. "If you feel the need."

Oh, he felt the need all right. He also felt a strong sense of wanting to avoid the room altogether. But his curiosity won through. With only a touch of hesitation, Liam opened the door and headed inside.

A huge bed dominated this room. Leather headboard and crumpled sheets. The vague stench of stale sex soured the air. Liam strode across a pale threadbare carpet to the window and pushed it open before he could even think about taking a proper breath again.

Once he'd filled his lungs with cleaner air from outside, he set about checking out the room in a bit more detail. Inside the top drawer of the nearest bedside table drawer, he found two tubes of lube, one a squeeze away from empty, and a strip of condoms. The sight of them lying there made his stomach lurch. But at least Martin was keeping himself safe against STIs.

"What you looking for?" Martin asked from the doorway.

"I don't know." Liam hadn't even realized he was seeking something, until now. Just some evidence that Roy was mistreating Martin. Something more than the bruises.

He pulled open a bedside table drawer. And did a double take.

"What the hell?" He pulled out a wad of fifty and twenty pound notes and held them up for display.

Martin broke into a proud grin. "Yep. First week's wages. Up five hundred on what he originally offered. Man's got it so bad for Button."

Liam dropped the money back into the drawer and closed it. "Looks like you're doing well for yourself."

"Now he finally believes me."

Believe and leave, was that the implication? Who was Martin, anyway? Just an irritating turd that had finally been flushed. Why rake the bowl in an attempt to drag him back out again?

Liam hadn't realized he'd sank down onto the bed until a firm hand pressed his knee. He lifted his head to find Martin kneeling on the floor in front of him.

"Roy's good to me, Liam, but only cos he has to be." Martin shifted his hand to Liam's thigh. "The only say he has in my life is where I sleep and how we fuck. Nothing else."

Liam thought that was more than enough control already, but there was no use pointing out the realities to Martin.

"I get it," he said, hearing the drawl of defeat in his tone. "You bank account is swelling at the same rate as your cock and you're happy playing the sex toy for as long as he wants you. What else do you want me to say? Congratulations?"

"Happy?" Martin snatched his hand away. "What gave you the idea I'm happy?"

Liam shook his head. "You just said as much. I get that you've got some twisted relationship going on and you're all nice and cozy—"

"Relationship?" Martin sprang to his feet. "With that piece of shit? No way. Liam, I ain't in no relationship with that piece of shit. I fucking *despise* him."

Chapter Twenty-Eight

"What?" Shock darkened Liam's eyes and made a pale mask of his face. *"What?"*

Strangely enough, the confession sent a shaft of light clean through the great black void that had been growing steadily wider and deeper ever since Martin had made the mistake of moving in here. No, the mistake had started farther back. Ever since he'd let Liam walk out on him at the hotel. He should have walked, too. "You were right about him. I should have listened to you, but I thought I knew him. I thought he was nice. Safe. Turns out, I know jack shit. As usual."

"You mean…?"

"Yeah. He sent them goons after me." Martin sat on the bed next to Liam. "Shaun's chief goon. There was another one, but he resigned when I outed him as a pedo back at the hotel." He grinned despite himself. "I should apologize. For not trusting you enough."

"It was him all along, and yet you're still here?"

There it was. The judgment, manifesting deep in Liam's eyes. A sort of disgusted horror that made him feel no better than a skid mark in a pair of second-hand underpants. "I've got plans."

"Yes." Liam rose too quickly from the bed. "So have I."

"Liam, don't…" He saved his breath. Liam wasn't leaving. Not just yet, anyway. Instead he moved to the wardrobe and threw open the doors.

"Are all these clothes yours?" He raked through the hangers, assessing the clothes like he was in the market for some new clobber himself.

Martin joined him at the doors. "Ain't none going to fit your wide arse, big man."

"Quit that. I'm not looking to wear them. Just pack them. You got a bag?"

"No." Martin squeezed himself between Liam and the clothes. "I ain't going nowhere. I can't." As long as he stayed here, Roy wouldn't go anywhere near Sandra. And by the time he was ready to leave, Roy wouldn't be able to threaten him anymore. Not when he'd have something of his own to barter with in return. "I told you I got plans."

"Yeah?" Liam swept out an arm, easing Martin to one side. "I like the coming home with me plan better. We'll stick with that." He unhooked about half a dozen new shirts from the rail in one scoop of his arms.

"No. Liam, I can't come home with you." It was a nice thought, considering what had already happened between them, that Liam still cared enough to want him safe.

"Why not?" The hurt was clear in Liam's tone. "Wouldn't you rather be there with us than here doing whatever it is you do with him?"

Martin gathered the clothing from Liam's arms and dropped it in a bundle on the bed. "None of this fancy shit is mine. It's Button's." He lifted a patterned silk robe between forefinger and thumb. "This fuck ugly thing is Roy's. All my stuff is still in my bag." He dropped the robe and gestured to where his bag sat in the bottom of the wardrobe, still packed with exactly the same things as when he'd left the hotel room with Roy. "Right there for when I'm ready to leave. Which ain't yet."

"What do you mean? Are you telling me you *like* it here? Being treated like a grubby secret? You actually forgive him for terrorizing you into coming here to be kept like a prisoner?" Liam abandoned the clothes and started pacing instead.

"No, I ain't okay with it. Which is why I've got something to fix this fucking disaster. And him, too, I reckon."

Liam stopped pacing. "What have you got?"

"Not much. Not yet. But I'll get more. When I do, it's payback time."

Liam stared at him. His lips flapped but no sound came out. He swallowed. "More of what? Poison?"

Martin laughed. "Yeah, that's right. I snuck out to B&Q and stole a job lot of weed killer to put in his tea."

"No need to take the piss. What is it, then? This thing you have?"

Martin shook his head. "Nope, I ain't saying."

"But it's something you have now? Hidden away?"

"This ain't twenty questions, Liam."

"Then tell me." Liam closed the distance between them. "You can trust me. You never know, I might be able to..."

Martin tuned out. He'd heard something. Just a click, followed by the gentle creak of a floorboard. Without thinking, he hurled himself at Liam's lips. They froze under his. That was okay. This wasn't supposed to be a kiss. Just a means of shutting him up. But then Liam's arms snaked around his hips and pulled him close. And Liam's lips started working against his own, devouring his breath, halfway to dredging up his soul.

Martin clamped onto Liam's shoulders and pushed until their lips tore apart.

Liam stared back at him, wide-eyed and panting. "What was —?"

"Wait here." Martin pressed a finger to his lips. Then he turned and stepped into the hall, closing the door behind him. "Shaun," he said, rather more loudly than he ordinarily would. Just to give Liam the warning. "You're supposed to knock."

Even with the front door still open, Shaun dominated the hall with lanky bones and his nicotine-scented aftershave.

"Why, when I've got a key?" He gave Martin a once-over with his flinty eyes. "What've you been doing all morning? Sleeping again?"

"What if I have?"

"Lazy little fucker." Shaun grabbed his jacket from the

hook by the door then threw it at him. "Put this on. We're going out."

"What for?"

"Boss says you need a haircut."

Martin clutched his jacket close. "I don't want my hair cut." He didn't want to go out, either. By choice, he'd have gone back into the bedroom and snogged Liam's face off again. But since when did he ever get offered any real choices?

"Didn't you already sell your right to an opinion?" Shaun stepped back outside. "Now get a move on. It's one of them fancy *ladies'* salons in town. They charge by the minute."

Martin clutched his coat close, digging deep in the pockets, trying to locate the key he couldn't find. Where the fuck had he put his key? He'd need it so Liam could get out. Otherwise he'd be trapped until Shaun opened the door again.

"Get a move on, kid." Shaun grabbed his arm. "I got better things to be doing than waiting on your overused arse all day."

Martin stumbled outside. He didn't have his key on him at all. Which meant it'd be in the flat. Liam would find it and let himself out. Unless, of course, he chose to remain until Martin got back. Which wouldn't be good for either of them.

"I'm going to tell Roy exactly how you speak to me," Martin said as Shaun locked the door behind them.

"Great. That'll give me the excuse to get your tongue trimmed at the same time as your hair."

Martin followed Shaun down the steps, resisting the urge to give the bastard a thorough push.

By the time he got back from wherever it was Shaun would be taking him for his hair cut, Liam would be gone. And that would be it. He'd have no reason to return.

Martin wished he'd had the chance to explain. That none of this was out of choice. But telling Liam one secret would only lead to revealing another, and another. By which time

Liam wouldn't simply not understand him. Liam would actively hate him.

* * * *

As soon as the front door closed, Liam made his way to the lounge and peeked through the balcony doors. He couldn't see much. The balcony got in the way. All he knew was that Martin had left with a goon to go get a haircut. A haircut he didn't want.

Liam found the key in the exact place Martin had dropped it. But he wasn't ready to leave quite yet, not with this perfect opportunity to explore in a little more detail. He made a start in the bedroom.

One place most people kept their secrets was usually under a shroud of dust on top of the wardrobe. Or in a shoebox under the bed. Martin's secrets hadn't had time to get dusty, either here or at home. He'd left nothing behind at the flat except his porn stills. But he'd brought his bag along and he'd practically told Liam that was where it was. Whatever 'it' was.

Liam took out the bag from the bottom of the wardrobe and placed it on top of the fancy clothing. He drew back the zip and delved inside. The first thing he brought out was Martin's scotch bottle. He was surprised Roy had let him keep it.

Next, he took out a few old T-shirts, a pair of jeans and two pairs of underpants. Martin's clothing rather than this new gear belonging to Button. Right at the bottom, he touched something soft and woolen. A sock? No. A hat. To be more precise, his black beanie. The one he'd left in the hotel room two weeks before. There was something inside, too. Something light but solid. He opened up the hat. Nestled inside was a phone. A cheap thing, which, surprisingly powered up pretty quickly when Liam switched it on.

Liam perched on the bed among Button's silky rags and scrolled to the contact list. Two listed. One of them was

Roy's. The other was just initials. OH.

Leaving the mystery of that particular contact where it was, Liam scrolled to the photos. Twenty in total. The thumbnails were explicit enough that he didn't need to focus on any particular one. They were all of Roy, naked, his flabby pink body on full display in the very bed on which Liam now sat.

He wished he felt more surprise. Or shock. Or disgust. But from what he knew of Martin, this was par for the course. One of Roy dozing. Martin's head on his chest, staring solemnly into the camera. Another was of Martin's lips over Roy's cock. Selfies, but not with Roy's approval. Or knowledge.

So, this was the sum of Martin's plan. Blackmail. God only knew what Roy would do to get those pictures deleted once he found out about them. This kind of material destroyed lives.

Having seen more than enough of Martin's camera work, Liam returned to the contact list. With his mind still scarred from those odious pictures, he called up the OH number.

The phone rang twice before a female voice answered. "Oakland House, how may I help you?"

Oakland House. Why did that sound familiar? Because he knew the place. A residential care home on the outskirts of town. A place that that cost a fortune to its mostly elderly residents. Why would Martin have that number? Who did he know there? And why on a phone filled with revenge porn?

"Sorry. Wrong number." Liam rang off then slipped the phone in his pocket. All the speculation in the world couldn't confirm any truth. The only way he'd get that was from Martin directly. And to do that he'd have to ensure Martin was given enough incentive to come to him next time.

For extra certainty, he grabbed the whiskey bottle, too. If, for some unfathomable reason, Martin could let the phone go, the same wouldn't ring true about his mysterious bottle.

Chapter Twenty-Nine

"Nice hair."

Martin climbed back into another of Roy's flash cars and glared at Shaun through the rear-view mirror. "I look like a fucking light bulb."

Shaun chuckled as he pulled out into the road. "Bayonet or screw in? No, wait. I think I already know the answer to that one." More laughter, though Shaun wasn't anywhere near as hilarious as he thought.

Martin pressed his lips together. Sometimes ignoring the bastard was the best thing to do. As soon as he got back, he was washing out whatever the sticky crap those women had loaded his hair up with. He'd requested a trim but, apparently, what he wanted didn't matter. Roy had rung ahead with instructions on what was to be done.

He'd had no option but to sit in the fancy massage chair in the fancy salon and let the scissors and the bleach do whatever the fuck Roy had ordered them to. Why should anything change? He did exactly the same in the bedroom.

When Martin pushed open the car door and stepped out, Shaun got out at the same time.

"What are you doing?"

"I'm picking the boss up in a couple of hours," Shaun called back, making his way to the stairs. "You might as well make me a cuppa before I go."

"No!" Martin dove for the steps and reached the top a second after Shaun. "You can't."

Shaun took out his key. "Why not?"

"Cos…I got no tea." Was the door still locked? If it was, that meant Liam was still inside. If it wasn't, then Shaun would know someone had been inside, because it had been locked when they'd left. Shaun had turned the key himself.

"I bought you some yesterday."

"I drank it."

"Forty teabags?"

"I like my tea like my sex. Strong and frequent." He tried a smile, but Shaun wasn't buying it. All Martin was doing was making himself look guilty. "Okay, so I don't want you coming in cos you're a cunt. That good enough?"

Shaun's expression remained blank. "No. It's not." With a sweep of his hand, he knocked Martin to one side and pushed the key into the lock. When he twisted his wrist, the key wouldn't budge. More than likely because there was another on the other side of the door.

"What's going on here?" Shaun withdrew the key then pushed the handle. The door yielded straight away. Before Martin could even think about running, Shaun grabbed him by the wrist and hurled him into the hall. "You stupid fuck." Shaun locked the door and shoved both keys into his pocket. "Boss will fry your balls and slice them up on toast when he finds out about this."

"About what?" Martin tried to calm his thrashing heart lest Shaun hear it. He'd admit to nothing and eventually Shaun might even believe the door had never been locked in the first place. "A key in a door?"

"No. A cock in an arse." Shaun shoved him aside and started throwing open doors. "More specifically, your arse."

When he disappeared into the bedroom, Martin chased after him. The clothes were still piled high, but now they were being raked through by Shaun.

"What are these doing here? You thinking of running off with someone?"

"No. I was having a sort out," Martin replied, knowing that this particular battle was already lost.

Shaun picked up a transparent shirt. "Boss only bought that for you last week." He tossed the shirt back onto the pile. "You'd better not be moonlighting. He's paying for sole use of that arse."

The edges of Martin's temper frayed. "You don't think I got anything else to offer other than my arse?" He stepped forward. "You're a fucking prick, Shaun. If I ever did have someone here, it would only be a friend. And nothing would have happened. I was fully dressed when you got here." Button had deserted him, but he didn't care. Squaring up to this skinny streak of piss was something he'd wanted to do for a long time.

Shaun snorted. "A, you don't have friends. B, boss told you no guests. C, either way, you're fucked." He stormed down the hall then and returned a moment later armed with a kitchen chair.

"What's that for?" Martin asked, still feeling a lot more confident than he should. "You planning to sit on guard duty 'til Roy gets here?"

"Something like that."

When Shaun slammed the bedroom door between them, he realized a second too late what the chair was for. He launched himself at the door. "Don't you dare shut me in!" When he tugged on the handle, it wouldn't budge. "I haven't done nothing, you fucking lunatic!"

"Shut up!" Shaun's voice hammered through the door. Then, silence. A moment later he spoke again, from somewhere farther down the hall. "Boss? Yeah, thought you want to know your *Shit* Tzu's been mixing with a mongrel or two in his kennel. What'd you want me to do, have him neutered? I got him locked in his cage, waiting for your instruction. Get back to me when you can."

Voicemail. Not that it made much difference. Roy would get the message soon enough.

It wasn't until he went to grab a couple of shirts that he noticed his bag on the bed. Wide open. The whiskey was gone. Not so much a problem. That bottle had never done him any good, anyway. Collateral damage. There was something far more important in that bag.

He turfed everything out on the bed, and searched through the lot. Twice. But there was no doubt that his second phone had gone. Such a lousy hiding place. Not only that, he'd practically invited Liam to have a snoop through. That phone hadn't even been password protected.

No use panicking. Too late for that. He took a few calming breaths and tried to think what to do next. Which would be exactly what Liam wanted. Call and beg for his property back.

He'd lie if he had to. Or he'd tell the truth. Half the truth. Whatever was needed short of the full and uncensored version. There was only one problem. And it was a big one. The phone Roy had given him was currently sitting on the coffee table in the lounge.

Chapter Thirty

"Button?"

Martin opened his eyes to find Roy peering down at him, looking neither pleased nor displeased. Just curious.

He sat up. The bedroom light was on and the curtains had been drawn across the windows. *Evening already?* His fuzzy head also confirmed that he must've slept for ages. "Roy. I—"

"I've sent Shaun to fetch dinner." Roy hung his jacket on the back of the door then loosened his tie. "Take off your clothes."

Martin rubbed the last of the sleep from his eyes. He hadn't planned on dozing the afternoon away. What he'd wanted to do formulate a half decent reason as to why the front door had been unlocked from the inside when there was no one home. He'd needed to invent a whole new person who wasn't Liam. But now he had nothing. And Roy hadn't even asked for an explanation. Just sex.

"Is there a problem?" Roy asked as he unfastened his shirt.

Could it be possible that Shaun had faked the voicemail? Roy's number one rule was no visitors. Well, number two rule. Just after sex on demand. Shaun was supposed to be in charge of ensuring he obeyed that rule. In which case, it made sense that Shaun wouldn't want Roy to know he'd failed.

"No." Martin forced Button to smile. "No problem."

"Then do as I've instructed." Roy pushed his trousers to his ankles. His cock stood hard and heavy, already flushed a furious scarlet. The veins were stark and ropey, almost pulsing with need.

Martin skittered off the bed, panic making him awkward and clumsy as he fought to remove his own clothing. Once naked, he looked up to find Roy staring at him. No, not at him. At his hair.

"I can fix this," he said, flicking back the fringe.

"It's very blond."

Yeah, practically luminous. "You don't like it?"

"It's...not what I expected."

"I didn't choose it." He pouted. The Button face disgusted Liam and angered Shaun, but never failed to win Roy over.

"It doesn't matter now." Roy slipped his shirt from his shoulders and hung it with his jacket. "Come here."

Martin inched across the space between them. Roy was hard as a rock, yet Button couldn't summon a twitch of arousal.

"You're quiet," Roy said as he stroked a finger the length of Martin's breast bone.

Martin stifled a shudder. "Would you prefer to talk?" He really hoped not. He could do sex on auto-pilot. Talking required a bit more thought.

"In time." Roy leaned close. His breath ghosted Martin's ear. "On the bed."

Martin cringed over to the bed. Until he knew for sure that this super-cool version of Roy was genuine, he'd rather not make a potentially volatile situation worse. Besides, it was only sex. Nothing he hadn't done a thousand times before.

Soon as he was settled on his back, Roy sank on top of him and pressed kisses into his neck. Polite little nips just sharp enough to leave marks. The kisses continued down his belly and only stopped when Roy reached the base of his flaccid cock. "Is something bothering you, Button?"

Martin swallowed. For a fraction of a second he considered replying with pure honesty. Something like, *Why should anything be bothering me? I'm locked up in a derelict flat and barred from having the slightest hint of freedom.* The words were there, but they weren't Button's. And Martin didn't exist in the same breathing space as Roy. He was pretty sure that was rule number three. "No. I'm just tired."

"Really? Tell me about your day." Roy shifted up to rest on the pillows. His fingers slipped south and gifted Martin's uncooperative shaft a light caress.

Martin's mind went blank. It had only been a couple of weeks and yet one day bled into another until he felt as though he'd lived here half a lifetime already. "I had my hair cut."

"I know about that." Roy engulfed Martin's left nipple with his lips. The gentle sucking, along with the hand rhythmically stroking his cock, had Martin writhing with the swarm of sudden, unwanted arousal.

He gasped. "Roy!"

Roy broke the suction, leaving a hot nub of burning flesh where a nipple used to be. "What is it?"

"Nothing." He sighed. A few more minutes and he'd be thrusting his hips into Roy's hand, desperate for release. But he didn't want this kind of a release. He didn't want to be here, in this bed. Doing what he was being paid to do. "Just...nothing?"

Roy paused a moment before working his cock. Up. Squeeze. Down. Squeeze. "You have nothing of any importance to say?"

Did Roy know he'd had a visitor after all? Something wasn't quite right, but how was he supposed to think like this? Even his hips had given up the ghost. They joined the rhythm, humping into Roy's hand like *he* was the punter. Sex was never an issue when the punters rarely touched more than his arse. When all they wanted was to get themselves off. But these sensations flurrying through his body made it impossible to switch off or take a trip to Tenerife or anywhere else. Whenever he was with Roy, he couldn't be anywhere but with Roy.

Roy peered down at him with oddly dark eyes. "Did you ever attend school, Button?"

Button might have tried for an education, but Martin had

skipped the place whenever he could. "Uh, it's the law. I had to." He closed a hand around Roy's wrist. "I'll come if you don't slow down."

"You won't until I give permission." Roy pumped a little faster. The bed started vibrating. "How about exams? Did you pass any?"

"W-what?"

"Look at me."

He tried to focus on Roy's face while clinging to Roy's ever-shifting wrist. There was no way he could avoid coming. He didn't have that much self-control. "I wasn't no good at school."

"Grammar not your forte?"

"N...No." He made the effort to form his words properly. Button was way more middle-class than Martin. The working-class punters liked to think they were corrupting the youth of the middle-classes and the middle-class punters didn't feel as though they'd dropped their standards too far. "Roy, I have to..." A sudden bolt of fire stole his breath.

"So very flushed. You need to come?"

He nodded. "Please."

The tight fingers unfurled from his shaft and transferred to his balls. "Don't you da — "

With the pressure released, Martin's climax roared over him without any hope of holding back. Cum spewed over his belly, leaving him gasping and groaning with each shameful pulse.

"I'm sorry," he said after he'd finally caught his breath.

"Are you?" Roy sounded unimpressed, but his fingers continued their work, kneading Martin's tender balls in a slow, regular motion.

"Yes." Despite the chill in the air, Martin's muscles had already begun to melt into the mattress. "I couldn't help — "

"Yourself?"

"No." His brain turned to mush as the effects of his orgasm coursed through him, powerful as a truth serum.

"So messy." Roy's fingers still cupped his balls. "And

disobedient." He looked up. "When you moved in here, you promised me obedience."

"I tried."

"Trying isn't good enough." Roy released his balls and traced a finger through the cum pooling on his belly. "Obedience and fidelity. Do you know the meaning of either of those words?"

The atmosphere had thickened, but Martin's body wasn't alert enough to take as much care over his words. "Yes. Just don't ask me to spell them." He risked a smile. A smile unreturned.

The finger shifted to his navel, tickling where it touched. "Who is he?"

The softness of the finger had lulled him slightly. That and the increasing pull of a sleep he really couldn't afford to indulge. The question, though, dragged him right back to acute consciousness. "Who's who?"

Roy pulled away to wipe his hand on the sheet. "The person you entertained here earlier. Shaun told me everything."

Fuck that shit-stirring prick. It had been too much to hope Shaun had kept his fat mouth shut. Now pleading ignorance would just make this worse. What had he decided to go with before Roy had arrived? Before he'd fallen asleep even? Just repeated exactly what he'd told Shaun, although the reality was Roy would be even less inclined to believe him.

"He was just a friend I met in town a couple of days ago. I mentioned where I lived and he just showed up. Unexpectedly."

Roy sat beside him, looming down as if to catch every lie as they left Martin's lips. "Really? Shaun didn't mention you meeting anyone in town."

"That's because Shaun didn't know. He was...um... waiting outside the shop I was in at the time. You know how he hates shopping." Grasping at straws now, but at least Roy hadn't called him out on it.

"And what did you two do when you met up in this...

shop?"

"We talked. He's straight, anyway, and I'm with you. There's no one else." As Martin presented the sweetest smile he could muster, Roy turned away to the bedside table.

"Turn over."

Okay. That meant it was time to fuck. The questions would now stop. Martin wasn't going to argue against that.

"I don't want you bringing anyone back here in future," Roy said, back still turned as he rummaged in the drawer. "Is that understood?"

Martin buried his face in the pillow and closed his eyes. "Yes." He sighed. So far so good. Seemed he had been believed after all.

The mattress dipped. Hot palms pressed down on the back of his thighs. "Open."

Martin moved both legs apart. At the initial invasion of a hot, determined fingertip, he tensed. But the finger had been well-lubed and Roy was always careful not to hurt him too much.

As Roy worked his hole, Martin rocked in time to the gentle thrust of the single digit working in and out of his body.

"Where exactly did you meet this friend?" The question dragged Martin back from the edge of a gentle doze. "Originally, I mean?" A second finger joined the first, pushing up inside him with only a twinge of discomfort.

Hadn't he already passed all lines of questioning? But then again, since when was Roy ever that easily convinced about anything?

"He was just an old school friend." It was the quickest reply he could think of. And who could actually prove him a liar?

A third finger joined the other two and angled up into him with more force. A sharp, not altogether unpleasant heat exploded inside him. Martin buried his groans in the pillow.

"You didn't let him fuck you?"

Martin lifted his head. "I told you, he's straight. Plus, he was only here ten minutes."

"Ten minutes is more than adequate for you, Button."

What was that supposed to mean? He wouldn't ask, positive already that he wouldn't like the answer. Instead he concentrated on the skilled fingers teasing his body. Again, he pushed his face into the pillow. Half in shame, half to muffle his own cries as the pressure of another orgasm reared inside him.

"Does he know how to excite you like this?" Roy's weight pressed him into the mattress, hot breath scouring the back of his neck.

"I told you," Martin muttered. "Nothing happened."

Roy withdrew his fingers and replaced them with the head of his thick, bulbous cock. Martin tried to relax. This was the easy part. The worst had to be over.

Roy drove in hard. Too hard. A piercing pain stabbed through Martin's pelvis. He muffled his cries into pillow, knowing by choice he'd rather have this than more questioning. Roy's panting breath beat against the back of his head.

He was barely aware when the panting changed pitch, became words, until a hard slap stung his backside.

Martin jerked his head off the mattress. "What?" he snapped, more Martin than Button. But the irritation burned through him, as scorching as the cock inside him. What could Roy possibly want to ask now?

"Your friend. His name." Roy slowed his thrusts, teasing a faint stir of pleasure to soothe the harsh burn of pain.

Roy wanted a name. Any name. It didn't matter which — as long as it wasn't Liam's. "Dave."

"Dave?" The name dropped like a stone. Heavy enough that Martin pushed his face back into the pillow. "Are you sure?"

He thought he had been, when he'd said it. Certain enough that Roy would accept it, anyway. But that disbelieving tone told him he was wasting his time. Hot tears prickled in his eyes. He let them fall into the cotton before lifting his face again. "Yes."

"I see," Roy said softly. He pulled back, withdrawing his cock to the head. "Dave, you say?"

Martin didn't bother to reply. He barely had time to take a calming breath before Roy forged into him again at a fresh angle. A flurry of sparks erupted inside him, shooting pleasure-tipped fire through his nerve endings. It didn't matter how much he didn't want to get off. His body always betrayed him, because Roy knew exactly how to make him feel whatever Roy wanted him to feel.

"Are you...quite certain it was Dave?" Roy panted, thrusting back and forth, little mercy now. "And not...say, *Liam*, for example."

Liam? Martin jerked up, despite the weight pumping away on top of him. Roy already *knew?* He had to. Unless it was just a guess. Either that or Button's lousy lies had been as transparent as the condom on Roy's dick all along. "Why would you think it was Liam? He...doesn't know where I live now."

"It would be such a pity. I mean, if it wasn't Liam."

"What do you mean?" Martin wriggled like an insect pinned to a corkboard. He clenched down in the hope he could end this more quickly. Too difficult to think with two distinct sensations rioting though him at the same time.

Roy froze, his cock buried deep. "Do that again."

Martin clamped down harder, picturing Liam inside him. The tighter he hugged, the safer Liam would be.

Roy let out a long low groan. "Yes. Exactly like that." The hip pumps softened. Something pulsed in Martin's body, flooding him with heat. The burn radiated through him, but something else did, too. An unpleasantness he hadn't endured in years.

The fucking bastard wasn't even wearing a condom.

Roy sighed. His cheek came down to rest on Martin's head. "You suck me right in as if you never want to let go."

"You didn't ask," Martin said, quietly numb. He never let anyone fuck him raw. Negative test result or no negative test result. Who'd tested Roy?

"Ask what?" Roy said, almost wearily.

"All those questions you just asked me and that one didn't even figure on your list. I never said you could fuck me raw."

Roy's chuckle ruffled his hair. "I always fuck you raw, Button. If you're talking about the lack of a prophylactic, well. You're mine. I can and will do whatever takes my fancy." He withdrew and rolled off, flopping one arm across the bed. "Cuddle into me."

Martin stayed where he was, on the farthest edge of mattress. Belonging to Roy was old news. Button might belong to him, but Martin Bailey didn't. And never would. "What did you mean about Liam? You told me I wasn't to see him again and I haven't."

Roy beckoned him with a wet, shiny finger. "Come here and I'll tell you."

Didn't matter that he would rather shove his now limp dick into a waste disposal than cuddle into Roy right now, he dragged himself across the mattress. He rested his head over Roy's breastbone and willed the solid thud of the heart beating beneath to stop.

"I'm really not sure about this." Roy plucked at his hair. "I asked for pale gold. And this, this is…"

"It's platinum." Martin sucked in a breath loaded with the scent of sweat and semen. "More expensive than gold." Not that he felt any more expensive. Worthless would be closer to the mark. "What did you mean about Liam?"

Roy was silent a moment. "For someone who means nothing to you, you can't stop repeating his name."

Martin lifted his head. "You said it was a pity my friend wasn't Liam. And I just wondered why you'd say that?"

"Does he have a brother, this Liam?"

"No." Martin had no idea if Liam had siblings. But he wasn't about to drag them into this sordid mess.

"A brother by the name of Dave, perhaps?"

"You knew it was him all along, didn't you?"

"Of course. I had Shaun check the CCTV."

CCTV? As in cameras? In here? Martin sat up. He scanned the shadows, looking for a lens. If Roy had cameras, it meant he knew about the phone. Roy had opened his bag and taken it. *Fuck the photos. What about Liam?*

"Not in the bedroom. There's a small camera in the porch. I thought we agreed you weren't to have visitors."

Martin concentrated on keeping his breath even. He could deal with this. Sort everything. Just as long as Liam was okay and continued to be okay. "He won't come back again. I'll call him and tell him to stay away."

As he made to get out of bed, Roy grabbed his wrist. "There will be no further contact with that overgrown wastrel."

"I didn't have contact with him. He came to me. I wasn't expecting him."

"Then how did he know where you find you?"

"He followed us when we left the hotel." Martin tugged his wrist free and ran both hands over his face. "I need to call him. Let him know he's not to come again."

"Not necessary. Shaun's taking care of the issue as we speak."

"Shaun?" Martin lowered his hands. He'd spoken too sharply for Roy, but he didn't care. "I thought he'd gone to get dinner?"

"And he has. Via flat number fourteen, Somer's Court."

"What?" Martin's heart dropped to his stomach. "Shaun's gone to see Liam? To tell him not to see me anymore?"

Roy's lips tilted to an oddly cold grin. "Let's hope he listens. Now come here. I miss your heat."

Liam wouldn't listen. Not to Shaun. Martin rose from the bed. He barely felt the cum trickle down his thighs. There wasn't time to wipe clean. "You can't intimidate him. He's bigger than Shaun. He could take Shaun no problem." He wished he sounded more certain than he felt.

"The matter is being dealt with. We agreed no visitors, and I intend to enforce that even if I have to confiscate your key. Do you understand me?"

Martin understood all right. He was to become more of a prisoner than he had been before. "I need some water."

He didn't. Not really. What he needed was his phone. After pulling on his pants and jeans, he limped from the room. Roy had probably checked it, but wouldn't find anything. Martin never used the phone to call anyone other than Roy or Shaun.

He'd memorized Liam's number a while ago. But it wasn't so simple to get Liam to pick up, leaving Martin with no choice but to warn him through voicemail.

"Liam, listen to me. Roy knows you came here and now he's sent Shaun after you. If you're at home, don't let anyone in. If you're out, then don't go home. Tell Katie not to either." Liam would hate him for putting Katie in danger. Katie plus baby, and not for the first time. "I'm sorry, big man. I wish now I'd left with you. I…"

"It's a little late for that."

Martin spun.

Roy stood in the doorway, draped in his silk robe.

"I've got to go." He rang off and clutched the phone. Just in case Liam called him back. "What do you mean, too late?"

"Why the melodrama?" Roy asked, idly fastening the robe. "I sent Shaun for a chat. Nothing more."

"Shaun didn't chat to me too well when you sent him after me."

"What happened to you was an unfortunate misunderstanding concerning boundaries. What did you mean when you said you should have left with him?"

"What do you think it means?" Martin made to pull away.

Roy caught his arm. "Did I mention I'm spending the night? Which means you'll credit me with your full attention."

Martin lifted his gaze from the hand on his arm to the

hardness in Roy's eyes. "What about Liam? Will you call off your goon?"

"The man needs to understand not to touch another's property. Shaun's taking care of it. Now answer my question."

What question? There had been quite a number these past few minutes. Martin had voiced a few himself, but it seemed only Roy's required answers. The last one had been about Roy spending the night. *Well, that was easy enough.* "Yeah, I guessed you'd want to stay over. And I understand about the no more visitors rule, too."

His apparent obedience had the desired effect. Roy's grip on his arm eased, and Martin pulled away. He collected his jacket off the hook by the door and put it on.

"Where are you going?" Roy asked as Martin stuffed his feet into his scruffy Button trainers. They sat next to a pair of Nikes Roy had bought him for the best part of a hundred and fifty quid.

"Out." Just to confirm the front door was locked, he tried the handle.

"Not tonight you don't. Shaun's fetching dinner and we'll eat together."

"No, he ain't. Shaun's beating up my friend."

"I thought you said he could take Shaun in a fight."

"In a fair fight. But I reckon an ambush hardly counts as fair. Unlock the door."

Roy shook his head. "It's late, you're not properly dressed and I have plans for you this evening."

Tough shit. Whatever else happened he was getting out of this prison. He stalked back into the bedroom and opened the bedside table drawer. Empty. *Would Liam have taken the money, too? No. This wasn't Liam's doing.* He turned to find Roy directly in front of him.

"You took my money?"

"You disobeyed me. I'm entitled."

Roy had taken the cash because he'd thought there was a chance Button was going to run. It didn't matter. He could always get more. There was nothing else here. Liam had everything that was important to him.

He gave Roy a wide berth back into the lounge and the only other route of escape.

"Button?" Roy followed him there, too.

Martin drew back the vertical blinds.

"I thought we might have a chat over dinner tonight."

"Yeah?" He unlocked the door and slid it back. A cold evening breeze whipped across his face. The street lights were on, beaming down the pavement to his left. Trees to his right and the side of another house straight in front. Beneath him, the carpark. That was where he was headed.

"Indeed. About your mother. I think it's time you introduced us."

Martin heaved in a breath of air, clean and fresh despite the faint grittiness of car exhaust and the distant hum of traffic from the bypass. He'd known that particular threat was on its way. Now he'd finally heard it, somehow it wasn't quite so chilling as before. "Why would you want to meet my mother?"

"Because she's important to you, just as you're important to me." Roy went to the sideboard and poured a whiskey. "I thought we might go together, perhaps on the weekend. What do you think?"

"Would it mean you calling Shaun off Liam?" It didn't matter whether it did or didn't. There was no way Roy was going to meet Sandra. He had to put up with Shaun taking him to the care home and back each time. That was as far as Button got into her life.

"Shaun's been gone a while. I dare say it's far too late to call anything off now."

"You said it was just a chat."

"Yes. Just a chat." Roy sipped his whiskey. "Come in and close the doors. The bed's getting cold and I'd rather like to warm it again before dinner."

Not a chance. He'd played the spineless toy for long enough. This would never end unless he ended it. What he had so far would have to be enough. Turning to face the dark air, he stepped outside and peered over the edge of the balcony.

The light behind him flickered on, throwing back the shadows, making the drop all the longer.

"Button." Roy came to the doorway. "What are you planning? We're two stories up."

Cold air bit at his nipples. He zipped up his jacket. "Last chance to unlock the door."

Roy downed the rest of his drink. He came forward, still in his dressing gown, and set the glass on the little plastic table. "I'm not going to do that—any more than you're likely to jump."

Martin turned back to the rail. "Suit yourself."

"Button." Roy's tone sounded a touch more urgent now. Finally, he was beginning to realize this wasn't a party piece. "This is pure disobedience."

Martin swung a leg over the rail, wincing at the flare of pain rocketing through his pelvis. "Yeah. Sue me."

"You won't jump. You'll break something."

"My face, with luck. Or my arse. Least then you wouldn't want me no more."

"But you want me to want you. You need me."

"I need you…" Martin peered over the edge, wobbled, and righted himself. "Like syphilis."

"Button. Don't you…"

Martin didn't catch the rest. His ears filled with cold air as the ground reared up to greet him.

Chapter Thirty-One

When Liam's phone rang, an unfamiliar number lit the screen. Probably Martin wanting his whiskey bottle and his phone. He wasn't getting either back, yet. Liam let the call go to voicemail.

"Who's that?" Katie asked, peering over his shoulder.

Liam angled the phone away and switched it off. "No one."

"Someone you're trying to avoid?"

"Nope."

"Is it the nurse?"

Damn Martin and his stirring by making up some fantasy girlfriend. Liam sipped his beer. "I told you before. There is no nurse."

"Whatever." Katie rolled her eyes. "And you accuse me of being secretive with relationships."

The pub was crowded for a Thursday. Someone had a birthday in the corner, and a round of congratulations followed the bringing out of a cake. Beyond the windows, boats bobbed on their moorings. A stuffed bird perched in a cabinet on the shelf behind him, glass eyes burning into his back. And then there was Robbie, whose eyes weren't quite as beady as the bird's, but whose presence was equally disturbing.

"Are you going to tell me what's wrong?"

"There's nothing wrong." Liam chugged another mouthful of beer. He was only here because Katie had insisted they go for a pub meal together, just the three of them. Or the four of them, since the bird behind the glass sat close enough to secure its own place setting.

"It's more than a sulk. You've had a face like a dropped Fray Bentos all week. Speaking of which…" A hungry grin lit Katie's face as the waiter arrived with their food.

Liam had never felt less like eating, even if it was steak and ale pie with chips. If he'd gone for a sandwich, Katie would have been more suspicious. She'd think he was pining over this fictional nurse, or reluctant about sharing space with Robbie.

"This looks good." Robbie picked up his knife and fork, preparing to dig into a plate full of crab salad. No wonder the bloke was weedy, to quote Martin's adjective. "You watch the match last night?"

Liam looked up from his insurmountable pile of chips. "No."

"Liam's not into sport," Katie answered for him. "He dabbles with the online poker every now and then. That doesn't count, does it?"

Robbie's eyes narrowed. "You're a gambling man?"

"Not regularly." He didn't know why he sounded defensive. He was beginning to see how Martin felt now. Their crimes were hardly comparable, but the sensation of being judged was probably close. Roy was probably looking at Martin that way now. Every time he let the Button mask slip.

"It's just my mates and I meet up for a few rounds of cards once a month or so. Nothing big, just a few quid here and there. You should come. It's always good for a laugh." Robbie smiled. He had a handsome face, too smug for its own good.

Liam snatched up his knife and fork. "I'll think about it."

"Yes. You two should totally go on a lads' night. That way you can get to know each other without me getting in the way." Katie smiled. "Oh. You could go after this. I fancy an early night, anyway."

Liam raised an eyebrow. "In your own bed?"

"Yes. In my own bed. That way Rob can stay over. What do you think?"

Katie's pupils glittered more than her eye shadow. She was desperate for him and Robbie to get along. Her best friend and her boyfriend. Another night, though. Tonight was for brooding alone. "I'll pass. I'm after an early night myself."

"Rob?" Katie downed the rest of her juice and handed him the glass. "Go get me another pineapple juice."

"You've already had two."

"The baby demands a third." She patted her belly. She was barely a month gone. No way that kid could be demanding anything yet. *That kid?* What was wrong with him that he'd level contempt at an unborn child?

Robbie took the glass and moved toward the bar.

Liam began to suspect a lecture was on its way.

"Do you have to be such a misery guts? Rob makes all the effort, and you blank him every time."

"I speak to him."

"One word answers? He invited you out and you sounded as if you'd rather boil your head."

"*You* invited us out. I don't know the guy." He forked a chip. "Why'd you think I'd want to spend time with him, anyway?"

"Because he's my boyfriend. The father of my baby." She wielded the knife in his air space. "And if you dare say she's not a baby yet, I'll —"

"You think that's the kind of thing I'd say?" The knife waving in front of his face he could handle. But her putting those kinds of words in his mouth couldn't go unchallenged.

Katie narrowed her eyes. "If you're in the right mood, yes. I do."

Liam looked away. He might not have said the words to her actual face, but he'd thought along those lines. In private. He set down his fork. "Sorry."

"You might have driven Martin out, but you can't use those same tactics with Robbie."

"I didn't drive Martin out." Hadn't he? He'd offered Martin money to disappear at one point. If he'd have been a little more sympathetic from the beginning, he wouldn't have virtually shoved Martin into Roy's outstretched arms.

He had to get a grip. Katie was with Robbie. That wasn't going to change. The sooner he accepted the reality of the situation, the better. "Look, I know I've been a…" He tried to find a word that wasn't 'prick' or a variation thereof, but he couldn't find one. "I've been a prick. But this time it's not about the two of you. I swear it."

"Right." Katie lowered the knife. "Then what is it? The nurse?"

The nurse who didn't exist. But since she didn't believe him whenever he tried to tell her that, he decided to go with the easy option. "Yeah. It's the nurse."

Katie shuffled her chair closer. "Tell me about her. Or is it a him?"

Liam cleared his throat. "The latter."

"Oh. So there's actual potential this time?"

He looked up. "Potential?"

"Yes, for something real. He obviously likes you if he's calling so much you switched your phone off. Remind me why you did that again?"

Liam hadn't said it was the nurse who kept calling. She'd assumed. And as he'd already cast Martin in the role of 'the nurse', she'd been right. "I have something of his and he wants it back."

Katie pushed her plate of pasta away and edged closer. "What's the something?"

"Doesn't matter."

"Was it something he gave you?"

"No." He might as well come right out and say it. The bar was busy enough to keep Robbie there for a while yet. "I stole it."

"Stole?" Katie peered at him, eye shadow glittering. "You're not a thief, so don't give me that. What's this really about?"

Liam's throat had dried out and suddenly his pint looked attractive again.

"Liam?" Katie grabbed his arm. "At least tell me why you took it?"

Liam set his glass down. "Because I wanted his attention and it was the only way to keep contact." He sounded desperate, little short of a stalker. Like Roy. He wanted something back from Martin, too. In return for that phone. Something other than 'Roy treats me good. My life is with him.' He wanted the reason why Martin would want to record their sex sessions for future blackmail fodder, if that was what it was. *What a mess.*

"He doesn't feel the same as you?"

Liam stared into his glass. "I don't want to talk about this anymore."

"This mood you've been in, it's nothing to do with Robbie and the baby. Is it?"

Not entirely true, but Liam didn't want to lie. He shrugged instead, though he might as well have said yes.

"God, I'm so sorry." She pressed a kiss to his cheek. "I know that must've come across as disgustingly arrogant." She rested her forehead on his shoulder. "What's the issue between you and him? If you both like each other, then what exactly is the problem?"

He didn't want to talk about his feelings. Not with Katie, and not when they were feelings he didn't want to have about someone he wasn't sure he even liked much of the time.

"There's someone else," he said. "Someone who can give him what he wants most in the world, and I can't compete."

Katie tilted her head, curiosity webbing a path across her brow. "And what is it he wants?"

"Money."

Katie blinked. "You've fallen for a gold digger?"

Liam shook his head. He wasn't sure what part he was denying. The 'falling for' part or the 'gold digger' accusation. "There's more to it than that."

He didn't think this was love. You had to know someone before that could happen. But there was just something about Martin that wouldn't let go.

"More to what?" At the sound of Robbie's voice, Katie pulled away. "Sorry, was I interrupting?" He winced then set down her glass. "I can go away again."

"No. Sit down and eat your dinner. Liam and I can talk later."

Liam busied himself by dissecting his pie. He wished he had some more hate to block out Robbie with. But every time he thought he had the guy figured as a wrong 'un, Robbie did something to contradict his opinion. Like apologizing for being here when Liam should be the one apologizing. Or at least making an effort to get along with him.

Liam set down his knife and fork. "Ah, about Katie's suggestion. Us going for a drink. I think we should."

Both looked up from their plates, both as confused as if he'd just spoken in Chinese.

"You sure?" Robbie's face broke into another wide grin. Whether it was genuine or not, Liam couldn't say. But if something had to change, it might as well be him.

"Yeah. It's about time we got to know one another, and Katie's not going to stop nagging me any time soon."

Katie laughed. "I didn't force him. Not entirely at knifepoint, anyway."

Liam didn't feel like smiling. He still had dinner to tackle. But if going for few beers with Robbie meant smoothing things over with Katie, as well as taking his mind off Martin, he'd give it a go. All the while, though, his phone was burning a hole in his pocket.

By the time he'd forced half his dinner down, both Robbie and Katie had finished theirs and were contemplating apple crumble for dessert. While they were distracted with the menu, Liam gave in to temptation and turned his phone back on.

One voicemail. If Martin thought that was all it would take, he was wrong.

"Liam?" Martin's voice sounded as fearful as the texts had read. "Listen to me. Roy knows you came here and

now he's sent Shaun after you. If you're at home, don't let anyone in. If you're out, then don't go home. Tell Katie not to either. I'm sorry, big man. I wish now I'd left with you. I..."
He breathed hard. There was another voice, undoubtedly Roy's, in the background, the words faint. Martin spoke again, more quickly. "I've got to go." And that was it. End of message.

Liam returned the call. Straight to voicemail. His thoughts buzzed. *What to do next? Call the police? And tell them what?* Martin hadn't been kidnapped, and he didn't want rescuing. Or so he kept saying, anyway.

On the other hand, Martin wasn't always the best judge of what was good for him. Actually, he wasn't the best judge full stop. If anything happened to him, Liam would never forgive himself.

First things first. He'd make his excuses to Katie while Robbie was up at the bar ordering dessert.

"The nurse called." He flashed his mobile at her, as if that were enough proof. "I've invited him round ours for a talk. Would you mind staying over at Robbie's tonight?" All nice and civilized.

"Liam, are you sure that's wise? If money's all he's interested in, he's not exactly onto a winner in that department with you. And you're way too good for someone like that." She brushed his cheek and he felt every bit of her love for him in the touch. She didn't even know this nurse and yet she wasn't putting Liam down. The way he had with her. And Robbie.

"I'm going to call him."

"About the something you stole?"

He hoped Martin wanted more from him than that and rescuing. "Yeah. I'll apologize to Robbie before I go."

"What for?"

"For being an unsociable git." Liam placed a kiss on top of her head as he rose. "I'll see you in the morning."

He took a wander up to the bar next to Robbie. "Take Katie back to yours tonight. Do not, under any circumstances, let her come home."

Robbie handed a twenty-pound note to the barman. "Why not? What's going on?"

"I've told her I've got company tonight." He could leave it at that, but Katie would find some excuse to come home just to meet the nurse. "It's the nurse who doesn't exist."

Robbie looked at him blankly. "Then there really is no nurse?"

"No. There is someone, but he's no nurse." Liam waited while Robbie collected his change. "It's Martin."

"Martin? Your ex-flat mate? The little blond guy?"

"Yes."

"He's your nurse?"

"In a way."

"You two have something going on together?"

"That doesn't matter now." There wasn't a chance of him discussing Martin with this guy. "As far as she's concerned, I'm meeting someone back there, someone who plans to stay all night. There are other things going on, possibly dangerous things I can't tell you about. Just keep Katie away from the flat. That's it."

"Dangerous things? Wouldn't it be easier to call the police?"

That would be the logical next step. But this was Martin. Logical and the police didn't belong in the same sentence with him. "I'll see how it goes first."

As he made to turn away, Robbie caught his arm. "You're not going back alone. I'll come with." He set down his bottle. "I've boxed in the past. I—"

"No." Katie would kill him if Robbie came home with a broken nose or a black eye, or damaged any of those other parts that Katie found irresistible. "I told you so you'd keep Katie away. I'll call when it's sorted." Again he made to pull away.

Robbie's grip tightened. "And when will that be? If the flat's not safe for Katie, she's going to want to know why."

"Don't tell her it's not safe. Just tell her I don't want to be interrupted."

Katie was watching them too keenly, but she didn't look concerned.

Liam pulled away again and this time Robbie let him go. He needed to call Martin back, out of range of Katie. He only hoped Martin would be in a position to answer.

He'd no sooner reached the street than his phone buzzed in his hand.

* * * *

Liam answered on the second ring.

Martin stopped walking and half collapsed against a chain link fence. Whether out of relief, or just because his ankle had given out, he wasn't sure. But he went with it, sinking to the ground as he pressed his phone to his ear. "Liam?"

"What's happening? Is Roy with you?"

Liam was okay. He had to be, since he was on the phone. He didn't much sound as if Shaun had hold of him, gun to his head, telling him what to say. "No. I got out."

"You walked out on him?"

"More or less." He didn't want to say exactly how he'd managed it. Not over the phone. He'd fallen heavily on the drop from the balcony, cracking both his head and his ankle in the process. But at least his phone had survived in one piece.

"Finally, you get yourself some sense."

He didn't like to point out the only reason he'd got some sense was because Liam had forced the issue. Otherwise, he would have still been there. Still seeking enough evidence to get rid of Roy for good, and saving his extra pay each week to disappear afterward. "Seems I did."

"Where are you now?"

"I got no idea. Have you seen Shaun? Where's Katie?"

"Katie's with Robbie. She's safe, and I'm safe. Our home might not be so safe, but I'll worry about that later. What about you?"

"I'm okay. Need my phone back, though." He took a breath. "I guess you know why."

"Yes." The tightness in Liam's tone suggested he'd already had a snoop through the contents. Of course he had. It was the reason he'd taken the thing in the first place. For what reason, Martin had yet to work out. If there was one time he was glad the phone had fucked up while filming him and Roy in the sack, then this was it.

"Could you bring it to me?"

A moment passed before Liam answered, "Did you call to warn me there was every possibility I was about to get my head kicked in, or was it just to persuade me to give you your phone back?"

Martin opened his mouth. No sound came out. Had he really given the impression that he didn't care? He must've, since he'd continued to do so right up until an hour ago. "As soon as Roy told me what he'd done, I called you. But I still need that phone. He'll never let me go, otherwise."

"If you want it that badly, then you're going to have to come and get it."

Easier than said than done. Martin shifted on the damp ground. A sharp flash of electricity flared from ankle to knee. He let out a tight cry, then immediately bit his tongue.

"What was that?"

"Nothing. Cramp."

"Has he hurt you? Martin? Is this another wind-up?"

"I'm okay." Martin wiped the wetness from his face. It was a combination of sweat and a fine rain. "I'll meet you someplace. Don't go back to the flat. Or to work. Shaun's a mean fucking bastard. He'll — "

"Have you got money for a train?"

Train? He didn't know how to get to the station, and wasn't sure he could walk so far even if he did. "Don't worry about it. I'll hitch." He knew how to get up to the bypass. He might have to crawl part of the way, but he'd get there.

"What can you see? Any road names?"

Martin squinted through the rain. "There's an industrial estate behind me and some houses in front. And it's pissing down." A shiver coursed through his bones. He wished he'd taken the time to put a sweater on instead of focusing purely on getting out. Roy wasn't Shaun. Roy was old and out of shape. With more stamina than any other punter he'd known. No, he'd escaped just in time. And no way was he ever going back.

"Is there somewhere you can go to get out of the rain? A café or a pub? Even bed and breakfast. I could book a room."

"This ain't no time to be arranging a dirty weekend, big man." When he didn't get a laugh, he sighed. They obviously didn't quite share the same sense of humor.

"Is there or isn't there?" Liam said, clipping his words. "Otherwise you can wait where you are. I'm going to be at least an hour."

"I told you I can hitch."

"Would you rather hitch?"

Would he? If he could get a lift off a woman, it might not be so bad. They tended not to want anything off him in return. Though women tended not to give random guys a lift at night. Even less than in the day.

"There's a B&B close by. Trinity House. I can get there." He'd passed the place several times in Shaun's car, and Roy wouldn't be able to get to him if he was physically off the street. "Look, Liam, I know I'm a weak stupid fuck who brought it all on myself. Just give me my phone. Then you don't have to see me again."

The line went silent long enough he suspected Liam had already hung up. "Give me an hour."

"Okay."

"And dump your phone."

"Why?"

"Because Roy gave it to you. He could have some tracking app on there you don't know about." He paused. "Just a thought."

A thought Martin hadn't had. It would be just the kind of devious thing Roy would do. The controlling bastard would know where he was every second of the day. Not that he ever went anywhere or did anything. "Yeah. I'll get rid of it. Thanks. Uh, Liam?"

"What?"

"I know I don't deserve no help. But thanks all the same."

"You know I want answers in return, right?"

Of course he did. And it was past time that Liam got them. Then, at least, the guy would give up on him. "I'll answer anything you want," he said quietly. Then hung up before Liam could take him up on the offer.

* * * *

"Liam?"

Liam spun. A slight figure stepped out of the alley, about half a dozen houses down from the bed and breakfast, indistinct as a ghost behind the sheet of rain. "Martin? What're you still doing out here in the rain?"

"Uh, because I'm kind of a mess." He stepped under the halo of a streetlamp, limping heavily on his left leg. "And I didn't think they'd let me in."

"What the...?" 'Kind of a mess' was an understatement. Aside from being soaked to the bone, his hair had turned white. Threaded through with pink streaks. Streaks that looked very much like... He touched a strand of pink. "Is this *blood*?"

"It's nothing." Martin flinched from the touch. "My ankle's worse. And my jeans are totally buggered." He grinned, but it was so forced that Liam couldn't tell if it was because he was in pain or he wanted his phone and to get as far away as possible.

"He did this to you?"

"Nah. He wouldn't let me leave, so I skipped over the balcony."

"Two floors up?"

"Better than twelve."

He had a point. *But still, two floors?* "What happened to your hair?"

Martin raked a hand through the wet strands. "It weren't my choice."

"It looks like your choice. You make so many bad ones."

Martin scowled then gestured to the bag Liam had brought along. "You got my phone in there?"

"Nope. Just toiletries and pajamas."

"So, where's my phone?"

"Safe."

Martin kicked at an invisible stone on the pavement. "You know what's on there?"

"Yes."

"Why'd you take it?"

"Because I was curious."

Martin looked up. "About how me and Roy fuck?"

A well-aimed verbal punch, but Liam wouldn't let on how firmly he'd been hit. "I wanted to know what you had on him. I want to know why you needed it."

Martin stepped back into the shadows. "Where's your car?"

"Close by. I'm answering your questions. Why aren't you answering mine?"

"I just want my phone, Liam." Martin scuffed a toe after the invisible stone again. He couldn't seem to support himself fully on that foot. "Give it back and we can both move on."

"Move on to where? Have you definitely left Roy for good?"

"Of course I left him." Martin's head snapped up. "He sent goons after you. Just cos you came to visit. He's got CCTV above the front fucking door to check if I leave the flat without permission. Or if I have any visitors. All this time I was doing exactly what he fucking said."

"Why?"

"What?"

"Why were you doing exactly what he said?" When Martin didn't answer, Liam gestured to the large terraced house behind them. "Why don't we continue this conversation inside?"

"We? I thought you'd just book me a room."

"And where am I supposed to stay? Your goon could be staking my place out."

Liam wouldn't have let that goon stop him from going home if he wanted. But right now he didn't want. He'd used this situation as an excuse to spend some time with Martin. Once they were safely in a warm private room, Martin was going to part with a few of those secrets he kept so close.

Martin kept staring at him. Not talking even to argue. He even seemed oblivious to the rain. His expression remained remain starched. No, frozen. And then it hit. Exactly what Martin was thinking.

"God, no." Liam raised both palms. "I don't want... I didn't get us a room for that. I mean, *that* is about the last thing either of us need."

Martin continued to stare. "Fucking me is the last thing you need? Or fucking you is the last thing I need?"

Liam suspected any answer he gave would be the wrong one, so he chose to avoid the questions altogether. "I'll tell you what. I'm going inside and spending the night here. I'll leave it up to you whether you join me or not." Without looking back to see if Martin was following, he started up the steps to the house.

A chubby, middle-aged woman answered the bell. As Liam explain who he was and what he was doing there, she was all welcoming smiles as she ushered him inside.

"I'm June. Your landlady. Now it's just for one night, isn't it?" June retreated behind a small old-fashioned desk to the left of the stairs.

The place smelled of roast potatoes and furniture polish. Homey, yet clinical at the same time. Not a particularly attractive smell, but better than being stuck out in the rain.

"My car's broken down," Liam explained. "We decided to stay over rather than take the train home." He didn't know why he'd rustled up that fairy tale, but at least she'd understand why they'd traveled light.

"Oh, I am sorry to hear that. Cars have a habit of breaking down at the most inconvenient of times and in the worst of weather." She passed him a form and a pen. "If you'd like to sign here, I'll give you a room key and a front door key in case you'd like to go out again this evening. There's a bar in the main lounge, which is through the door behind you, and…" Her words faded. Liam looked up to find her staring at the front door.

Martin stood at the top of the steps, face contorted in pain as he more or less dragged himself through the front door.

The landlady eyed him like he was a sewer rat strolling in to warm by the fire.

"He's with me," Liam said quickly as June shifted out from behind the desk. She looked very much as though she was preparing to quietly usher Martin back through the door. Not that it would have been quiet, if she had got around to trying.

"You realize you booked a double?" She looked from one to the other. Her face hardened. The welcoming smile was snuffed out. "We have no twins."

"We're not twins," Martin said, the weariness dulling what he clearly intended as sarcasm.

"I mean our available beds are doubles. Not singles."

"That's not a problem." Liam signed the form and passed back it across the desk.

Martin shuffled closer. "Why'd you assume we'd want singles?"

Liam sighed. He was not in the mood for this. "We'd prefer singles, naturally. But we'll make do seeing as we're both tired and we need sleep."

"Naturally?" Martin arched an eyebrow. "Would it be, like, totally unnatural for us to share a double?"

"No. It was a figure of speech."

Martin eyed him a moment longer, before returning his attention to the landlady. "Don't worry, Grandma. We're not going to be corrupting none of your beds anytime soon. Liam's straight. Can't you tell by looking at him?"

Liam glared at Martin, willing him to shut up, but Martin had other ideas.

"Bet you wouldn't have said a word if Liam was a girl."

Liam opened his mouth. He was about to ask why he would have to be the girl, but changed his mind. It wasn't important enough to query.

"Now here's your key." Rather than handing it over, June set the key on the desk. "Room three, up the stairs. Breakfast is served from seven."

Liam watched the smirk rest on Martin's lips. It beat the rising blush on June's. He wasn't much bothered about a homophobic landlady. She wasn't that much of a 'phobe to not accept his money. And Martin looked very much like someone who'd be prepared to take things to the press if she turned them away.

Liam took the key from the desk. "I'm not straight, for the record."

June started tidying things on the desk that didn't need tidying. "That's none of my business, I'm sure."

"You got that right, Grandma." Martin waited until they were out of earshot before he vented. "Was the confession for my benefit? Cos it don't change nothing. You're still a closet case."

Liam decided to ignore anything that could be considered inflammatory, which was probably ninety percent of what came out of Martin's mouth. "You want help getting up the stairs?"

"No. I ain't sure I'm going up yet. I might walk for a bit. Your car can't be that far away."

"With your ankle? I don't think so. Why are you so interested in my car, anyway?"

"Because that's where my phone is."

"Why'd you jump to that conclusion?"

"You saying it ain't?"

"What I'm saying is, your phone is in Robbie's car."

"Robbie's car?" Martin paused at the bottom of the stairs. They kept their voices low, but that didn't stop June from homing in from her place at the desk. "Robbie, as in Robin? As in the guy you hate most in the world?"

Liam thought back to how Robbie had offered to help him with the goons, though he was far from deserving of Robbie's help considering how he'd treated the guy. Robbie wasn't even so bad. He was always so attentive toward Katie, too. The way he touched her, like she was something precious. And the way she looked at him in return. The way, when they were together, Liam might as well not be present at all. "Yes. That's him."

"Why?"

"To keep it safe."

"But you said you had it."

"I do have it. Just not on me." He slipped his arm around Martin's waist. "Don't worry, I'm not touching. Just helping you up the stairs."

Martin tensed but didn't object. He placed his good foot on the first step, then dragged the other up to join it.

A yelp rocked his body. He fell back, losing his balance. Liam caught him and swung him up in both arms. A soggy streak of hollow bones, rigid with attitude.

"What the fuck are you doing?" Martin asked, his cold wet arms clinging to Liam's neck.

"Don't cause a scene," Liam said, as he climbed the stairs. "This doesn't mean you're the girl instead of me."

"I don't care right now. Just don't drop me." Martin dug his fingertips into the back of Liam's neck. "The only reason I ain't fighting this is cos I'm too knackered. Well. That and the expression on that old turkey's face. She looks like we just shat all down her stairs."

Chapter Thirty-Two

"Martin?"

"Hmm?"

"You're alarmingly still. And quiet."

"I ain't dead. Just thinking."

"About the easiest way to avoid answering my questions?" Liam stopped walking. "Silence won't be the easiest way, believe me."

Martin opened his eyes. They'd stopped outside a door. Room three. "The interrogation chamber, I presume."

"Would you rather be back at Roy's?"

"No." He shivered. Half from the chill, half from the thought of being sent back. "Here's good."

"Keep your weight on your good leg. I need to open the door." Liam's strong arms carefully lowered him to the carpet. Gray with pink flowers. Yep, a makeover was sorely needed for this place. "Lean against me. I don't want you putting any weight on that ankle. It might be broken."

"It ain't broke." Martin steadied himself on one foot while clinging to Liam with both hands. "I'd still be under that fucking balcony if it was."

"Not necessarily." Liam sounded ridiculously calm, like the voice of reason that wasn't worth arguing with. "Was there no other way out?"

"He took my door key. Think he was going to keep it, too."

Liam unlocked the door. "What happened to him being good to you?"

"You turned up." Martin looked up to find Liam staring down at him. "I'm glad you did."

"You are?"

"Yep. Now help me to the bed?"

The room wasn't anything special, but Martin wasn't bothered about the chintzy curtains or the mismatched cushions scattered on the double bed. He was free and he felt safe, despite the 'phobe downstairs who'd probably be up later with a glass against the door listening out for shenanigans. And an excuse to boot them out. She wasn't going to get lucky tonight, any more than he was. Right now all he wanted to do was sleep.

Liam helped him hobble to the bed, and once he was settled went back to close the door.

"I'm going to look at this ankle," Liam said, kneeling at his feet. "If I think it's broken, we're going to the hospital. No arguments. Okay?"

Martin nodded. He didn't feel like arguing. What he felt like doing was sleeping. After he'd had a long hot bath to rid himself of all traces of Roy. He must reek of sex, but Liam was obviously too polite to pass comment.

After removing the shoe, he gently examined Martin's ankle as though he was a fully trained medical doctor with a wall full of certificates. "It's swollen all right. Hardly surprising considering what happened." He gripped the heel and pressed down on Martin's toes. "Tell me if this hurts?"

Martin jolted. Pain pulsed all the way from foot to thigh. He held the evidence in a single breath, then shook his head.

"Liar." Liam gently removed the other shoe, grasped both ankles and lifted both legs onto the bed. He piled a couple of cushions at the end and rested the bad ankle on top. "We'll see how it is into the morning. The last thing either of us want is a stint in A&E."

Martin raised his head from the pillow. "I thought the last thing you wanted was sex with me."

"Need, not want." Liam fixed him with that heavy gaze. The one that pinned him to the spot, although the spot right now happened to be a relatively comfortable bed.

"Is there a bath or just a shower in there?" Martin nodded to what he assumed must be the bathroom door. "If there's a bath, can you run me one?"

Liam's glare morphed to a frown. "You know your obsessive washing rituals aren't fixing the cause of why you always feel so unclean."

"I ain't obsessed. I'm soaking wet and freezing cold and these blankets ain't getting any drier with me lying on 'em like a soggy piece of seaweed."

"Yes, okay. You may have a point." Liam opened the bathroom door and switched on the light.

Bath. Perfect.

This was nice, being taken care of by someone he cared about. And he did care, no matter how many times he told himself or Liam he didn't. Rather than think too hard on what he couldn't let himself feel, he started taking off his clothing.

"Right, it's running." Liam emerged from a puff of steam, drying his hands on a towel. "You need some help getting—?" The towel dropped to the floor. Liam was staring at him. "You said he didn't hurt you."

"Huh?" Martin followed the line of Liam's stricken gaze. The reddening bruises marking his body looked way worse than they were. They didn't even hurt. "No. He was just a bit full-on tonight. That's all."

"But—"

"I didn't tell him he couldn't. Okay? And I ain't going to lie just to make you feel better." He unfastened his fly and pushed his jeans to his knees. Rainwater wasn't the only thing that made them damp. He sat back down on the bed, holding his jeans to hide what he didn't want Liam freak about. He'd been bleeding. That had never happened before, not with Roy. "If you get my phone, you can get rid of me easy as."

"I don't want to get rid of you," Liam said quietly, eyeing him like he was a teddy bear with a ripped-off arm.

"You should. Roy might be a bit of a sadist, but you've

got all the signs of being a raving masochist."

"Don't compare me to him." Liam offered out his hand. "You want some help getting in?"

Martin shook his head. "I can manage."

"You sure? Remember the last time we were in this situation?"

Martin swiped the offered hand aside. "Will you stop being nice to me? I dumped you for two grand a week. For a bloke I fucking hate. A bloke I let you offer yourself up to. I *chose* him."

"You didn't have a choice," Liam said, still infuriatingly calm. "You said so yourself. Either he had something over you, or turning him down would turn out a hell of a lot worse than taking his offer."

Martin shoved his jeans to his ankles. "Don't look." He waited until Liam had returned to the bathroom before taking them fully off. They would require a thorough scrub before he put them on again. Maybe the old lady downstairs had a washing machine he could use. Or he could ask Liam to lend him the cash for a new pair. No. Not that. The only people he ever took money off were punters, which was something Liam would never be.

The underpants were beyond rescuing, and no amount of washing would make them clean again. For now, he kicked them under the bed. *Out of sight, out of mind.*

Liam came back armed with another towel, which he offered out as he swept the jeans from Martin's hand.

"Wait!" Martin lunged, but already they were out of reach.

"I'm going to put them on the radiator to dry. You don't want damp clothes for the morning, do you?" When Liam lifted an eyebrow, Martin shook his head. Because who would actually say yes to wearing damp clothes for the morning? He let Liam get on with draping the jeans on the radiator. As dirty as they were, he didn't think any evidence of what Roy had done to him carried through.

To distract himself from the possibility, he focused on

arranging the towel over his hips and thighs. Trying to make himself decent, if such a thing were even possible. As he tried to stand, a vicious flame seared a path from his ankle all the way up to his knee. A cry escaped his lips before he could bite it back, and Liam was by his side in a moment.

"Yeah, okay." Martin forced a shaky smile. "So I could use a little bit of help."

"Hold on to me." Liam slipped an arm around his shoulder, and took most of his weight as he rose.

Martin gritted his teeth, and, holding the towel to his junk with one hand, he clung to Liam with the other. Dignity wasn't something he had much use for, but somehow it seemed to matter in Liam's presence. Together they made their slow path to the bathroom, and only then did Martin relinquish his hold on both the towel and Liam's body.

Once he was safely settled in the bubbles, he relaxed back into the hot water and sighed. "Best. Bath. Ever."

"Don't try to get out by yourself," Liam said, sounding more like a parent than his friend. "I'll just be outside. Give me a shout when you're ready. We've got all night to talk."

Martin closed his eyes. The defense mechanism in his mind was already constructing elaborate lies to fob Liam off with. But he wouldn't be using any of them. Liam deserved the truth. If he'd been more honest in the beginning, they wouldn't be here now. No, if he'd been that honest, then Liam wouldn't have bothered with him at all. In fact, Liam would have handed him to Roy on a velvet cushion.

Chapter Thirty-Three

Liam perched on the edge of the bed and stared at the closed bathroom door. Since Martin had said he hadn't been assaulted — *raped* — then Liam would have to take his word for it. Even if he didn't fully believe it.

Beyond the bathroom door, the gentle splash of water reassured him that Martin was doing okay. He could be hours in that bath yet. That was how it had usually gone at home. Liam used to think it was because he spent all that time tarting himself up for his clients. Now he knew that not to be true. But the kind of dirty Martin felt went far deeper than the skin he spent so much time trying to scrub clean.

Once he got out of that bath, whether of his own accord or Liam going in there and prying him out, he'd need some ice for that foot. And some painkillers, too. Liam wasn't about to leave the building to find a supermarket open at this hour, so his only hope was the landlady.

He found her tending the small bar in the lounge room, and politely enquired about a bag of ice. She handed one over as tentatively as if he were the local satanic cult leader and the ice her newborn child. She didn't have any painkillers, or so she claimed. Hopefully Martin could manage without.

Back upstairs, he wrapped the bag in a spare towel, which he placed on top of a cushion at the end of the bed. Where Martin's foot would rest. Then he tapped on the bathroom door.

"You almost done in there?" He pressed an ear to the wood. He hadn't heard any splashing for a while. Come to think of it, he hadn't heard anything coming out of that room in a while. "Martin? You want a hand getting out?"

"Go away. I'm sleeping."

"You're stalling, more like." Liam grabbed the door handle. "All right if I come in?"

"Why? You want to join me?" There was humor there now, and life was always simpler when Martin was amiable.

"I'll pass for now." Liam opened the door and stepped inside the steamy room.

He was still soaking in the bath, eyes closed, up to his neck in bubbles.

"Enjoying yourself?"

Martin cracked open an eye. "I was." He drew up his knees until they were sticking up out of the water. "I reckon there's room enough for two. Get in."

Liam shook his head. "No thanks." He took a step back and noticed a robe hanging off the bathroom door. "You ready to get out now?"

Martin opened his other eye. "You don't fancy stewing in Roy's sloppy seconds?"

Liam decided against answering. Some questions really were meant to be rhetorical. He moved to the side of the bath then leaned in. "Wrap an arm around my shoulder. I'm going to lift you out."

"You really get off on carrying me about, don't you, big man?" Martin's eyes danced with mischief. But not enough to banish the shadows beneath.

"I like to keep you close because it's the only time I stop worrying about you."

Martin's grin vanished. "Don't say shit like that. Not to me."

"Why not?" They were close now, their faces only inches apart. Martin's full lips were slightly open, but relaxed. And not, for once, pouting.

"You know why not. Save it for someone you really care about."

Liam leaned even closer. He lowered his voice to a

whisper. "I did."

"Then you're a fucking idiot." Martin lowered his voice, too. "But I'm glad you are."

"Me, too." Liam stayed close enough to accept another kiss, if Martin were to gift him one.

"I reckon I'm ready now."

Liam's heart lurched. "For what?"

"To get out this bath."

Not for the kiss, then. Which wasn't for Liam to take. In fact, not touching Martin at all would be the wise thing to do. He wasn't sure what had gone on with Roy, but it had been bad. Something Liam would ensure never happened again.

"Okay. Hold on tight." He curled an arm around Martin's waist, instantly soaking his sweater sleeve. The other arm he slipped under Martin's raised knees. Both sleeves now equally waterlogged, he lifted Martin from the water. Once out, Martin balanced on one foot while Liam grabbed the robe off the hook on the door.

When he turned around, he was treated to the sight of hot soapy bubbles cascading down Martin's back and arse. So lean and smooth, his body sleek as water. Except for the bruises, which Liam quickly covered with the robe before helping him to the bed.

Once Martin was settled, Liam placed the injured foot on the towel-wrapped ice.

"Can you put the telly on?" Martin asked as he munched through a biscuit he'd somehow nabbed from the complementary tea tray on the desk.

"No."

"Can you make me a cup of tea so I got something to dunk these in?" He raised another handful of biscuits in the air.

"Nope."

Martin slumped into the pillows. "Whatever."

"Who do you owe?"

Martin turned his head away. He didn't speak.

"Look, Martin, all I want to do is help." Liam hoped he

sounded more persuasive than patronizing. "If you tell me what's going on, between us we could find a way out. I don't just mean from Roy. I mean a way out of being Button, too."

Martin pushed himself up against the headboard. "There ain't no way out for me, big man. And I can't think about letting there be one, neither."

"Why can't you?" If using these vague answers as stepping stones got them to the number one question again, it was worth taking the extra time to get there.

"Because Button is what I do. What I have to do." He nodded over at the tea tray. "Talking's thirsty work. You can always raid the mini bar if you want to buy yourself a little patience."

More likely he wanted to buy a little time to conjure up ways to get out of answering. Liam wasn't going near the mini bar, not after the last time. He got up and grabbed the kettle off the tray.

"I'm still waiting for the second half of the answer to my first question." When he returned from filling the kettle at the bathroom tap, Martin was lining up the biscuits along the quilt, like soldiers. Drawing his battle lines. No. His defenses. "I should have booked two nights here, the way you're going."

"You think I'd mind being holed up here with you an extra night? Is that the greatest form of torture you can imagine to make me talk?"

Liam plugged in the kettle. "No. But while you're with me I can keep an eye on you and hopefully stop you from jumping headlong into yet another disastrous mistake."

"Why bother?" Martin dropped the final biscuit on top of the others. "If you give me my phone, you can go back home right now. Once I send a couple of them pictures to Roy, he won't bother either of us no more. All you're doing is delaying shit cos you like to spend time in my company, huh?" A sly grin worked across his face. "If you want to fuck again, there ain't no need to make out like you care 'bout me. I'll do you for free in exchange for my phone."

He yanked the bathrobe open and grabbed his flaccid cock. "Forget the tea. You got condoms in that stash you bought?"

Liam's bones suddenly felt a hell of a lot heavier than they had a moment ago. He'd known this would be tough going, but he'd had no idea how much Martin didn't want to talk. "Sugar?"

"Huh?"

"In your tea." Liam turned back to the kettle.

"No. Would it help if I compared you to a porn star again?"

"No, it wouldn't." Liam loaded the cups with a teabag each. "You could try answering one of my questions by giving me a satisfactory answer. That might go some way to persuading me."

Martin drew his robe closed then settled back into the pillows. "Most of what you think you want answered, you really don't. But by the time you realize you don't, it'll be too late cos I would've answered them."

"Does Roy know?" Liam set the cups down on the bedside table. "About your big secret. Have you told him?"

Martin opened his mouth then closed it again. He looked away.

"That's a yes." Liam took a seat amid the crumbs on the duvet. "Roy doesn't hate you, though, does he? He knows your secrets and he's still as obsessed as ever."

"That's cos he ain't got no soul." Martin folded his arms over his robed chest. "And the only reason he knows anything is cos he was having me followed. He knows where I go twice a week, and who I go to see. Nothing else."

"Wouldn't be to Oakland House, would it?"

Martin looked startled. "How'd you know that?"

"The number's in your phone." Liam picked up his tea, trying to keep things casual. The last thing he wanted was for Martin to feel cornered and clam up again.

"Did you ring them?"

"Yes. I was curious."

Martin scowled. "About all aspects of my fucking life.

You're as bad as Roy is with Button."

Liam set his tea back down. "Ouch."

Martin unfolded his arms. "You know I didn't mean that, right?"

"You should stop saying stuff you don't mean. Even I have limits as to what I'll take."

Martin grinned. "But you ain't reached them yet."

Liam shrugged. "I almost did, when you chose him over me. But I got over it because I needed to make sure you were okay."

Martin glanced over at the window. The light had faded a while ago. He clicked the lamp on. "Why?"

"Why what?"

"Why'd you care 'bout me? I ain't given you no good reason."

"You're the first person who's interested me enough to take my mind off Katie. And I know there's something there, with me and you. Even with Roy and all your secrets, I'm not wrong. Am I?"

Martin smiled again. This time it was warm, natural, without an ounce of smirk. His defenses were down again, for now at least. "I've always thought you was hot. Right from the first moment I saw you. I assumed from the way you looked at me that you was straight."

"Because I didn't find you irresistible?"

"Yeah, if you like. I felt safe cos of it, though. Still do." He folded his fingers around Liam's. "If things were different. If I—"

"You said that before." Liam turned his palm so that it rested under Martin's. A subtle way of showing he'd follow Martin's lead.

"I know. And I owe you an explanation. But if I tell you everything, as in all my secrets, then you won't let me hold your hand like this. You got your morals and your principles and that all stuff. What I did, you wouldn't be able to see past it."

Liam didn't believe that. Martin wasn't capable of doing

something so bad that he couldn't be forgiven. But even if he was, it wasn't Liam's place to forgive. Just to understand, which he was fully prepared to do. "Tell me."

"You heard what I said."

"Yes. You want rid of me. You also want your phone back. Tell me your secrets and, apparently, you'll get one hundred percent what you're after. Why are you holding back?" When Martin tried to tug his hand free, Liam covered it with his other palm. "No, you don't get to pull away. Just talk to me. I promise I won't judge you."

Martin's eyes shimmered. "You can't make that promise without knowing what I did."

"Then give me the chance to prove you wrong yet again, and tell me."

Chapter Thirty-Four

"Her name's Sandra." Martin finally managed to pull his hand free then reached for his cup. Not because he wanted tea, more because he could use the process of drinking as a distraction.

"Who?" Liam asked softly, because evidently he'd already forgotten one of his own questions.

"The person I owe. My mother. She's a resident at Oakland House. Has been for almost three years now. Ever since the accident."

"Wait." Liam raised a hand. "You told me you had no parents."

"That's cos I don't. Not like how you mean. Not someone who cares about me. Sandra don't know what day it is most of the time, let alone remember she has a son." Martin took a sip of tea. He'd just told a lie. And he'd already promised himself he wouldn't do that. "No. That ain't true. She does know who I am. She recognizes me. She smiles at me and sometimes she even holds my hand."

"You said she had an accident?" Liam's voice was softer now. More sympathetic.

Martin didn't deserve any sympathy, but he took it anyway. Clutched it close while he still could.

"Yeah. She got distracted one day and walked out in front of a van." Martin looked away. He didn't want to catch the pity written all over Liam's face.

"And you kept that a secret from me, why?"

Scratch pity, there wasn't any. Just hurt and a touch of irritation. Martin refocused on his cup. "Because it's my business. No one else's."

"Least of all mine?"

Martin made to set his cup back on the bedside table. His hand trembled so hard that tea dribbled down the sides and splattered on the sheets. It was Liam who finally took the cup from him and set it safely down.

"I have to move." He swung his legs off the bed, ankle heavy as a log smoldering in a grate. The ice had gone some way to calming the flames, but he still had to grit his teeth and limp toward the window.

"Martin..."

The curtains were open. Beyond the glare of the streetlamps, spooky shadows danced in the road. If he homed in on his reflection in the glass, he'd discover the specter of a guilt he could never lose. But he didn't focus on the glass. Instead he fixated on the house across the road.

"Sandra had me when she was young. Like, thirteen. And she never really got on with her parents, which meant we were on our own most of the time."

"What about your dad?" Liam asked. "Wasn't he around?"

Martin shook his head. "He was some kid from Norway or Sweden. Someplace cold like that. An exchange student. Long gone before Sandra even found out about me. I used to wonder about him sometimes, though."

"But not anymore?"

Martin looked back at Liam still sitting on the bed. "I'm long past needing a dad, Liam." He adjusted the foot he balanced on and returned his attention to the window. "Me and Sandra did okay on our own. We had this one-bedroom place from the council for a while. Was a bit awkward whenever she had boyfriends stay over." He paused, realizing how that must sound to Liam. *Boyfriends,* like there were countless dicks through the door at all hours of the day and night. "When I say boyfriends, there were only a few. And she didn't often bring them home. She tended to stay at theirs."

"You had a babysitter, though," Liam said. More statement than question.

"Nope. Ain't like I ever needed one. Sandra left me out food and most of the time she was back before I woke up. Just means I learned to take care of myself faster than most kids. Nothing wrong with that." He checked back over his shoulder.

Liam was biting his lip so hard, his whole face had flushed red.

Martin turned back to the window. "When I was nine, she met this one guy. Ian. He was older than her. With money. Proper money. He had his own business and his own house. Plus, unlike most of the others in the past, he liked kids. He liked *me*." He switched his focus to the more solid reflection beyond his in the glass. Liam was watching avidly. He didn't speak, though, which was good since things were only going to get more difficult from here onward. "Then they got married and everything got all fucked up."

"Fucked up? Do you mean Sandra's accident?"

Martin closed his eyes. If he told the story as if it belonged to someone else, some friend of a friend of a friend he didn't have, then it would be easier. But it would be a lie. The story was his. His responsibility. It would be cowardly and unfair to pretend otherwise. "I was eighteen when it happened. Her accident, I mean. And it happened cos of me. Cos I did something bad."

"What kind of something bad?"

"The unforgivable kind." Martin pressed his forehead to the cool glass. His thoughts raced in circles, like an unmanned speedboat with a burning engine. "Me and Ian. Both of us. Mostly me. I made the first move. Actually, that last time I made every move. And Sandra found us. Together."

"Found you?" Liam sounded closer than before.

"Yeah." Martin kept his eyes closed and his forehead pressed to the window. He thought he might be sick if he moved. That and he was too much of a coward to open his eyes and catch Liam's reaction in the glass.

"You mean, she found you in bed with your stepfather?"

Martin spun. The room tilted. He staggered against the window still. "That fucker is not my…"

He half-coughed. His throat filled with bile. He tried to swallow, but the sour liquid scalded his tongue. He managed to choke it all back down. No way was he puking in Liam's presence. He might as well not bother arguing about Ian's connection to him, either. Legally, that was exactly what Ian was.

"It weren't a bed. It was the living room sofa." He paused, knowing that the next thing he said would thump the final nail in his own coffin as far as his relationship with Liam was concerned. "I planned it that way."

Liam stood in front of him, white-faced, eyes as black as the shadows lurking beyond the window. "Planned it?" He spoke so softly, but his words were stiff and hard. Like the knotted fists at his sides. "You mean you *wanted* her to find you two together? Is that what you're saying?"

It sounded cold and calculated from Liam's lips. But his reasons hadn't been cold, or calculated. He'd been desperate. He hadn't thought there was any other way.

"That's what I'm saying. Can I have my phone now?"

"Why?" Liam wasn't talking about the phone. Pretending that he had been would delay the inevitable. "Did you think he'd leave her for you?"

"Fuck no!" Had he given Liam that idea? Wasn't he being clear enough? He didn't know. Things were a little hazy in his past. Because most of it he'd prefer to forget. "I thought she'd kick him out. That's what I wanted. I needed her to see what he was. The guy she worshipped like he was the entire world. She chose him. Over me. And I couldn't let it happen."

Liam was looking at him now like they'd skipped back a couple of weeks. The contempt was right there as if it had never really gone away. "You were *jealous?*"

Martin shook his head, more to clear his mind than deny the question. "Of what?"

"Of your mother's relationship with your stepfather. Or

of his relationship with her?"

No. That wasn't it. It wasn't about jealousy. Was it? "I was trying to do what was right. That's all. He got her pregnant. And it'd never even crossed my mind before. I thought she was too old for all that. I never wanted to think of Ian and her…having sex."

"They were married. It's what married people do." Liam was rigid with hostility and disgust, yet there was nothing to be done but forge ahead. The sooner this story was out, the sooner he could get that phone back. The sooner Liam would hate him again. Like when they'd first met, only worse. Because he'd done worse than sell sex. Which was all Liam had needed to hate him the first time. That and his friendship with Katie. Which probably didn't exist anymore, anyway.

"I didn't do it cos I was jealous. I did it cos I couldn't let it happen again."

"Let what happen again? Am I missing something? You were having an affair with your stepfather and yet—"

"It wasn't a fucking affair! Liam, you ain't listening to me." His head throbbed with pressure now. But there was no not telling the rest, even though Liam misunderstood at every turn. How could he be clearer? Was there any point? "If you give me my phone, you can think what you like."

"If it wasn't an affair, then what was it? Because putting on a display so your mother would find you and end her marriage? Sounds like a despicable thing to me."

"I warned you it was. I told you that you wouldn't want to know. I as good as killed my own mother now she's locked inside her own brain forever. I deserve Roy. You should keep the phone and use it to call him. His number's in there. Will that make me any less despicable?"

"No. But you're most of the way to bringing it on yourself."

"I know that, you stupid fucking…" The will to fight seeped away. "Get me my phone. Please." He sank to the carpet and brought his knees to his chest. His head pounded harder than his ankle now.

"If it wasn't an affair, what was it? A casual fling? A boyfriend you never said you had?"

Martin looked up. "I didn't want any part of it. I had to drink a ton of whiskey before."

"Now you were drunk?"

"Of course I was fucking drunk. It was the only way I could stomach him touching me. He didn't even want to. He hadn't been interested in me for years. I near enough had to force him just to let me suck him off."

"Years? Wait." Liam scratched his head. "How old were you?"

"I told you. Eighteen."

"No. When it first started?"

Martin thought back. He couldn't remember. Might help if his brain wasn't trying to pound a hole in his skull. "I dunno. Just after we moved in with him. No. No, before then. He used to take me swimming. Every week. Just me and him."

"Age, Martin."

"I told you already." Hadn't he? Martin ran both hands over his face. Hard to remember what he had said, but if Liam wanted to hear it again, it was only a number. Just one word. "Nine."

"*Nine?*"

Martin opened his eyes and squinted until he made out Liam's vague outline. The light was dazzling bright all of a sudden, and the shadows way too dark. "Nine to fifteen. Then it just stopped. It only happened that last time because Sandra said she was going to have a kid and I couldn't risk it happening again."

When Liam didn't say anything, he realized he'd done enough to break whatever it was about him that had held Liam's interest. Might as well make the rest brief. "Sandra didn't believe a word when I tried to tell her. Ian said I was just trying to stir up trouble. He was so good at that. Twisting things until I got to doubting myself.

"He always said I had the choice. That I was in charge. I

could say no if I wanted. But he said so much about how he was only doing it cos he loved me. He said if I loved him then I needed to show that I did. I got so confused over what I was supposed to feel. And then I couldn't come up with any reason good enough to keep hold of the no he said I could have." Martin swiped at his eyes. It was the headache, blurring his vision.

Liam moved closer, stopping a few short paces away. Big and broad and silhouetted against the glare of the too-bright light. He'd frozen solid that way. Fists clenched though at his sides. Not yet flying. "Give me a minute."

Martin barely had time to register the request before Liam took off and shut himself in the bathroom.

* * * *

"Liam?" Martin rapped on the door. "You made me tell you. I said it was better if you didn't know."

Liam sat on the tiled floor, ignoring the chill cutting up through his backside.

"Look, I get it. You can't hate me more than I hate myself. But I can't change nothing about what I did. I just want my phone. Tell me where Robbie lives and I'll go ask him for it. You don't have to see me again. I can leave right now. Liam? Please."

Nine years old. The age rolled in Liam's head like a pair of dice where every combination added up to a nine-year-old Martin. Martin thought Liam was in here because of what had happened. The accident. Setting that pervert up. *Oh, fuck.* He wasn't to think that a moment longer.

Liam got up and opened the door.

Martin stared up at him with big shimmering eyes. He frowned. "What?"

"Permission to touch." Liam's throat was gravel, but he got the words out.

Martin retreated half a limp back to the window. "You ain't going to hit me, are you?"

Liam grabbed him then. Martin resisted, but only half-heartedly before he melted into Liam's chest.

"What's going on?" Martin peered up into Liam's face. "You got tears. Why?"

"Do you really not know?"

"I thought…I dunno. You got what I told you, right? You understand it was me. I set him up. Sandra walked in on us, exactly what I planned. Except the part when she got run over. That wasn't planned. And it's why I need the money. Because I want her to have the best care in the world."

The money? Liam had forgotten all about that. That had been the main thing he'd wanted to know, before this. "You pay for her to stay at Oakland House?"

"About thirteen hundred a month, depending on what treatments she has."

Liam held him tight and ignored his squirming. "But it's not right, that you should pay these fees. Who left you to foot the bill?"

"I needed Ian out of our lives. And he couldn't wait to go. I made him put thirty grand into her account first. That was the deal. And her safety net, in case something happens to me."

"As well as your life insurance?"

Martin sighed against him. "Yeah."

So much to be said, but where to begin? Something had obviously gone wrong in a system that in no way should leave Martin paying thousands a month for a service that should be free. But Martin was too tired to hear it right now. In the morning, they'd talk. Make plans. Go home. Find out about getting Sandra funding for her care. Pack Button's bags and kick him out of Martin's life. For good.

When Martin started to sag in his arms, Liam helped him to the bed and got him settled under the covers. "Rest for now. Okay?"

Martin gave a vague nod. His eyes closed. Liam secured the covers around him then edged toward the door. He got most of the way there before Martin started talking again.

"You're not running out on me, are you? Ain't like I can go after you. But I'd rather know now if you're not coming back."

"I'm not going anywhere." Liam offered him a smile. "Not after all the trouble I had getting you back."

"Is that why you stole my phone? So you could tuck me into bed?" Martin was obviously trying for funny, but his words were slightly slurred. The night had got the better of him and what he needed now was to be left to sleep.

"That's exactly why I took it. And the bottle. Which you haven't asked about once. It was his, wasn't it?"

"Yeah. Helps me keep focused." Martin's eyes fluttered closed again. "Want it back, too."

He'd get it back. But only when Liam was ready to let it go. Without letting Martin go at the same time. "I'm just going downstairs to get a drink. And maybe a snack. You want anything?"

Martin shook his head on the pillow. "Just...hurry back."

"I will." There was no fear of him not hurrying back. The less time Martin spent alone right now, the better. But he had no intention of stopping by the bar for food or drink. That was just an excuse to leave the room for ten minutes.

On his way down the stairs, he found the land lady fussing about behind the check-in desk once again.

"Everything okay for you?" she asked, as he made to pass by pretending he hadn't seen her.

Liam stopped. He'd had the art of good manners drummed into him for so many years as a child, that he couldn't just blank someone who'd asked a perfectly pleasant question. "Yeah, thanks. I'm just going for a walk." He lifted his hand and gestured toward the front door. *As if she needs showing where her own front door was.*

June frowned, her gaze fixed to his outstretched arm. "What happened there, then?"

Liam at once lowered his arm. The sleeve was still wet and evidently noticeable enough that a hint of suspicion had worked a path into June's tone. "Oh, that. Nothing really. Just had a bit of a mishap with the bathwater."

"A mishap?"

"Yes."

June's silence was just long enough that Liam understood it was an explanation she was after. Nosy bitch.

"A mishap where my friend lost the soap." He met her confused gaze and held it. "Took a bit of finding again, I can tell you."

When he flashed her a fake smile, something must've clicked in June's head. Her face flared bright scarlet. She shot him a glare, then hurried away into the room across the hall faster than a gust of autumnal wind.

Liam walked the puddle-strewn streets until he found his car, then popped the boot. He took a bag from the back. A bag containing two items. A half-drunk bottle of supermarket whiskey, and a cheap pay-as-you-go mobile phone.

He took out the phone then returned the bag to the boot. Sitting on the tailgate to protect himself and the phone from the drizzle, he switched the phone on and brought up Martin's bedroom pictures onscreen.

After selecting a couple of the clearest shots, he found Roy's number. Then, before he gave himself time to think twice and change his mind, he hit send.

Martin wasn't on the bed when he returned to the room, but running water sounded from the other side of the bathroom door. Was Martin washing *again*?

Liam sat on the bed, trying to settle his nerves. What he'd just done, what he'd had to do, it was ripping the situation from Martin's hand and taking it into his own. But if this were down to Martin, he'd want to act alone. And he'd been alone for way too long as it was.

The water stopped, replaced by a harsh, abrasive gasp. A sound that was more than familiar. Katie threw up practically every morning on the days she was home.

Liam pressed an ear to the door. "Martin? You okay?"

"I don't know. I…" The words were cut off by another

vigorous retch.

Liam tried the handle. It wasn't locked. He opened the door.

Martin pulled his head out of the toilet. "Been sick," he said, looking up with bloodshot eyes. "Something I ate, I reckon. What did I have?"

"A couple of biscuits."

"Oh, yeah. Well, they were off."

"Can you stand?"

He shook his head. "I thought I'd stay down here. The floor's nice and cold. And I don't feel too good."

"I noticed." Liam squatted at his side. "But you can't stay here."

"Why not? Ain't no rule that says I got to use the bed. And that old bat downstairs would prefer I keep my homosexual arse on the floor."

"Doesn't matter what she thinks." Liam tried to at least appear outwardly calm as he slipped an arm under Martin's shoulder. "The floor's not the best place for you to be." He applied enough pressure that they rose together, although Martin staggered back against him with a sharp cry.

"Liam, I'm okay." He was slurring every word now. Alcohol wasn't an issue, so something else was making him this way. He'd probably hit his head a lot harder than he'd admitted to before.

"Quit struggling." Liam held him tighter, wrapping both arms around his chest from behind. "Or do you want me to call an ambulance?"

Martin immediately stilled. "Why? What's wrong with me?"

"Concussion, I'd say," Liam said, trying to make the diagnosis seem like it was no more serious than a grazed knee or a twisted ankle. Turned out that ankle hadn't been so much the problem after all. "You'll be fine, but we need to get you checked out. No problem with that, is there?"

"Checked out where?" Martin turned his head, trying to peer at Liam over his shoulder.

"Just the hospital. A quick trip to A&E."

"But I ain't ill. I just feel sick." He didn't resume his fight. Instead he slumped back into Liam's arms. "I just need to sleep for a bit. That's all."

"You can sleep in the car on the way there." Once again, Liam hoisted Martin up in his arms. This time there was no argument at all.

Thankfully it was late, and everyone appeared to be in bed when Liam headed downstairs. Including the landlady, whose main complaint would more than likely be that they were trying to steal one of her bathrobes.

Chapter Thirty-Five

"You won't leave me?" Martin's grip was so tight that Liam's fingers burned with a pressure that had barely let up since they'd arrived at A&E. "Will they let you stay?"

Liam shook his head. "I shouldn't think so. It's two in the morning."

"Is it? Are you sure?" Martin searched his face as if seeking the joke. He might be confused for a while yet, according to the doctor. In the morning, they were going to see about a CT scan.

"I'm fairly certain, yes." Liam placed his free hand over Martin's, sandwiching them together. "Listen, I've been thinking. About what happens when you get out of here. I think you should come straight home with me."

"Home? No, I can't. Roy won't let me. Y'know he's asleep in all them pictures. I was holding out for better."

"They're good enough. I've seen them, remember?"

Martin's eyes closed. The doctor had told him he could sleep. He needed it. And he'd be safe here. Or as safe as he could be with Roy and the goon on the prowl. But that was something Liam was going to deal with as soon as he could leave here.

"Liam?" Martin half-cracked open an eye. "Will you do me a favor? I know I got no right asking, but there ain't no one else."

Liam leaned closer. "What do you need me to do?" *Fix things with Roy. Number one priority. Or just fix Roy. For good.*

"If I die, will you visit Sandra? She don't get no other visitors. Just me. If anything happens —"

"Nothing's going to happen." Liam forced humor into

his words, in the hope of making Martin feel that little bit reassured. "You've got a slight concussion and a sprained ankle. You heard what the doctor said. Forty-eight hours and you'll be home. With me. And we can visit your mother together. Sound good?"

Martin's other eye opened, half-lidded and glassy. "Too good."

"No. Just good. Because it's happening. I'll also start looking into some proper funding for your mother. Which is something you should have done years ago."

"No, she can't get it." Martin's voice waned. Fighting through the layers of sleep. "Ian had too much...too much money."

"Yeah, well. *Ian's* not around anymore, is he?" If he was, he'd get what was coming. Which was a bullet he'd dodged for too long.

In time, Liam was sure he could convince Martin to go to the police about what had happened throughout most of his childhood. But there was a thought for the future. For now, this was about Martin. And Button was the immediate threat here, not Ian or even Roy. "Do you want this to happen again? Some punter threatening your mother? Or worse. For all your life insurance, money won't make up for losing her son."

Martin's mouth twitched. He lowered his gaze. "Later, okay? Ain't fair to expect me to do this now." His eyes drew closed. The platinum strands swept across his forehead, washing out his already pale skin.

"At least agree that when you get out of here, you'll come home with me, if only until you're properly well." By which time Liam would have exhausted every possible persuasion technique to get him to stay. Hopefully that would be enough.

This time Martin's lips did drift into a smile. "Thanks, Liam. You're the best mate I ever had."

* * * *

Back at the B&B, Liam watched TV until seven a.m. Then, he took a brisk shower and drank an even brisker coffee. After dressing in the same clothing as the night before, which meant rolling up the sleeve still slightly damp from Martin's bathwater the night before, he cleaned his teeth and ran a comb through his hair.

At approximately quarter to eight, he collected the rest of his things and bagged up the clothing Martin had hidden under the bed. Muddy jeans and sticky, bloodied underwear. Liam's initial rage at finding them had cooled now. Toward Roy he felt nothing. But he was prepared to do whatever it took to ensure that vile, sadistic pervert never went near Martin again.

He checked out with minimal words to the landlady. And she appeared only too pleased to see the back of him without having to cook him a full English beforehand. Liam had other breakfast plans, anyway.

He'd found the restaurant via an app on his phone. A quiet but public space open for breakfast at seven. Roy was already seated at a table when he arrived. The goon was probably loitering close by, but not within easy sight.

Roy barely glanced up from a plate of cooked fish as Liam pulled out a seat. "You're late."

"I know." He'd purposely showed up five minutes late, in the vague hope it might lend him the illusion of power. He was, after all, supposed to be the one in charge.

"Is Button with you?"

"No."

"Then where is he?" Roy looked up, his gaze hard enough to sear a hole through a church wall.

Martin's bruised hips flashed into Liam's mind. He held no doubt Roy could be a relentless lover. How relentless he'd be as far as recovering his 'property' went remained to be seen.

"Somewhere else." Liam grabbed a menu. The images of a bruised Martin morphed into memories of himself, laid out flat and naked on a hotel bed. He might as well have had a two-hundred-pound price tag hanging by a string from his toe. The thought made him blush, but didn't carry enough shame to distract him from what had to be done.

"Where, exactly?

Liam lowered the menu. This couldn't be done any other way than face to face. "All you need to know is, he's not coming back. Not to…" A waitress approached the table. When she looked at him, Liam faltered. He wasn't here to eat. He didn't think he could keep anything down anyway. "Just coffee. Thanks."

The waitress jotted the order down then left.

Liam cleared his throat. "He wants you to know that it's over. Whatever it was between you two." It was safe to say so. Martin had said he wasn't going back. Ever.

"If Button wishes to discuss our arrangement, I'll do so with him and not his…what are you, exactly?"

Good question. Friend didn't cut it, and they were far from lovers. Complicated, that was what they were. But now wasn't the time to discuss his and Martin's relationship. And Roy definitely wasn't the person to be discussing them with. "There's no chance of you getting anywhere near him."

'Over my dead body' would have been a better comeback, if not the most original. But Liam wasn't sure how much of a gangster Roy was, or if he even was one. Or how great the possibility of Liam's dead body becoming the preferred option.

"On whose word? Yours?"

"Ours." Liam sat back as his coffee arrived. The waitress unloaded the pot and cup from the tray to the table. "His and mine. Together."

Roy waited until the waitress had moved out of earshot before speaking again. "He's due a payment this week. Tell him if he wishes to collect, to come and see me. In person."

"You don't get to give the orders anymore. Unless you want your wife to see some of those pictures. There's a video too, if you're interested." It didn't show much. The phone had slipped sideways and showed nothing beyond a shirtless Roy walking out of shot toward the bed. The sound was better, but not really something that could be used as blackmail fodder. "All you have to do is leave him alone. Agree to that and we'll trash the phone and everything on it."

Roy set down his knife and fork neatly together on the plate, the fish half-eaten. "Inform Button I'll see him at noon. Either here or at his mother's."

"His mother's? Why?" Liam should have expected this, but he hadn't. Not for Roy to bring Sandra into this. Not yet. Not when he had the photos. This wasn't a part of the plan.

"If you have to ask, you obviously don't know the boy as well as you think you do." Roy drew out his wallet. "Noon. Sharp." He tossed a twenty-pound note on the table then rose to leave.

"Wait!" Liam reared up out of his seat. Roy wasn't supposed to offer up an ultimatum of his own. "He can't get there."

Roy paused, one palm pressed to the table. "Why can't he?"

Because he's languishing in a hospital bed. As much as Liam wanted to tell Roy exactly what his obsessive behavior had led to, he couldn't. "This wasn't his idea. He doesn't know I'm meeting with you. I'll have to call him."

"Do that. Because If I don't see him today, Mr. West, I'll definitely see his mother. Make certain he's aware of that." Roy strode toward the lobby, leaving Liam speechless and an early chill of defeat running through veins that should have been hot and buzzing with triumph.

Chapter Thirty-Six

Lumpy porridge and burnt toast for breakfast, all washed down with a lukewarm cup of tea. If the doctors thought he was going to spend another thirty-something hours in this place, they had another think coming.

Martin lay in bed listening to the goings-on beyond his room. The scuffed footsteps, squeaky trolleys and occasional laughter. His sleep had been interrupted several times by various nurses prodding him with equipment and there wasn't even a clock to let him know the time.

Visiting hours weren't for ages. He'd checked with a nurse, and he wasn't sure Liam would come anyway. If their roles were reversed, he'd probably take this as a lucky escape. But Liam wasn't him. Liam had voluntarily stepped into the center of the shit that was Button's life. *His* life. Liam was more than a friend. Way more.

Martin shifted in the bed, trying to find a more comfortable position. His ankle had finally quit smoldering now it had been bandaged up and subdued by painkillers. His headache hadn't gotten any worse, either. His thoughts were clearer this morning.

At least Roy would never think of looking for him in a hospital. Wasn't even Liam's hospital, so he was doubly safe. But Liam wasn't. He'd already had a restless night thinking of various scenarios, and in all of them Liam came out worse off.

It wasn't like he could walk out of here. He didn't have his clothes or his shoes. He had nothing. No. A few days ago, he'd had nothing. Now he had Liam.

A light tap sounded at the door. Not a nurse — they tended

not to knock. The words 'come in' locked in his throat. He clenched the covers at his waist. He didn't want whoever was on the other side in here. Not if it wasn't Liam. Because if it wasn't a nurse or a doctor or Liam, then it could only be the one other person who wanted to see him.

The door opened. Liam came in. He met Martin's eye and stopped. "What?"

"Nothing." Martin loosened his grip on the covers. Why had he doubted? The one thing Liam would never do was let him down. "They said you couldn't come until three."

"I told them it was an emergency." Liam shut the door behind him then set a carrier bag on the bed. "I brought you some things."

"Thanks."

Liam pulled a plastic chair from the corner of the room and took a seat. "You thought I was him, didn't you?"

Martin dragged the bag toward him. "Who?"

"Roy."

He shrugged. "For half a second. I wasn't sure you'd be back. I was thinking, since you had the chance to run, you'd take it."

"The only direction I run in is towards you. Or haven't you worked that one out yet?"

Martin had worked that one out for himself a while ago. The one thing he had yet to learn was why. "You're a fucking loony tune coming here, buying me more shit I don't deserve." He opened the bag. There were new pajamas inside. Toiletries, too. Not that he'd need them, since he was discharging himself at the earliest opportunity. "You bring my phone?"

"How're you feeling?"

"Fine. Did you bring it?" Martin emptied the bag onto the bed and raked through the contents. "It's not here."

"What did the doctor say? Did you get the scan?"

"Yeah. No brain damage. My skull's too thick." He looked up. "Where is it?"

Liam sat forward in the chair. "When did they say you

could leave? Tomorrow?"

"No. Today." Martin began to load the things back into the bag. "So this was all a waste."

"Today? Are you sure?"

"Yeah. Course." Martin focused on repacking the bag and hoped Liam couldn't read the lie in his voice.

"That's funny, because when I came in the nurse said you'd be grateful for the pajamas. She mentioned how you'd been whinging about the air-conditioning tickling your arse. I'm thinking she wouldn't have said that if you were due to be discharged."

Martin smoothed a hand over the bulging plastic bag. "I can leave when I want." Liam studied him with a keenness he didn't much appreciate. "Did you bring my clothes?"

"No, I...uh...I had to bag them up." Liam lowered his gaze. "They need washing."

Fuck. He'd meant to toss those pants in the bin at least. But he had nothing else except these pajamas Liam had bought for him. Would the hospital even discharge him with only pajamas to go home in? *Home. With Liam. Yeah.* He'd go naked if he had to. "What about my phone?"

Liam stared at his hands. "There's something I should explain about that."

Martin sat up straighter. "I told you things last night I ain't never told anyone before. You said you'd give it back if I did. You said—"

"I sent a couple of those pictures to Roy."

The words were so random, they took a moment to sink in. "My pictures? But...my phone's in Robbie's car. Did you go and get it?"

"No, it's not." Liam lowered his gaze. "It was in my car all along. I'm sorry."

Martin's stomach dropped straight through the bed and splatted on the hard floor. "Why are you sorry?" Liam couldn't deal with Roy on his own. Roy could out-manipulate the pair of them. Easily. He had been doing exactly that for weeks. Longer. "What did he say?"

Liam ran both hands over his face. When he lowered his palms, he looked as if he'd been told his entire family had burned to death in a house fire. "He said if he can't see you today, he'd see your mother. So what you need to do is contact the home. Tell them not to let him in."

"I already did that. I called them before I tried you again yesterday. Have you at least got your phone on you?"

"Why?"

Martin pushed back the covers and swung his legs out of bed. Including the swollen, bandaged one. "I'm going to do what you wanted me to do in the first place. I'm calling in the police."

Liam sat back in his seat. "I don't think that's a good idea."

Martin froze. Had Liam actually just said that? Not a good idea? Two weeks ago 'calling the police' had been the most popular phrase in Liam's vocabulary. He thrust out a hand. "Give me your phone."

Liam made no move to do so. He stayed where he was, calm as fuck, hands resting in his lap. "Roy won't harm your mother. He's all talk. For starters, if anything happened to her, he knows you'd never forgive him. And he'd know you'd be straight on to the police."

"But he could go there. He could easily find a way. And then he'd tell her what I am. What I do. She ain't a fucking vegetable, Liam. She understands what's said to her. She'd understand if he…"

A wave of tingling dizziness swept over him. He tipped forward. From nowhere, Liam's arms were suddenly around him, holding him, guiding him back into bed.

"He won't get the chance to see her," Liam said softly.

"I can't risk it. You're the one who keeps telling me to call the cops." He struggled feebly against the strong arms that held him. "Now you're going to get your wish, so give me your fucking phone."

"Do you trust me?"

"It ain't about that." His struggle died away. What was the point? He wasn't supposed to be fighting Liam anyway.

279

He'd done that for too long already.

Liam's warm lips pressed against his ear. "Do you?"

"I ain't never trusted anyone else as much. But you ain't no match for Roy. No one is."

"If we call the police, Roy could use those pictures I sent him. He could say we set him up. None of them show him awake. He could say you drugged him."

He could. But that wouldn't even matter. Once the police were made aware then Roy wouldn't dare touch Sandra, or go anywhere near her.

"Martin." Liam's voice was sterner now. "If you'd wanted to call the police before I sent those pictures, then I'd have gladly dialed the number for you. But now...I'm just warning you what he may do. It's up to you. Whatever you think is best."

"I don't know what's best, do I? I've fucked up my entire life. I think you know best. I should listen to you more. You're my best mate. Actually, you're my only mate."

"Mate doesn't quite cover us," Liam said quietly.

No, that was true. Liam wasn't a mate. He was the most solid and trustworthy presence Martin had ever had in his life. And the one thing he'd learned was that Liam always knew better than he did. "If you think it'll work, I guess I'll meet him." Martin slumped in Liam's embrace, relieved to give up the pretense of a struggle. "I'll show him what I've got. Let's hope it's enough. Cos I can't take much more of this."

* * * *

At quarter to three that afternoon, Liam was outside the restaurant where he and Roy had met that morning. When he'd made the call for this meet up, Roy had still insisted on noon being the preferred time. It had taken a bit of persuading to get him to change his mind. Visiting hours at the hospital didn't start until three, and Liam wasn't giving away Martin's location until the very last moment. Because there was every possibility Roy would send in Shaun the goon while Liam was hanging about out here waiting for a white Rolls-Royce.

When a blue Lexus pulled up two inches from the end of his toes, Liam skipped back but didn't think too much of it. There were arseholes everywhere and he had more important matters on his mind. Then the window buzzed down.

"Get in."

Liam dipped and peered through the window. Roy sat behind the wheel, gazing back with an expectant tilt of an eyebrow.

"Where's your driver?" Liam scanned the street. No sign of him. Could be this *Shaun* was closeted away close by, ready to steal Martin back. Well, that wasn't going to happen. Roy didn't know their destination yet.

"Otherwise engaged. Come along, Mr. West. Unlike you, I don't have the entire day to waste."

Liam straightened and moved back. Roy was trying to control the situation. Martin had pre-warned him already. Roy liked to be in charge of every situation. "We'll take my car."

"Don't be ridiculous." Roy revved the engine.

"Go ahead. But you won't find him without me." Liam stood back and crossed his arms. If he didn't let Roy intimidate him, then he'd remain strong. Right there was fifty percent of the battle won.

"Suit yourself." Roy switched off the engine. He got out of the car far more elegantly than was typical for a man of his size and followed Liam to the dusty Vauxhall parked farther along the street.

Roy gave the car a double take. "*This* is yours?"

"Yes." Liam wasn't ashamed of his car. He owned it and it had never yet let him down. In his experience, the flashier the car, the more time it spent in the garage getting fixed. "Why?"

"No reason." Roy gave the car a once-over, barely

suppressing a shudder. "I'd just assumed this area to be a recycling drop-off point."

Liam tightened his grip on the key. Anger counted as weakness. He was in control here. "Don't tell me, you've got socks that cost more."

Roy continued to eye the car. "Undoubtedly."

"The important thing is, Martin chooses to be with me. And a whole fleet of expensive cars won't change that." Liam pressed the key remote and the car opened with a beep. "Get in."

Roy stared at him, the distaste for the car transferring along with his gaze. "Will I require a tetanus injection?"

"You buy vulnerable young guys for sex and terrorize the ones who refuse you. I reckon it's the car that needs the tetanus shot." Liam climbed behind the wheel. His heartbeat was hammering through his skull but, apart from that, so far so good. More so when Roy eased into the car as though the seat might bite him on the arse.

"Button chose me, if I remember rightly. Easy to miss the truth when you're riding high on a steaming pile of self-righteous bullshit, isn't it?"

'Bullshit' didn't sound right sliding off Roy's tongue. But he'd uttered it simply enough as he reached for the seatbelt.

"If you say so." Liam pulled out into the road. Something told him this short drive was going to feel more like an epic road trip with severe toothache. And heartburn. He hoped the end result would be worth it, for Martin's sake.

"Where are you taking me?" Roy flicked at an invisible speck of something on his jacket lapel. "Or is this to be a complete mystery tour?"

"You'll see when we get there." Liam checked the rear-view mirror. No snow-white Roller following, but then, Shaun could be driving anything. The more inconspicuous, the better.

"The mystery tour, then." Roy settled back in the seat. "As long as Button's waiting at the end of it, I'm willing to humor you."

Liam said nothing. The less conversation they shared, the less chance he had of losing his temper. He took a couple of deep breaths instead. His nostrils itched with the stink of pungent aftershave and he had to lower the window in the quest for fresher air.

"He was perfectly content," Roy said, "before you showed up."

Liam focused on the road ahead. "You think?"

"He wanted for nothing, just as I'd promised."

"Yeah, the place you had him stashed away wasn't bad. For a prison cell."

"Is that what he told you? That I'd been keeping him prisoner?" A soft chuckle breezed from Roy's lips. "How you were able to enter the cell if he wasn't supplied with a key?"

"Was he allowed out without the guard?"

"The correct term is chauffeur. Why would he need to go out alone?"

"Why wouldn't he?" Liam turned the car toward the hospital and hoped Roy wouldn't guess too soon where they were headed. "Chauffeurs don't usually try to drown their passengers." Liam glanced over. Roy was studying the houses and the hedgerows beyond the side window. "Martin had reason enough to leave you. You should start thinking about that, before I let you see him."

Another chuckle, this one harsher. "You wouldn't know the first thing about keeping a boy like Button. You have neither the funds nor the experience."

Liam turned off onto the road that led directly to the hospital. How familiar was Roy with these roads? If he'd already guessed where they were headed, he didn't seem concerned. "Like I said, we're friends. Money doesn't matter with us."

"Of course, you don't satisfy him sexually. No matter what he might tell you to the contrary. You wouldn't know where to begin."

He spoke as if Liam had shared a bed with Martin

multiple times. And yet it had only been the once. Liam was pretty sure he'd satisfied Martin. There would never be any bruises when they had sex in future. Or if. They were still, very much, an *if*. "It's not about sex," Liam said quietly. "Unlike you, I actually care about him."

"You've been inside him and you expect me to believe it's not about sex?" Roy released another sinister chuckle.

Liam tightened his grip on the wheel. *Why'd you assume I was inside him?* How he itched to pose that particular question. But he refrained. He would not get drawn into that conversation. Thankfully, he didn't need to. The turning for the hospital proved an adequate distraction.

"The hospital?" Roy leaned toward the windscreen. "Why bring me here?"

Liam made the final turning into the car park of the squat, nineteen-sixties style building, and carried on to the more modern wing behind.

"What have you done to him?" Roy punched the dashboard. "Stop the damn car!"

What had *he* done? The man thought he'd had something to do with the reason Martin was here? Liam pulled up in one of the last remaining bays, glad of having something other than Roy on which to focus. Otherwise he would lose it. He'd done so well so far, too well to wreck things now.

Before Liam could cut the engine, Roy had unsnapped his seatbelt. He made to open the door. When it wouldn't budge he turned to Liam, dark eyes flashing pure rage. "Open the door."

"In a minute." Liam sounded calmer than he felt, especially since he'd been accused of being the reason Martin was here. "I brought Martin in because he has a head injury. From when he jumped the balcony trying to escape you."

"Is he all right?" The rage drained to something like genuine concern. "Is it serious?"

"Serious enough. Which means you say nothing to upset him. You don't touch him, either. I'm going to be with him throughout to make sure."

Roy's glare darkened again. Here was a man well used to playing alpha, but didn't have a clue about how to conduct himself at the other end of the spectrum. "What do you imagine I might do to him in a hospital bed?"

"Given the opportunity? Everything."

Roy drew himself up. "Button sold himself to me, Mr. West. 'Everything' is what I'm entitled to take."

"I need to get a ticket." Liam pushed the door open and got out into the cleaner air. As he strolled to the meter, he naïvely assumed Roy would wait for him to return. He didn't realize his mistake until after he'd paid for his ticket and turned around. Roy wasn't sitting patiently in the passenger seat. The man was already most of the way to the hospital doors.

Chapter Thirty-Seven

Martin felt the sickest he'd been since Liam had brought him here. He'd refused another dose of painkillers because of the nausea roiling in his belly. He didn't think his sudden deterioration had anything to do with his injury so much as the time.

Liam had said he'd bring Roy at three. It was almost that already. Martin flicked back the blankets and checked his mobile. It was all he had. And he wasn't kidding himself that it was much. If Roy asked to see all those pictures in detail, then he'd be fucked. But whatever happened, he wasn't going back. Even if it did mean Sandra knowing what he was. And the cops knowing how he made his cash. He'd prefer jail to Roy's flat. He was almost sure he would.

A knock at the door broke his dark thoughts. Liam came in, red-cheeked and slightly breathless.

Martin sat up straighter in the bed. "Is he...?" No need to finish the sentence. Roy stepped through a moment later. Neither red-faced nor breathless. He might as well have stepped out of a business meeting, dressed in his crease-free suit and shiny black shoes.

"Good afternoon, Button," he said with that particular smile that left no doubt as to who was in charge. "You're looking healthier than I expected."

"I've got a concussion." Martin touched his head then gestured toward the end of the bed. "And a sprained ankle."

Liam closed the door behind them. "I've already explained."

Roy meandered around the room, checking out the cold green walls. "Not so much as television to keep you entertained. This really isn't good enough. I'll arrange something private for the rest of your stay."

"Don't bother." Martin hitched the blankets higher. "I'm leaving tomorrow."

"Excellent. I'll have a car waiting." Roy took a seat on the hard plastic chair by the bed. The chair Martin had come to think of as Liam's.

"No. I ain't going nowhere with you." Once again, Martin found himself grabbing the blankets. He didn't even know why he did that. It wasn't like Roy was actually going to physically drag him out of here. "I'm going home with Liam."

"You are?" Liam stepped forward, his eyes wide with way too much surprise.

"You said I could, didn't you?" Or was his head playing tricks, inventing a conversation they'd never actually had?

"Of course I did." His surprise surrendered to a smile. "I just didn't dare hope you'd come to your senses so quickly."

"It wasn't quickly." Martin forced himself to relax his grip on the blankets, yet at the same time couldn't quite persuade his fingers to release them completely. "I need you to keep me safe, don't I? Or else I just keep making all these really bad decisions."

"Yes." Liam's smile was incredibly smug, considering their situation. "You do."

"Aren't you both forgetting something?" Roy interrupted their moment. Martin had almost forgotten he was even here, and much preferred gazing into Liam's eyes and seeing a future there. "I'm not prepared to lose you, Button. You bring me far too much joy."

"Well, you don't bring me none."

A smile curved Roy's lips. "An untruth if ever I heard one."

Martin fought the blush crawling up his cheeks. Wasn't his fault Roy knew exactly where and how to touch him to draw every last tingle of orgasm from his body. But the last time hadn't been good at all. And that was what he'd focus on.

"Now to business." Roy crossed his legs. "Revenge porn. That's what we're talking about here, I presume?"

He sounded far too calm, not in the least afraid. Or threatened. If anything, amusement threaded his tone. Like he was just here to humor them.

If the pictures didn't work, what else was there? The options were the same. Go back to Roy, or risk Roy telling Sandra what he was, or even worse. Roy would send someone to actually hurt her. And it wouldn't matter how many calls he made to the home about other visitors, or even if he called the feds — Roy would find a way, because no one got the better of him. Not Button and not Liam. They were out of their depth.

"Well? May I see these photographs, or am I going to have to take your word that they exist in the number your... friend claims?" He threw a disdainful glance at Liam.

Martin slipped a hand beneath the blankets and located the phone. "There's twenty. And a video. With sound."

Roy held out a palm. "Show me."

So he was expected to drop his phone into that palm. The same palm that had pinned him to the bed and held him down. The same palm that had often given a pleasure Martin had never even wanted. And the pictures on the phone, they still weren't good enough. And all he had was one last ditch attempt to find something that actually would be.

But he dropped the mobile into Roy's hand just as though they were.

"Martin..." Liam stepped forward. He looked desperate to pluck the phone from Roy's palm.

"It's okay." Martin offered a smile. The photos didn't matter half so much as they had. Not now.

"We've got copies," Liam said as Roy focused on the screen.

Had they? Martin hadn't made any. He didn't have Wi-Fi at the flat and the phone had nothing on it to back up to.

"Of course you have," Roy muttered, his attention fixed to phone.

Martin met Liam's confused gaze. There was anger there, but Liam didn't understand. There hadn't been time to tell him. Martin had only just come up with the solution himself. And only then because the thought of Roy's ruthlessness had been enough to give him the idea in the first place.

"Well, these are somewhat...anti-climactic." Roy finally looked up. "Which isn't something I'd ordinarily say to you, Button." He tossed the phone back onto the bed. "A toddler could have taken a better shot."

"Watch the video," Liam said, grabbing up the phone. Clearly something he'd been wanting to do since Roy had taken possession. "We could call up your wife right now and let her have a listen to—"

"Then do it." Roy plucked out his own mobile from the depths of his jacket. "Would you like her number?" He tapped the screen a couple of times then offered the phone to Liam.

Liam immediately stepped back like the phone was radioactive. "You're bluffing," he said, though by his tone he already knew Roy wasn't. And that really was his wife's number on the screen.

"My wife is more than aware of my penchant for beautiful young men, Mr. West." Roy continued to hold out the phone and Liam backed away another step. Roy knew Liam's last name. Martin hadn't told him. He must've done some investigating. Or, rather, more investigating. As if more were needed. "She won't appreciate your call, of course, but if you think you're about to impart any sort of revelation on our marriage, then you'd be completely... disappointed."

"There's always social media." Liam turned to Martin. "We could post those pictures all over. Send a few to wherever it is he works. We—"

"And he'd call the cops." Martin sighed. "Them pictures don't matter, Liam. Just delete them."

"*What?*" Liam clutched the phone close. "I'm not doing that. We can still—"

"We don't need them." Martin settled back into the pillow. His head had started throbbing again, but the atmosphere in here was far too tight. Stifling, even.

"Good. I'm pleased this little business meeting has reached such a swift and mutually agreeable conclusion." Roy tossed the phone back on the bed and rose. "I'll have that private room arranged for you, Button. And when you're discharged, Shaun will take you to the flat. I—"

"That ain't happening, though." Martin raised his voice to carry over Roy's. "Cos I've got your DNA inside me, haven't I? And too many bruises the docs have already called me out on. So now you got no choice but to leave me alone. Me and everyone I care about, including Liam and most of all my mother."

"I feel as though there's an 'or else' in there somewhere." Still Roy was humoring them. Well, that would end. In a moment.

"The 'or else' is obvious." Martin blew out a sigh and opened his eyes a touch wider, just so he could properly see the reaction on Roy's face. "If you don't leave me alone— me and everyone I care about, that is—I cry rape."

The word sent an instant chill through the air. Roy's face was stone. "You wouldn't *dare.*"

"Liam's got my clothes all bagged up, ready for the cops. I know I'm just a whore, Roy. But rape is rape, according to the law."

The fiery rage in Roy's eyes burned away. All Martin could see there now was blackness. A void he couldn't begin to read.

He turned his attention to the bedsheet. No way did he want to look any deeper into Roy's psyche. "Can we agree, then? Cos my head is banging and who knows what I might have to tell the nurse next time she comes in for checks. I say stuff when I get tired, stuff that may or may not have happened."

"Agree? I would never... You'd do this to me? After everything I've given to you?"

"You've given me nothing. I've been your fucking prisoner. And if you go anywhere near my mother, ever, if you even take your fucking cars down the same road, I call the cops. There ain't no time limit on rape, Roy."

Roy paled to the same shade as his crisp white shirt. "Whatever else I might have done to secure you, I wanted you happy. Clearly, you weren't." Roy sounded as though the reality bothered him. As if he honestly believed being told what to wear and how to dress and what hairstyle to have was all done out of some twisted act of affection.

"No. I wasn't." He nodded to the phone in Roy's hand. "You can keep that. Delete them or keep them as a souvenir, I don't care. We haven't got copies. Nothing will come back to haunt you. Not if you leave us alone."

Roy rose from the chair, stiff-backed, face tight as a pinch. He turned to Liam. "I wish you luck with him, Mr. West. You're obviously going to need it." With that, he turned on his heels and strode from the room.

Liam took a seat in the recently vacated chair, still warm from Roy's arse. In other circumstances, that second-hand heat would have bothered him enough to move to the bed. Now it hardly mattered at all.

"Martin? I need to ask. Did he?"

"Did he what?" Martin's eyes fluttered open. They stuck halfway, his lashes shadowing the cheeks beneath. He looked exhausted, just a pale scrap in a hospital bed.

"You know what I'm asking. Did you lie to me before? About what he did to you?"

"No. Them pictures wouldn't have worked by themselves. I needed to make sure he got the message, and that was the only way I could think of."

Ordinarily, Liam wouldn't have approved of those kinds of tactics. A false allegation like that ruined lives. But as it was Roy, he almost hoped Martin would take it further.

Go to the police. Report Roy. Report the monster Martin's mother had married. But he already knew that wasn't going to happen. And if it did, he wasn't sure Martin would be strong enough to go through it. Not yet.

"I think it worked," Liam said as the shadows fell away from Martin's face. Wouldn't be much longer and he'd be asleep. A long, peaceful sleep, which he was more than overdue. "I'm going to shoot off home in an hour or so. Just to check Roy's goon has been called off. Katie's at work and Robbie said he's picking her up. I can't call him until it's safe."

"Robbie again?" Martin's eyes opened fully this time. The haze had cleared from their blue depths. "You two sound like you're bezzies or something."

"Not quite." Liam managed a smile. "But he's the first bloke of Katie's that didn't turn out to be a loser."

"Ain't no need to say that for my benefit. I already know the score between you and her."

Liam ran both hands over his face. How were they ever going to move on? What could he do to convince Martin his fantasies about Katie were gone now? *Almost* all of them.

"It's all right, big man." Martin slid a palm across the mattress toward him. "Ain't a deal-breaker, since I know how desperate you are to get me home."

Liam took the offered hand. "You actually want to come home, then. It wasn't just something you said to Roy to… you know. Get him to back off."

Martin gazed steadily back at him. He looked sickly again. Frail. Now all his strength had drained away, leaving him worse than before. "You're the only person who gives a shit about me. And I like how you make me feel."

"How do I make you feel?" Liam was genuinely interested. Martin had never talked about his feelings before.

"Like I'm worth more than Button. Even after what I did." Martin squeezed Liam's hand. "But if I'm coming back with you, we got to get real. I'm going to need a job, cos I'm pretty much skint since Roy took all my cash. And fuck knows who's going to give the likes of me a chance when the only qualification I got is in shagging. I can't even spell proper or nothing."

Liam had noted his literacy could use some work. But that wasn't really an issue. Neither was Martin getting a job straight away. "I can take care of us both until you're feeling better at least. Then —"

"I ain't living off you, big man." He tried to tug his hand back. "I pay my own way."

"I said until you're feeling better, didn't I?" Liam tightened his grip. He wasn't losing this rare moment of closeness to a misunderstanding. "And we can get you signed up to a few of those free courses at the college. Maths and reading skills. While you're looking for work as well, that is."

Martin's gaze was loaded with doubt. "What about Sandra? She needs to stay where she is. And that ain't cheap. It's the only place I trust. And if I can't get no funding —"

"One step at a time. And we can make Sandra the first step. I understand how important her welfare is. And I know someone at work who can help out with the application for funding. And a proper care assessment. Okay?"

The doubt was still rife in Martin's face. But he no longer tried to pull his hand away. Neither was he arguing anymore. His lips twitched like he had something more to add, but when he spoke again it wasn't about his mother at all. "What about me and you?"

And that was, perhaps, the most challenging question of all. Liam cleared his throat. "Let's see how we go living together as friends. Before we think about taking things a step further."

"Does that mean you get to neck off with randoms behind my back? Are we going to be that kind of friends?"

Even now, Martin's trust wasn't fully there. Liam didn't let his sudden anger show. It wasn't Martin's fault. He'd been let down and used so many times, no wonder he still had doubts about someone's intentions. Even if that someone was Liam. "After all I've gone through to get you to agree to come home, do you really think I'd want to risk us by getting myself involved with randoms?"

Martin looked at him then bit his lip. "I don't know. Maybe. Like, a female random. So no one would know you was at least half queer."

"With you, Martin, I'm pretty sure I'm fully queer, so you don't have to think about someone else who doesn't even exist. Okay? All I'm saying is, let's see if we can live together first as friends. Just until you know what it is you want."

"But I know what I want. You."

It wasn't so simple, and Martin must know that. With his past, he'd never had the chance to have a relationship. He needed time to sort his head out. And learn that his body was his own. No one else's.

"Does friends mean there no kissing allowed, neither?"

The question fetched Liam from his thoughts. "I was hoping for kisses. But if it's not something you —"

"It is. I mean, if you were going to ask. It is something I want." Martin tugged his hand. "We could start now."

Lim rose from the chair and leaned toward Martin's lips. They were warm and dry, but soon opened beneath his own.

"When I get out of here —"

"You're coming home." That much at least had already been negotiated.

"Yeah. But on the way, could you do me a favor?"

"I thought we weren't doing any more favors."

Martin lifted a shoulder. "I just want you come and meet Sandra. I'm due to see her tomorrow anyway, and I reckon she'd like you. But don't feel like you have to. I can —"

"Yes." As if there would be any question he wouldn't want to meet Martin's mother.

"You sure?"

"But you need to do one more favor for me in return."

A flicker of dread passed across Martin's face. "What?"

Liam was sure he'd never actually asked a favor that

would warrant such a look, but he grabbed the carrier bag he'd set out of sight down by the bedside locker. "This isn't something I'd ordinarily bring in for a patient, but you really need to deal with this sooner rather than later." He set the bag on the bed and waited.

Martin peered in and drew out the bottle of scotch. "What'd you expect me to do with this?"

"I'm just returning it to its owner." Liam sat in the chair. Whatever Martin did with that bottle now would go most of the way to indicating whether or not he really did want to come home. "I know how much it means to you."

Martin studied the label, like it was a completely new bottle. A completely different brand.

"You realize you can't bring it home. Not with what it represents."

Martin finally turned to Liam, eyebrow cocked. "What if I say that I won't come home without it?"

"Then that would be a deal breaker."

"No it wouldn't. You've gone to way too much trouble to just mug me off now."

Despite the inelegance of the phrase, the sentiment was exactly right. Martin was actually beginning to realize he was cared about. Which was a good thing. But that bottle was still going to have to go.

"I'd be disappointed in you, then. Instead of proud."

Martin narrowed his eyes. "Ain't no fucker in existence who's ever been proud of me."

"Then I'd like to be that first fucker. If that's all right with you."

Martin thrust the bottle toward him. "Here, then. Tip it down the bog."

Liam shook his head. "This is something you have to do."

"Man, you just want an excuse to carry me again. You so get off on the feel of me in your arms."

There was some truth in that, more than Liam was prepared to admit. But that had nothing to do with why Martin had to do this himself. Or very little to do with it.

"You could always get the police to return it to its rightful owner. I think I'd prefer that option."

"I ain't talking to the cops. If that means you're disappointed in me for life, then I'd rather that than..." He swallowed. "Sorry."

"It's not for you to be sorry." Liam shuffled this chair closer. He touched Martin's arm, the one still attached to the bottle. "All I want is for you to leave Button behind, and come home to start over. You and me, Katie and her new bloke—"

"Robbie."

"Yeah. And her...*the*...baby."

"*Their* baby," Martin said quietly.

Liam sighed. "I'm trying, Martin. Do you think I could have something back in return? Please?"

Martin looked no less exhausted, but his eyes were brighter now. Was getting rid of that bottle still such a big deal for him? Did Liam have any right to insist he leave his entire past behind? No matter how bad those memories were, they were still a part of him. "If you can't do this now, that's okay. You can always—"

"No. I want to." Martin pushed himself up against the pillows. "You're right. You always are, but you're extra right about this. I don't want to be Button no more. I can't be him. Not to let anyone who wants in. Cos, you know, I'm in here too, and no one even notices me." He looked up. "'Cept you."

Liam rose from the chair and leaned in. He placed a gentle kiss on Martin's lips. A brief kiss Martin didn't flinch from. And when he pulled back, a tear trickled down Martin's cheek. A tear quickly swiped away.

"Here. Take this a minute." Martin offered out the bottle. When Liam took it, he pushed back the covers and swung his feet out of the bed. "You're going to have to give me a hand. They're giving me crutches, but I haven't got them yet." He quickly rubbed at his eyes again then sniffed. "Don't mean to say I want to be carried, though."

"You can walk. That's not a problem. Put your arm around me."

Martin did so, for once without argument. Liam had the bottle as they headed to the small bathroom. Martin wobbled a little and trembled a lot, but they managed to get there.

"Do you want some time?"

"I don't think so." Martin looked up from the toilet bowl. "I'm trusting you now, big man. Like, completely. With Sandra, too. It ain't just me. It'll never just be me."

"I know that. Here." He uncapped the bottle. The contents smelled worse than the hospital disinfectant bubbling in the toilet.

Martin accepted the bottle. He slowly tilted his wrist until the scotch trickled then flowed into the bowl.

More books from Pride Publishing

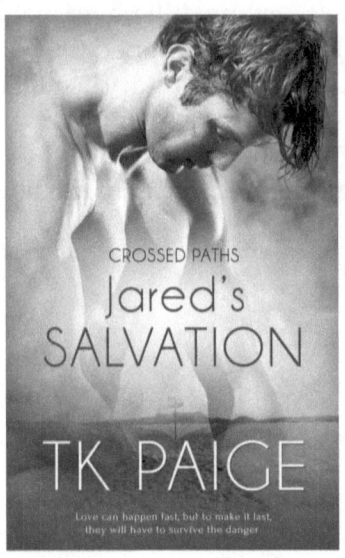

Book one in the Crossed Paths series

Love can happen fast, but, to make it last, they will have to survive the danger that is coming for them.